Y0-BQB-408

"Imagine how ambitious a task it would be to write a historical novel set 500 years ago, written in three distinct first person voices, demanding a convincing demonstration of cultural authenticity in more than one culture and then to weave a compelling narrative through it all. Vlach has done it and managed in the process to provide us strong characters, conflict, love, self-doubt, psychological understanding and a rare quality of mysticism that melds itself seamlessly with the reality of life in the most difficult of times. A compelling read."

—David Watts, author of
Bedside Manners and The Orange Wire Problem

THE GOLDEN CHALICE
OF HUNAHPÚ

THE GOLDEN CHALICE
OF HUNAHPÚ

A Novel of the Spanish Attack

on the Maya

WILLIAM VLACH

Full Court Press
Englewood Cliffs, New Jersey

First Edition

Copyright © 2014 by William Vlach

All rights reserved. No part of this book may be reproduced
or transmitted in any form or by any means electronic or
mechanical, including by photocopying, by recording, or by
any information storage and retrieval system, without the
express permission of the author and publisher, except where
permitted by law.

Published in the United States of America
by Full Court Press, 601 Palisade Avenue
Englewood Cliffs, NJ 07632
www.fullcourtpressnj.com

This book is purely a work of fiction. Names, characters, places and
incidents either are the product of the author's imagination or are used
fictitiously. Any resemblance to actual persons whether living or
deceased, events, or locales is entirely coincidental.

ISBN 978-1-938812-33-0
Library of Congress Control No. 2014942730

Cover painting by Emmanuel Paniagua

*Editing and Book Design by Barry Sheinkopf for Bookshapers
(www.bookshapers.com)*

Colophon by Liz Sedlack

FOR NORITA

We the indigenous peoples of Guatemala declare and denounce before the world more than four centuries of discrimination, denial, repression, exploitation, and massacres committed by the foreign invaders and continued by their descendants down to the present day. The suffering of our people has come down through the centuries, since 1524, when there arrived in these lands the assassin and criminal, Pedro de Alvarado.

—*The Declaration of Iximché*, February, 1982

*My sons! Newest generation of this ancient city of Thebes!
Why are you here? Why are you seated there at the altar, with
these branches of supplication?*

*The city is filled with the smoke of burning incense, with
hymns to the healing god, with laments for the dead. I did
not think it right, my children, to hear reports of this from
others.*

*You, old man, speak up—you are the man to speak for
others. In what mood are you sitting there—in fear or resig-
nation? You may count on me; I am ready to do anything to
help. I would be insensitive to pain, if I felt no pity for my
people seated here.*

—Sophocles, *Oedipus the King*

Book 1

OH, MY SONS!
1510 TO 1525

1

HERE IS THE STORY, OH, MY SONS! the story of our people. Here is the history of our people, our family. This is what happened to the people who originally came from the place of reeds, from Tulan. The story of K'umarcaaj, now Utatlán; of Iximché, now Guatemala. This is our story. Here is your history.

This is the story of your father, Belehé Qat. The story of the rabbit and the loss of the rabbit. The story of Hunahpú, who still lives. Lives here. Lives now in Christidom. This is the story of your mother, Xtah, now Lucía, and your father, Belehé Qat, now Francisco. It is written so that you may know that the Spanish are men, wooden men, men waiting for black rain. This you will learn. This story is how you will learn.

Before I learned to write as Tunatiuh taught us, before I learned to write as the Spanish taught us, before I saw the faces of the Spanish, before I saw the gods of the Underworld, oh, my sons! before all this, I saw the messengers of Mexicu warning us, telling us of signs and portents. Signs in the stars, portents in the bowels of the sacrificed. They feared, they predicted the return of Quezalcoatl.

Before the arrival of the Mexicu, I thought all that existed were the Kaqchikels and the K'ichés. That is all I thought there was in the world. Two great nations, foreordained to war. That the most powerful man in the world was my grandfather King Hunyg, one of the dual kings of the Kaqchikel.

I thought the world of the K'iché and the Kaqchikel was the world. But when the ambassadors of Mexicu arrived from Tenochtitlán, they came in great numbers. They came to us dressed in feathers. They came with the countenance of greatness and even superiority. And when they came, I was frightened, oh, my sons! I was frightened and hid behind my mother, behind my mother's skirts. They came to warn us of the arrival of the gods.

They came to our city. Our world. They came to Iximché. We watched them arrive. My cousin, Zorach, and I watched the ambassadors of Mexicu arrive. I am not ashamed to say that we were afraid, oh, my sons! We stood half way up the great pyramid of Awilix and watched. We watched them walk with flags and banners and smoky incense along our Kaqchikel roads, through our ravines, up through our hills and pine trees, along the white rock causeway.

THE BEASTS AND BIRDS PAID THEM RESPECT. The stones and the animals paid them respect.

When they came, there were many of them. Multitudes of them. Zorach and I ran down the pyramid to be with our mothers. The royal wives and children stood at the bottom of the pyramid and watched as my father, your grandfather, the Ahop Achí Balam, opened the great obsidian doors for the procession. We hid behind our mother's blue skirts as they entered our city. They were given great respect by my grandfather, King Hunyg. He bowed and showed them the respect I thought only gods received. He honored them as they walked into Iximché.

The front rank of ambassadors wore the green and red feathers of their supreme god, Huitzilopochtli. They were followed by a row of lords dressed as hummingbirds and eagles, then warriors dressed in the skins of wolves and jaguars. Slaves carrying boxes of jeweled gifts and supplies followed.

From the back of the Great Hall we watched as they gave our fathers and grandfathers many tributes. Our royalty gave them Pipil slaves. The slaves were old and sick.

I was ashamed.

After the ambassadors and our royalty went into the purple chambers, and I ran from the Great Hall to the ball court. All the families were gathering for a game to be held in honor of the messengers. Zorach and I became legendary ball players. We played ball with a pine cone. As the families began to join us I looked to the seats and saw my little brother, Ahmak, sitting in our mother's lap, admiring us. Whenever I kicked the pine cone, Ahmak bounced up and down, then laughed and drooled all over her white huipil.

I was taller than my cousin, I was stronger and had wider shoulders. I laughed and ran. We were the same age, but he was smaller. He yelled, Belehé Qat! I yelled, Zorach! We were both boys and we played war by the ball court. We were ten years old and were destined to become great leaders. Our family told us this. This was our fate.

In the midst of our battles, I smashed Zorach with the pine cone. Blood gushed from his face. I kicked my pine-cone ball at him, and he was hurt. I felt something a warrior cannot feel. There was no name for what I felt, or where that feeling came from. That moment was the beginning of my journey. I felt his blood to be my own. I felt my own skin tear, and I felt his blood on my cheek.

I wanted to heal his face. I wanted to heal my eyes. I wanted to tell the story of how my pine-cone ball had hurt the both of us. I looked at my family.

My mother smiled and Ahmak laughed and cheered.

Zorach cried.

THE NEXT YEAR, WE WENT TO WAR with the K'ichés. My grandfather, King Hunyg, and your grandfather, the Ahop Achí Balam, made war on the K'ichés. They did not become great by starting this war, oh, my sons! This was one of the many wars that occurred after our people had freed themselves from the law of the K'iché.

"Do the K'iché bleed?" I asked Zorach. "Do they have families and clans and gods? I want to see them."

"Let them bleed," my cousin said. He did not like it. He was my cousin and my friend and I miss him, but he was afraid. In the end, he agreed. We would find some K'ichés. We would look at them. We would look at the enemy. I wanted to attack them, kill them, bring them shame. They were not Zorach.

I am old, but I was young once, oh, my sons! I was young and free. If I wanted to attack the K'ichés, I would attack the K'ichés. Who was there to stop me? The gods did not argue. Hunahpú was busy fighting the lords of the Underworld, Xibalba. My parents did not argue because they did not know. Who was there to argue?

As the sun came up, Zorach and I left the gates of the city. My cousin, Zorach, and I were cold. Our city, Iximché, the city of the Kaqchikels, sat on the plateau of a great hill. This was our great defense and fortification. We walked down the side of the hill. Frost lay on the pine trees. Green brush spread out before us to the ravine below.

Two white butterflies fluttered around my legs. A broken tree lay in front of us. It became a fallen K'iché. The wood inside the split bark was red. I spit on it. I spit on the wound of the enemy.

We marched through the brush and trees into the ravine as the sun began to warm us. We saw tiny yellow and white daisies. Blue flowers hung from their narrow stalks. They had become the enemy armies. The entire hill was covered with flowers. We stopped again, and this time there was not the silence. The hum of bees and flies surrounded us. Enemy war songs! I looked closely at the blue flower enemy. A yellow-and-black bumble bee landed on one, then slowly flew from blue to yellow to white flowers.

Suddenly, through the trees and brush and flowers, a huge bright red flower appeared: the king of the K'iché. I wanted to run over to it, beat it, but the brush was thick, and I was a boy. In shame I couldn't get through the brush. I saw another, closer this time. The red flower was deep, dark red. Zorach and Belehé Qat, your uncle and your father, attacked and destroyed this enemy king. The massacre of the flowers raged as we became dazzled by the red flowers, the bees, and the trees and the humming green brush.

I told Zorach to stop when we reached a clearing. We looked out over the territories of the Kaqchikels. From that clearing halfway down the ravine, we saw the hills and valleys and villages that paid allegiance to our people.

As we walked down to the valley, we passed the tribes and subjects and slaves that had come to Iximché. They came to Iximché to help my grandfather make war on the K'ichés. I smelled the pine, I saw the smoke in the air from the morning fires, I heard the women chattering as they cooked. Zorach and I walked past these royal vassals.

We walked out of the Valley of the Kaqchikels. We left the valley and we began to climb the hills on the other side of the valley. We became tigers and monkeys, and made the sounds of tigers and monkeys. On the far ridge beyond the sight of Iximché, beyond the sight of the valley, Zorach became afraid. He was afraid because he had never faced the K'iché. He had never walked this far from our city without his father. He did not know if he existed this far from our people.

Zorach sat on the ground under the trees by the bushes. He said he would not continue. The sun was directly above us. He looked like a small clump of white rags my mother might have thrown out. White rags with a small brown boy hiding in the clump.

My impatience ended quickly.

We heard, oh, my sons! the sound of the K'iché drum. We heard the sound of the K'iché flute. We heard these sounds from beyond the bushes, beyond the trees.

We heard the sound of the K'iché, and Zorach wanted to flee. My good friend and cousin wanted to escape. We had come all this way, and he wanted to flee. I told him no. We had not come all this way to run like babies, to run from the music of the K'iché. These were not flowers, not bees. This was what we had come for. We had come to see the K'iché. All we had done was to hear them. We must now see them.

Had I listened to him, our story would be different.

He glared at me, then agreed.

Zorach and I crawled through the bushes. We crawled like crabs in the ocean. We crawled so that we could not be seen or heard. We crawled and became two crabs with shells to protect us. We crawled to see the K'iché.

As we crawled, the K'iché music came out to meet us: *dum dum didi dum*; *loow loow li low*. But the music could not find us because we were crabs and had shells. But we could hear the music. But the music could not find us.

We came to the end of the bushes. We came to the end of the bushes and the beginning of the K'iché. They were there. The K'iché walked along the paths in bushes as my father and my grandfather walked. They wore K'iché black short jackets and black long pants. They walked beyond the bushes as men and not as crabs. There was a drummer and a flute player. The K'iché musicians played.

The music found us. We were no longer crabs. We had turned back into mere Kaqchikel boys. The music found us and told the K'iché men that we were who we were.

Through the bushes we ran. We ran because we could not become crabs. We could not become invisible. We could not crawl. We had no shells. We had become human and could not change back into crabs. As we ran we wanted to change into birds, but we were too young to know how to change into birds. We were boys and had to remain human.

The K'iché ran through the bushes and they turned into jaguars. They turned into cat-humans. They became as the wind and we were but small boys. I'll ask you now my sons—When can boys outrun a jaguar? When can the fastest man outrun a jaguar? Is not a jaguar a god? Can a man outrun a god? Can a boy?

Zorach was grabbed by his black hair. Belehé Qat was grabbed by his neck. Boys can fight, but not even a man can fight against a jaguar. A man can fight against a jaguar, but I ask you, will the man win? The boys relented and let themselves be taken by the K'iché. We were taken, but we were not humiliated. A boy cannot be humiliated when taken by a jaguar. They played their flute and drum: *dum dum didi* dum; *loow loow li low.* All along the way they talked and laughed at us. We walked and did what they told us to do. We were now slaves of the K'iché.

We walked for three days, we were captives of these K'iché musicians for three days and three nights. We climbed through the K'iché trees and green mists until we came to the plateau of their city. Around us, like at our city of Iximché, were many pine trees.

Gray moss hung from the green trees. There were fewer flowers by their city of K'umarcaaj. I saw the deep red one, but only a few others. The musicians walked and we walked through the drizzle. The climb to their city was even more steep than the climb to Iximché. The K'iché capital was safer than our city, better fortified.

WE ENTERED THEIR CITY, K'UMARCAAJ, AT MIDDAY. We entered their city, oh, my sons! as slaves to the K'iché. We entered their city of council buildings, their city of palaces, their city of temples. The light hit the rain as it fell on their temples, turning the drops gold and silver.

We entered their city, and I whispered to Zorach, "Our city is bigger than theirs. Our city is more magnificent." He would not look at me. His fear had become anger. But it was true that their entrance was better fortified than ours.

The musicians stopped at the edge of the market. The K'iché market looked like the market of Iximché. Mats lay on the ground, covered with red glistening tomatoes, green limes, feather necklaces, and medicinal herbs. Women in purple and green dresses argued over the value of their fruits and vegetables while children darted through the busy crowds. We were ignored.

The K'iché flute player leaned down and picked up a tomato from a carefully stacked pile. A woman with a purple shawl wrapped around her shoulders started to protest, then smiled a wide toothless grin.

The drizzle stopped.

The K'iché flute player's word for "mother" was the same as our own.

"Look," I said to Zorach. "His mother is wearing red diamond emblems on her huipil."

"They wear what women wear," he said, dismissing me.

"Like our women's dress, the diamonds are the unity of sky and earth. There is a tie between the Kaqchikel and the K'iché."

"They are our enemies, and they will kill us," he said.

As we left the market, I saw five men in tassels and feathers, at the far edge of the mats, watching us.

Mexica. I am not ashamed to say were frightening, oh, my sons!

We walked away from the five Mexica. In relief we walked by the K'iché ball court. It was the same shape as ours. Ours was not a unique ball court. Past the ball court was the plaza of the gods. In the plaza were altars, dance platforms, brilliantly colored mortar houses, and temples. These K'iché were closer to the gods than our people. You could tell from their temples. The K'iché flute player spread his arms and said, "K'umarcaaj."

He named each temple at the plaza: Awilix Temple, K'ucumatz Temple, and Tohil Temple. At the base of the temple of Tohil were jaguars. Painted jaguars glared at Zorach and me as we faced the temple. They were orange and yellow, and I felt their power to leap from the walls of the temple. These jaguars commanded us to look at all the aspects of the temple.

We stood at the base of the stairs and looked up to the heights of the temple. White-robed priests walked up the steps to the peak of the temple of Tohil. Flags and banners waved at the top.

A wood terrace stood at the top of the temple. Priests were gathered on the terrace under the flags. I looked at their temple, and I thought of our own. I thought, Yes, these K'iché were closer to the sun than the Kaqchikel.

We could see, above us, on the temple terrace, a naked man lay on a stone. His hair was tied with dark vines to the wall of the pyramid. His arms and legs were stretched out in different directions, each tied to a ring on the temple floor. Smoke from the incense burners swirled around him.

A tall old priest lifted a black stone knife high into the blue air then brought it down into the man's chest. Zorach turned away from the sacred sight. I saw the red blood spill onto the stone altar. The priest lifted out the man's heart and held it up to the sky, held it up to the K'iché god, to Tohil, to the sun. He placed the heart in a large red bowl.

The other priests cut off his head.

The priests stuck his head on a pole. From the pole the head looked down at us. Zorach held me. This was not the way of the Kaqchikels. This was not the way of the moon goddess, Awilix. Was this the way of the Mexica? Had they taught this form of sacrifice?

They took us inside. They took us, oh, my sons! inside the great palace of the Cawek family, the Cawek clan. Inside, the K'iché flute player gave us as a gift. He handed us over to the guards of the palace. As he handed us over, this man who had become a jaguar looked down at us. He looked at my white shirt and pants and red woven belt and said, "Tell them you are Kaqchikel royalty. Insist on that, and you will live."

He left. Our captor went back to his drum player. How strange were these K'iché musicians. They became jaguars, capture you, bind you to them, then save you.

Two Cawek guards carrying long lances pointed to the center of the palace. Zorach and I walked slowly to this open plaza. Now we were watched by the court.

At the far end of the plaza was a waterfall. The guards motioned us toward it. As we walked forward we saw slaves on the floor above pouring pot after clay pot of water onto a ledge. The water poured from the ledge in an even flow. That flow of water became the waterfall. After the water splashed onto the floor in front of us, it drained down to an inlaid shallow round pond to the right. Slaves dipped pots into this pond, then ran to the stairs. More slaves carried the pots upstairs to begin the pouring again.

We stood in front of the waterfall. Both of us felt a slap on our backs. We fell to the floor. Zorach hid his face. I looked up. Just beyond the water flowing down in front of us sat a great gold chair. Sitting in the chair, covered with long green quetzal feathers and red jewels, was an old man. He seemed half asleep. His image wavered in the waterfall.

"Bow your head to Three Quej," one of the guards said. I tried to stand up, to tell this ruler that we were also royalty. The guard hit me with his lance. This blow knocked me to the ground. I looked up again. Through the water, I thought I saw this old man smile.

"Tohil," Three Quej ordered.

The guards marched us back to the temple of the sun, to the house of Tohil. We marched past the cylinder shaped K'ucumatz temple. We were marched through the market, so that all could see us. This time everybody watched. We were captives of the House of Cawek now, the first Kaqchikels captured in the war. We were marched to the Tohil temple. This was the temple of sacrifice.

2

A SMALL WHITE BUILDING WITH A THATCHED ROOF stood
next to the great temple. An old man walked slowly out
of this building. His hair was gray, intertwined with black
and white feathers. They marched us to the building and gave us
to this old man, Laughing Falcon. They gave us to the priest who
had already sacrificed once that day. By our slender brown arms
he took us into the building. It was dark and smoky inside the small
room. It smelled of incense. There were others there. Zorach and
I looked around and could see other boys our age in this house of
Laughing Falcon.

"I am Belehé Qat, son of the Ahop Achí Balam and grandson of
King Hunyg," I said with defiance. "This is my cousin Zorach." I
stood small in front of this old priest and told him we were
Kaqchikel royalty.

Laughing Falcon sent us to a corner of his house. He sent us
through the other boys to this corner. As we walked, the boys

played with us. A tall boy named Yellow Deer led the others in their play with us. They hit us and scratched us and pushed us.

When we got to the corner, the K'iché boys stopped and simply looked at us. They stood around us and stared at us. They grew tired. Yellow Deer spat at us and walked away. The others did the same.

Zorach and I whispered to each other.

"Belehé Qat, will you let yourself be sacrificed?" Zorach scratched at his right arm in fear.

"What can we do? These K'iché can sacrifice anybody and anything."

He began to cry. I was angry at him. I did not want the K'iché to see sons of the Kaqchikel cry. We were to be warriors. He would not stop. I looked away from him. I looked out at the room. Smoke drifted through the room. Orange light reflected up from the small candles. I heard the music of the flute and the drum outside. As we waited, he cried.

One of the older boys, almost a K'iché man, grabbed us by our Kaqchikel arms and dragged us to the doorway of the building. We stood in the light, no longer protected by the building and the incense.

In front of us stood twelve chanting K'ichés. In the front of the procession was Laughing Falcon. Now he was dressed in sacredness. He wore many different-colored feathers, pendants of gold, images of the sun.

Yellow Deer told the K'iché boys to hold us, and Laughing Falcon chanted. He finished chanting and there was silence. He pointed to us and cried, "*Wak-ko! Wak-ko!*"

As he screeched, I heard the laughter of the falcon. I felt the falcon in my bones. I saw the falcon gliding in the air, seeing two tiny field mice. He dove down through the air. Laughing Falcon plunged through the sky for the two mice. He screeched and laughed as he descended.

Laughing Falcon screeched, "*Wak-ko! Wak-ko!*" as he snatched these two field mice. He carried them high into the sky, high above the pine trees, high above the mountain gods, high up to the highest peak. He dropped them into his great nest. There they were dropped. There they would stay. They would not fall. They would stay in his nest. Why didn't he eat them? Why didn't he feed them to his young?

The procession marched around our building to the Tohil temple. Zorach was shaking. I told him we were safe. The K'ichés had decided that we were the sons of royalty, that we would not be sacrificed, that we would be trained to be priestly assistants. The call of the Laughing Falcon did this. I did not know this by language. I knew this by the cry of the falcon.

The K'iché flute player had saved our lives.

Zorach kept shaking and scratching at his arm I wondered about these strange men. And I wondered how I could learn so much from the cry of a falcon.

THE PRIESTS BEGAN TO TEACH US the ways of the Tohil temple. They taught us to light the fires. The fires of the temple burned because of us. We lit them and maintained them. Laughing Falcon allowed us to hear the ancient prayers.

"I want to use their own magic against them," Zorach said. "The more we know, the more we will be able to destroy them."

After one week, after thirteen days, we saw soldiers and tribes and villagers coming to the city to assemble, to gather, to destroy our people.

There appeared to be thousands of them, and I trembled for our people. There were hundreds of tents for the officers. Red and blue and green flags flew from poles on the fields outside of K'umarcaaj. Each group had different designs and images. Drum and flute music floated everywhere, interweaving with the smoke from the incense burners.

These were the K'iché that wanted to destroy our people. These were the K'iché that were close to the gods of Tulan.

"We have to join the fight," Zorach said. "We must fight against the K'iché."

"How? I don't know how," I said.

That night and the next and the next, we talked about how to join the fight. Each day there were more sacrifices. Each night there were more heads on the skull rack in front of the temple. We did not want to be sacrificed to their gods, but we had to fight. We had to become child warriors.

We knew in the morning this would be the day that the K'iché and the Kaqchikel would do battle. We knew it would be this day. How did we know? Music played before the sun came up. Not just flutes and drums, but also shells. Many different kinds of shell horns made music.

The boys of our little house stood outside to watch. We stood in front of our little house as the sun, Tohil, swept orange light across the temple. We stood in line and watched the soldiers march to the Cawek Palace. They stood in line and waited. We stood in line and watched.

"Your people will be destroyed on this day," Yellow Deer laughed. Yellow Deer had narrow yellow eyes.

Out of the Palace came the military officers. They joined their men. Each held a shield or a lance or a bow. The lords of K'umar- caaj walked slowly down the stairs of the palace. They were as fierce as anything I had seen at Iximché. Behind the guards were the litter carriers, the litter, and the K'iché king, Three Quej. He was carried on a litter down the steps of his palace. He would lead the K'iché in battle against our people. He was not old on that day.

They formed a procession. The king sat on the litter in the front surrounded by his guards, the lords, the officers, then the soldiers. The musicians were last. They marched toward us.

As they came closer I could see the king more clearly. I could see Three Quej. His crown of gold glistened in the orange sunlight. Light reflected off his body so that we would have to shield our eyes. Flashing crystals covered him.

Zorach and I watched this king who wanted to destroy my father, the Ahop Achí Balam. Who wanted to destroy our grandfather, King Hunyg. Who wanted to destroy our city of Iximché. Zorach and I looked at each other.

In that instant, I knew what to do. It became clear. I told Zorach.

As the procession drew closer, we ran to the skull rack. All eyes were on the king as we stood behind the skull rack in front of the Tohil Temple. Just before the king was to pass in front of us, we pushed at the skull rack. At first it did not move, then it cracked and fell forward.

Nine skulls crashed onto the streets of K'umarcaaj. Nine skulls rolled on the streets of K'umarcaaj. Nine skulls rolled in front of the litter bearers. Nine skulls rolled around the feet of the lords and warriors. The king glanced down at the nine skulls.

The procession marched out of K'umarcaaj.

AFTER YELLOW DEER AND THE OTHER BOYS beat us, Zorach saw his own death.

"When the men come back, we will be sacrificed. Belehé Qat, we will be taken to the sun and we will be killed." Blood ran from the worried scratches on his arm.

"Laughing Falcon has protected us," I said. "We won't be offered to Tohil." I remembered Laughing Falcon's cry.

While we waited for the return of the warriors, we were allowed to walk around their great city, K'umarcaaj. We walked by the houses of the lineages, of the families of the K'iché. We walked by the temples of the K'iché.

We walked by the temple of the teaching room of the girls. The girls laughed and ran. They were happy. They knew their fathers were running through the pine trees with lances and shields. They knew that their fathers were butchering my people. And so they ran and laughed and played.

"Girls are a species apart from us," Zorach said. "They are as different from us as snakes from birds."

"You are wrong," I said.

One girl had a radiant smile. She seemed a little older than me. She smiled and ran. She wore red and blue and green, and she was bolder than the rest. She smiled at me, and one of her front teeth was missing. She smiled and ran. She peeked out from behind their teaching room to show her heart to me again. She was playing a game with me.

She darted away, and I followed. She ran, and I ran, and she ran faster than me. For a moment I thought I would feel humiliated, but then she appeared again and ran from me. I ran after her. She hid. This was the game I played while my parents were at war. This is the game she played while her parents were at war. She ran, and I ran after her. I wanted to play this game forever.

WE HEARD THE DRUMS, OH, MY SONS! We heard the drums outside the city of K'umarcaaj. We heard the drums of the returning soldiers and lords. We heard the drums of the return of the king. We heard the drums, and Zorach and I thought of our people. Would my father come back as a slave? Would our grandfather, King Hunyg, be among the captured?

They returned. There were not as many as had marched out of the city. The women and the children were on the streets of

K'umarcaaj. We were in the plazas of K'umarcaaj. We watched as they entered the city. There were no slaves, and there were no spoils. The drum beat the sound of death, not the sound of celebration. There were tears in the streets of K'umarcaaj. The women cried for the loss of their men and sons. The children cried for the loss of their fathers and brothers.

Zorach rejoiced. He hid his face from the K'iché, but he rejoiced. He was happy with our people. He was pleased with the war. Zorach felt the right way about the return of the K'iché lords and warriors. He stopped scratching.

Since I had smashed my cousin, Zorach, in the face with the pine cone, since I had seen the blood on his face, I could not feel the right way. It was not available to me. I felt many things, but I did not rejoice.

I hid my face in shame.

I looked at the crying in the streets of K'umarcaaj. I looked at the little girl with the tooth missing. I looked at her crying and holding her mother's skirt. I looked at her twisted and fatherless crying face, and I remembered Zorach's cheek. I saw her crying and I did not rejoice. Which of my people had caused this?

Nine skulls had crashed onto the streets of K'umarcaaj. Nine skulls rolled on the streets of K'umarcaaj. Nine skulls rolled in front of the litter bearers. Nine skulls rolled around the feet of the lords and warriors. Three Quej had looked down at the nine skulls.

Could such a thing have caused the despair of K'umarcaaj?

3

THIS IS HOW I BECAME A MAN, MY SONS. This is that story. This is the part about how your father left childhood and grew into what he had to become. We stayed with the K'ichés, oh, my sons! We stayed with the K'iché for many years. We dreamt of our families, we dreamt of our homes, but we could not leave. We were K'iché hostages. For many years we studied and were not sacrificed.

During this time, the artisans worked on rebuilding the spirit of K'umarcaaj. They repainted the murals and images. They repainted the drawings of monkeys and rabbits, night bats and dancing gods.

Zorach said they were painting lies for the people. He chose not to look at the drawings. Zorach learned to be a potter. He said that was closer to the truth. His pottery was like no other in K'umarcaaj. His was of ancient gods playing with their long pottery penises.

One warm K'umarcaaj morning, I watched the K'iché artisans. I wanted to understand not how they did their work, the materials they used. I wanted to understand what their work said. What their work meant. Who were the rabbits and bats they drew on the walls of the temples? Who were the dancing gods?

I entered the teaching temple. I watched the animals and the gods in the flickering light of the teaching hall. Laughing Falcon grabbed my shoulder. In fear I turned to face him.

"Belehé Qat wants to understand our paintings," he said.

"I was just looking."

"What right does a Kaqchikel boy have to look at sacred drawings?"

"I wanted to see."

"Belehé Qat is bold."

With those words I came under the tutelage of Laughing Falcon. He laughed the falcon's cry, "*Wako-ko! Wako-ko!*" I saw who I was, who I was meant to be. I was a small rabbit. Here in the face of Laughing Falcon's cry, his laugh, I had become a small bunny.

I sat cross-legged. I was bent over. What was I doing? I could not see. I wanted to see, not only who I was, but what I was doing. I could not see. Laughing Falcon stopped the falcon's cry. I was left with an image of identity. I was left with the echo of the falcon's laugh, the falcon's cry.

"My little bunny rabbit, my little hopping animal, my little furry creature, you at least know what you are. I have named you, so you know what you are. You know where you are. Do you know what you do? Do you know what the gods have decided that you will do? What is the small rabbit doing?"

I looked at the floor of the small building. I looked down as I should have. I looked down because he was right. I did not know this. This is what I did not know.

"My little bunny hops but does not understand. My little rabbit does not know where he is going. He could fall into a river just like that." He snapped his fingers.

"A coyote could come up and eat him. Then where would the little bunny be? He'd be with the lords of Xibalba, that's where he would be."

I looked up at him. His hair was gray, and he had as many wrinkles as my grandfather. But he was different from my grandfather. My grandfather knew thoroughly of this world. This man knew of other worlds.

"I will someday see," I said defiantly, "I will someday become what I should become. I will become a human being who can see. I will become a rabbit who knows what he is doing."

Laughing Falcon squawked, then stretched his arms out like wings and screeched. In the screech I saw myself as a man. I was a man and I was holding you. I was holding my sons.

I WENT DOWN TO THE BATHING PLACE. I left Laughing Falcon and went to Tohil's Bath. Usually, I would go with Zorach, but on this day I went alone. I left the city and went to the river to think and to understand the rabbit identity that had been given to me. It was late afternoon. We were passing through the summer of the K'ichés. I lay on the sandy bank of the river with my eyes closed. In my eyes I could see the red of the sun, the red of Tohil. This red must be the reason they painted all their sacred buildings red, I thought. Tohil's red.

I heard chatter from across the river. On the other side were two girls from the girl's teaching house. I looked at them, and they did not see me. One of the girls had been the child who had one tooth missing. The girl I had played with when I first came to K'umarcaaj. The girl who had lost her father to our people. We had seen each other through our years at K'umarcaaj. But we could not speak. That was forbidden. With our eyes we had sung and danced together.

This girl who had one tooth missing had become a maiden. She had become a beautiful deer. I watched as they talked and played on the sand by the river. Her friend was small and round and giggled. They threw sand at each other, ran, and laughed. They played, and their rainbow blouses shimmered in the late sun.

In the orange light, they undressed themselves. In the orange light they became naked in front of me. I did not move. I watched as they entered the water.

They splashed each other. The giggling girl saw me. She yelled and ran out of the water. The girl who had had a tooth missing did not leave the water. She smiled. Her laughing friend put her blouse and skirt on, turned to the river, and called, "Xtah!"

Xtah waved her away. The girl on the river bank giggled again, then ran into the trees.

Xtah turned her back to me and stretched her arms up in the air. Her brown back glistened in Tohil's light. She turned, faced me, then smiled as if she were playing our childhood game. I walked, then ran, across the sand. To my great surprise, this time she did not run.

I joined her in the water. In that orange light, on that late afternoon, I became a man. I became a man not just in the sense of the sexual. I became a man because I let the K'iché maiden enter my heart.

She allowed me to forget who I was and to remember who I was going to become.

There in the river and then on the bank, I was no longer Kaqchikel. She was not K'iché. We were neither. We were animals. We were human beings. We were gods.

As we lay on the sand by the river, she told me her name was Xtah. She touched my Kaqchikel skin, touched my Kaqchikel heart. She heard the loss of my family, my people, my city. I heard her loss of her father by my people. In our loss we found each other. We also found that which is inexpressible.

I met this girl whom I had played with, I met Xtah, many times by the river. I went to Tohil's Bath many days. I did not need to be cleansed, and I would still go to the river.

When I met her, when I met Xtah, all the trees of the forest, all the animals of the land, all the birds of the air celebrated us. They were no longer divided up into warring groups: animal versus animal, plants struggling against trees, tribes against tribe. They were at peace, and the meaning of the peace was clear. It was an enlightened peace. It was a peace to celebrate what had been at war.

In the stillness by the river, hummingbirds flew past us, then returned to glorify our love by floating slowly over our bodies. The trees around us joined together to protect us from intruders. Butterflies and ladybugs landed on our bodies giving us blankets. The river sang to us.

I THOUGHT WE WOULD BE KILLED when Laughing Falcon found out about Xtah. I was supposed to be pure in my training, in my education. That is what Yellow Deer told me after he had told Laughing Falcon. He had now become even taller. He was K'iché, through and through.

"I saw you by the river, Belehé Qat," he said. He had never liked Zorach and me because we were Kaqchikel. He especially did not like me because Laughing Falcon loved to tell me stories of the history of our peoples when they were joined as one.

"I told Laughing Falcon about your impurities," he said.

I beat him. I beat him, so that he had one tooth missing. I beat him so hard that he would have been happy to have given his heart to Tohil. In this way he would have had some relief from his pain.

Laughing Falcon called me. I sat in front of his sacred chair. I am not embarrassed to tell you, oh, my sons! that I trembled as I sat there. I saw my Xtah heart being ripped out at the temple. I saw my head on the skull rack. I also saw that it was worth it. How many men have a love that is protected by hummingbirds?

"This has happened before, my young rabbit with a penis pointing to Tohil," he said. "This is not the first time."

I started to protest that I had never made love before, it was not just because of my penis. It was more than that. He waved my mouth shut with his hand.

"It is time Belehé Qat became a man," he said.

Xtah understood. I could see her, but we could not talk. We could not venture near Tohil's Bath. I learned new prayers. I chanted and prayed more than ever before. I began the purification. I fasted. I took enemas. As the holy day approached, I felt lightheaded. I took the sweat baths until I came back to my body. Then I turned my body black with smoke and soot.

Zorach did not encourage me. "This is wrong," he said. "You are Kaqchikel." He thought it was a betrayal of our people to undergo such a ritual at K'umarcaaj. He rubbed his arm where he had, as a young boy, scratched at it.

He was wrong. The ritual was from a time when our peoples were joined. At Iximché I would not have been allowed to enter such a world. My world was supposed to be that of the warrior king. Laughing Falcon knew this.

I shook as I walked to the sacred center of the city. I walked with Laughing Falcon, I walked with Zorach, I walked with three of the K'iché boys who had become my friends. Yellow Deer was not there. It is true that I walked in fear. I walked and I shook. I walked to the temple in the earth. I walked to the goddess of the moon, the underworld, to Xibalba. The ritual to my becoming a man began at the temple of the moon. The temple waited for me. She was pale green. I looked at her. I chanted of Xtah. I chanted of my mother. I chanted of my grandmothers. My grandmother's grandmothers.

We walked up the steps. The first step was the beginning of all things. The next nine were the levels of the Underworld, of Xibalba. The final thirteen were the layers of the heavens. We walked up the steps to my adulthood.

We were greeted with prayers at the top of the pyramid. I glanced over the sides of the temple. The city of K'umarcaaj was beneath us. The city below was beautiful that morning: long narrow streets, palaces and houses of warriors, in the distance green hills and green trees.

As we sang and as we prayed, I wanted to see. I wanted to see the four corners of the world. I wanted to see as the first men had seen. I wanted to see unencumbered. So that I might see, I entered the darkness. We walked into a small room at the top of the temple.

In the blackness there appeared Laughing Falcon, the priest of the Nijaibs. The musicians were also there. The drummer and the flute player played for us. They were no longer jaguars. They had found us so they were responsible for us. Candles were set in the four directions. The musicians played. The beat and my breathing became as one.

Small gourds were brought into this sacred room. Each of us received a gourd. I held the gourd. I listened to the music. I wanted Zorach with me. I drank from the gourd. It was warm corn mash. I drank the sacred maize so that I could see. It was warm and sweet to the taste.

I drank and the musicians played. I put the gourd down on the floor of the dark room. When I put the gourd down, it fell to its side and the corn mash spilled out. It was then I thought my ritual would lead to my death. I had spilled the sacred drink. We were in a temple of sacrifice. I sat in stillness not knowing what to do.

"Spilling the sacred drink will not help you become a man," Laughing Falcon chuckled. He picked up the gourd from the dark floor of the temple. Two of the Nijaib boys cleaned up the mess. Laughing Falcon returned with the gourd. It was full again. You can not measure my gratefulness, oh, my sons!

Laughing Falcon and the priests led me down the steps of the temple. They left the boys by the temple. They led me to the edge of the K'iché city of K'umarcaaj. Chanting, they led me down a narrow path, down the side of the great hill of K'umarcaaj. This was the hill that the city sat upon. I thought of the hill of our Kaqchikel city, Iximché. Through the trees I could see a slight rainbow. We went down. We walked slowly because of the mud.

Laughing Falcon directed that the ritual take place in the tunnels below K'umarcaaj, at the heart of the earth. In the temple, above ground, my ritual would have ended with my Kaqchikel sacrifice.

We walked down to a clearing of rising smoke. Several women stood in a circle with their small children. In the middle of the circle lay a wide round pile of ashes. In the middle of the ashes, a small fire burned copal. In front of this fire circle there was a sooty black cave opening. Laughing Falcon and the priests directed me to enter the cave, to enter the doorway to Xibalba.

I entered.

The cave soon gave way to a carved tunnel barely wide and tall enough for a Kaqchikel boy to get through. I looked back. All was black except the cave opening. In that faint light I saw the orange of the sacred fire, smoke rising, and the K'iché priests chanting and praying.

Candles flickered from tiny indentations lining the rocky walls. I walked, oh, my sons! I walked to face two tunnel paths. Each led off in a different direction. Flowers surrounded candles in the right path. The left path smelled of skunk. I entered the right path.

Bread, flat chocolate, and sugar lined the dark floor of that path. At the end of those offerings was a hole. I peered down. It was dark and deep. I thought of the entrance to Xilbalba. I thought I could see an end to the hole, but perhaps not.

I heard chanting and prayers echoing behind me. In the darkness, in the flickering light, I began to see. As I began to see, I heard Laughing Falcon.

"The little bunny will see. He will see the world as it really is. He will see as the first four men saw. He will see as Jaguar Quitze saw. He will see as Jaguar Night saw. He will see as Mahucutah saw. He will see as True Jaguar saw.

"There will be no limit to his vision. He will see to the four edges. He will see to the four corners of the earth. He will see to the four corners of the sky. This is our request. This is our prayer."

I SAW.

I had entered the cave; I now entered the realm of Xibalba. I fell into the black hole. I was not pushed. I simply fell.

As I fell, thousands of bats attacked me, bats of hell. These were the bats I had seen on the walls of K'umarcaaj. This was my greeting. This was my welcome to Xibalba. I did not see them at first. I only heard them. I heard their screams. I heard their shrieks. In the blackness there was only my travel downward, my descent and the screams of the bats. They became a part of me. I became their scream.

The concerns I had from the beginning of my stay at K'umarcaaj evaporated. I was no longer worried about my family, my mother, my father, my little brother. I was no longer worried about my people at Iximché. I was no longer worried about my betrayal of my people. I was not worried about Zorach. I was no longer thinking of Xtah. This was all gone. There were only the incomprehensible screams of the bats. As they flew at me, screeched at me, I saw their red eye sockets.

At first there were just a few of these empty orbs screaming past. Then there were more. Then thousands. The black shifted slightly to gray. In that light I saw the hideous monsters of Xibalba. Their wing span was immense. There were incomprehensible designs on their wings. Each wore a collar. On the collar was the eyes of the bat. And their noses were knives. Each screaming bat had a snout that was as long as a knife. As they screeched past I could see the sharp edges of their knife noses.

They tried to slice me. They tried to cut me. I was to be carved by the bats of Xibalba.

I descended into the purple light of Xibalba. In that strange light the bats began to halt their pursuit. They grew weary. They seemed afraid of the light. I passed them in my falling, and they quit scratching and stabbing at me. I entered the land of Xibalba. The screams were gone. I entered Xibalba with the memory of the drum and flute from the temple of Awilix.

Laughing Falcon's voice was in me. I heard his voice. It was without words. His voice was my voice, and it encouraged me on. I was encouraged to discover the Underworld, to discover myself.

I fell to the ground. I bounced. It did not hurt. I looked down. I was a rabbit. I twisted my leg around to scratch my long white ears. I hopped onto the beginnings of Xibalba.

I came to a river. I came to the bank of a river that ran red. I looked into the river. The contents were crimson. In the river ran blood. All there was was blood. I found a small wooden boat. I crossed this river, but did not let the red touch me.

I came to a second river. This river flowed yellow and white. This was Pus River. Both Blood River and Pus River were evil. I knew this. Laughing Falcon was telling me this. I crossed Pus River on a small wooden boat.

I hopped out of the boat to the rocky bank. Here were four

roads. One was black, one red, one white, one yellow. I sat at the crossroads. I looked at the directions.

"I am your road," the black road called out. "I am the road you will take. You will walk me, and you will find what you are looking for. I am the road of the lords. I am your road."

I stood in front of the black road. Laughing Falcon squawked. I stepped onto black road. I hopped into Xibalba.

4

AS I SCAMPERED ALONG THE BLACK ROAD, four owls circled in the air above me. They circled in the gray light watching me. I saw them and kept hopping.

The four owls landed on the blue rocks by the road. One owl had piercing talons. One owl had only one leg. One owl had a red back. And one owl had a head and wings but no legs.

The owls spoke to me. "We bring a message from the lords of Xibalba. We bring a message from One and Seven Death, from House Corner and Blood Gatherer, from Pus Master and Jaundice Master, from Bone Scepter and Skull Scepter, and from Trash Master and Stab Master. The message from these, our lords, is that they welcome you to Xibalba. We would like you to follow the road to our judgment palace."

This was the message given to me from the owls. This was the message from the lords of Xibalba.

I declined.

The four owls swooped down on me and, with their talons, picked up this rabbit, flew this tiny rabbit through the air, through the night air of the Underworld. They dropped me through the roofless judgment hall of Xibalba.

I fell onto the black marble floor. I scrambled to my haunches and scratched my ears. The lords of the judgment hall looked down at me.

They sat in ascending rows. Each was monstrous: purple and green skin, protruding bones, and bloody blisters. Each rattled his bones and sang, each carried on with wild screams and confusion. They laughed and stank of sulfur. Each of the lords sat in a chair made of green jade tied together with black hair. I heard Laughing Falcon's voice introducing each to me: Blood Gatherer and House Corner, Pus Master and Jaundice Master, Bone Scepter and Skull Scepter, Trash Master and Stab Master. They sat in rows of judgment. They were to be entertained before they judged.

Huge fireflies flew slowly back and forth carrying torches, lighting the hall.

An enormous red dog trotted out onto the floor. He carried his own decapitated head in his paws. He threw the head into the air. His red hairy body twisted around to catch it. He missed catching his head. It fell to the floor and rolled to me.

I kicked it back to him.

This headless red dog rolled his head to his back haunches. He turned and picked up his head as the lords screamed and hissed. This red headless dog retreated from the hall holding his head as the lords threw flaming garbage at him. He left the hall with his fur on fire. Tortured cries came from the dog head he carried.

A great mosquito slowly walked out to the judgment spot in front of the lords. He wore a headdress of orange and purple feathers. He stopped in front of the lords, stood very still, then made grotesque slurping noises. He bowed and walked away. Blood dripped from his anus.

The lords cheered and laughed and rattled their chairs.

I, the bunny, wanted to flee the judgment chaos, but I only twitched.

A god walked out to the center of the hall. His skin glistened brown. He was a strong and beautiful man. From somewhere in me, I heard Laughing Falcon's voice: "This is Hunahpú."

The god Hunahpú turned his back on the lords. He turned to me. He smiled at me. His face was thin, with high cheekbones. His hair was pulled back, tight, in the ancient way. He wore a black loin cloth. He moved his hands in delicate ways, rhythmically, making circles with his fingers, moving his hands like ripples in the rivers, leaves in the wind. On each finger was a turquoise and silver ring. He danced with his whole thin body.

The dance was fine, and smooth, and graceful. Feline. His skin changed from deep brown to gold. The color pulsated— bright, dark, and bright. He turned, gracefully turned, again and again. He leapt into the air, then floated to the floor. As he danced, each muscle of his long body stretched and defined itself.

I rested my furry chin in my paws and watched, enchanted.

Two of the lords descended from their chairs. Each wore robes of bloody jaguar skin, and a mask of jaguar paws and tails and noses.

They grabbed him, pushed him to the ground, made him squat on the judgment hall floor. They held him down. They pushed his head down, too. They held him. They hacked at his head with an ax until blood spurted out and spread on the white floor. His head came off. The lords of Xibalba cheered.

How could they do this to a god, my sons!

One executioner lord dragged his beautiful body out of the palace. The other kicked his head toward the doors of the hall. The lords cried and cheered and laughed.

The head of Hunahpú rolled out of the hall. As it rolled, it chanted, "The sacred. The sacred. The sacred."

It was my turn, oh, my sons! How did I know it was my turn? It was my turn because the owls lifted me, my bunny self, from my place by the wall and dropped me on the judgment floor in front of the lords. I looked up and saw two bleached white men standing at each side of the rows of the lords. These bleached men stood on stilts. They carried long horns. They played a noise, a racket, that echoed through the hall.

Sitting on tall chairs above rows of the lords were two skeletal men. They looked like men, but they also looked like bones. They were the leaders of Xibalba. They were One and Seven Death. They smoked cigars.

"Dinner," said One Death.

"Stew," said Seven Death.

"Wait," I said. "I am a human being."

They laughed. "Human?" cried One Death.

"You are hardly a rabbit," said Seven Death.

"I am," I said, "a human being." The lords on the rows below them laughed. They knocked their bones against each other. The horrible sounds of the knocking echoed around the hall.

"You are like the beings the gods made when they first tried to make humans," said One Death. "They could not name the gods. All they did was squawk. Is this the way to name the names of the gods?"

I sat and looked at him. My nose twitched.

"They did not name the names or keep the days of the gods. The gods made them beasts and let their home be in the trees. You are no more than that," Seven Death said. "You did not keep our names."

"I am more than that," I said. The hall floor glistened white except for the pool of the god's blood. The walls and columns were as black as oil. The yellow light from the fireflies moved the shadows back and forth across the floor. I smelled the copal from above.

"You are no more than the gods' second try at creating humans," One Death said, blowing smoke and fiery sparks at me from his cigar. "This was a being made of earth and mud. It made no sense. Its body was all twisted around and dissolved in the rain. So we made them only a thought. You are merely thinking. That is all you are. You are no more than that. You are mud."

"I am more than that." The lords laughed. They spat blood at each other.

"Then you must be one of the wood men," Seven Death said sarcastically. "There was nothing in their hearts and nothing in their minds. They just went and walked wherever they wanted. They took whatever they wanted. They thought they were free from the gods." The lords shook their heads. "You are wood."

"The animals destroyed them," he said looking at the smoke and sparks from his cigar. "Their eyes were gouged, their heads were snapped off. Their flesh was torn open. Their cooking pots and tortilla griddles insulted them, then destroyed them. The earth was blackened because of this. The black rainstorms began, black rain all day, black rain all night. That is who you are. You are no more than that."

"I am more than that," I said. "I am human, and my children will be human, and their children will be human." These are you, oh, my sons!

The lords were quiet now.

"I don't know if you are more than that," said One Death. "If you are more than that, then you are human. You are a human being."

"I am a human being," I insisted.

"If you are a human being, you are descended from Jaguar Quitze, from Jaguar Night, from Mahucutah, from True Jaguar," they chanted. "You are their descendant."

"I must be, because I am human."

"If you are human, we should destroy and eat you anyway," they howled and laughed. The lords below them cheered. They clapped their bones against their chairs.

"The humans do not keep the days of the calendar," One Death said, shaking his head.

"They do not pay homage to us. They have nothing in their hearts, they have nothing in their minds," Seven Death nodded.

"We shall cook you and eat you," they chanted together. "And then we shall have the cooking pots and tortilla griddles attack the humans, and there shall be another great black rain that will wipe you from the face of the earth."

I saw Xtah, and I saw Zorach, and I saw my fathers and my mothers and my little brother and all the cities of the human beings facing the attacks of the black storms.

"I will warn them. I will tell them," I said, scratching my ears again with my hind leg.

One Death laughed so hard his bones rattled. "You cannot even hold your paw to your nose. How do you suppose you can warn the humans?"

"If I show you, will you free me?"

Seven Death blew more smoke and sparks. "Why not, you rodent with long ears."

"Why not, you ridiculous vermin," Seven Death said.

I hopped, oh, my sons! I scampered to the pool of blood of the god, Hunahpú. I did this to save you, so that you could exist. I plunged my paw into his blood. My rabbit paw became red in the god's blood.

I sat again in front of One Death and in front of Seven Death. I held my red paw up to them. The lords' laughter echoed through the hall.

"The little rodent stepped into a blood bath," One Death said.

"I can warn the humans," I said. They blew sulfur smoke into my fur.

On the floor of the great hall, I drew. I put my paw on the white marble floor and drew red pictures. On that floor I wrote. I drew the magnificent Hunahpú being sacrificed. I drew humans ignoring the calendar. I drew pots and griddles attacking them. I drew a great black storm destroying them.

One Death and Seven Death were astonished. The lords were astonished.

"Now we have to let him go," said One Death.

"Now he can escape," said Seven Death. "You have written what has been secret, you have proclaimed what can not be proclaimed."

"Yes," I said as I hopped, then ran out of the palace. I ran with two human legs up from the abyss, up through the cavern, out from the black cave, out to the sacred copal smoke and to Laughing Falcon.

A HUMAN BEING AGAIN, I STOOD facing him, facing my teacher, facing Laughing Falcon. In the clearing in front of the cave, in front of the entrance to Xibalba, I was a man now. There, under the heavens and above Xibalba, Laughing Falcon placed a silver chain over my head. Hanging from the chain was a gold image, a gold pendant. I recognized it. I knew it. I held it in my human hands. This was the profile of a head made of gold. His fine hair was pulled back in the old way. He had high cheekbones.

"You have earned the golden head of Hunahpú," Laughing Falcon said. "You have earned the gods' respect. Now you may dance your own dance, you may write your own story."

5

AS A YOUNG MAN I HAD WORKED to accept the rabbit, to accept that spirit. But neither a man nor an animal could prevent the destruction of the K'iché. As a man and as a rabbit, I witnessed the destruction of K'umarcaaj.

"They have invaded our lands," came the cry from the K'iché spies. They told the boys in the building by the temple. They told the young men preparing to become priests in the secret room of the temple. They told the women at the market.

"They have arrived at Xepit and Xetulul."

"They went around the mountains. They came along the water."

"They've brought with them warriors from Mexicu. We could see Tlaxalan, Cholultec, and Mexica soldiers. There were 400 of them."

"There were 120 soldiers of Quetzalcoatl. These gods have light skin."

"We could see 135 men riding on beasts. They are not one

monster as some have said, but men sitting on top of monsters."

"The beasts pulled four metal things. We could not understand what these things were to be used for. These gods value them. They guard them at night."

"This is all we could see."

Fright was in the face of children. Fright was in the face of the old men. Warriors were everywhere, building, practicing.

Rumors rumbled through the marketplace. The gods were going to cause an earthquake that would destroy K'umarcaaj. The gods were marching against the K'iché because of misdeeds of the women. These men with white skin were really Kaqchikels in disguise. There was despair and panic in the market. There was little hope.

I had now entered the third rank of training to be a priest. Zorach spent his time making penis pottery and sleeping with the young men of the warrior class.

A new rumor swept the market. All was hope and salvation. The ruler of Xelaju was going to join the K'iché in the battle.

Tecún Umán was the most powerful warrior-captain in all the lands. He possessed magic, he had military cunning, and he commanded total loyalty. This was the captain of the Tzijbachaj, the fiercest of all the tribes of the K'iché. This was the captain who would save K'umarcaaj from the god Quetzalcoatl. The people waited for his arrival into K'umarcaaj.

Three spies returned from the pale gods. They had been captured. To their surprise, they had not been killed instantly. To their surprise, the god Quetzalcoatl was not there. The leader was an emissary from Quetzalcoatl. This god was huge, with light hair and a red beard. His bright face was like the sun. The Tlaxalans called him Tunatiuh. This was their name for the sun. He was Tunatiuh Avilantaro. Now, oh, my sons! I know him to be the assassin and criminal, Pedro de Alvarado. But then, we called him Tunatiuh Avilantaro.

These spies came back with a message for the rulers of K'u-marcaaj. The message was the demand to surrender. A demand to accept the religion and rule of Tunatiuh. No message was sent back. There was no response. K'umarcaaj would not answer the gods.

The next day, Tecún Umán came to K'umarcaaj. Fear was washed from the face of the children. The rushing and swirling stopped. The people looked at Tecún Umán. His arrival gave the people hope. His arrival gave the people a vision of defense and victory.

I stood with the other apprentice priests half way up Tohil's pyramid and waited for his entrance. Next to me was my Poko-mam slave. He smiled and giggled and jumped up and down. He was young. We waited as Tecún Umán completed his purification rites at the gates of the city.

As we waited I looked up, beyond the palaces and the temples. I looked up into the ice blue. There were no clouds, there was only the winter chill. I looked up at the sun. I looked at Tohil. I looked up and felt sad.

At the base of the temple, the skull rack was full. Celebrating Tecún Umán's arrival, the priests had sacrificed many slaves the day before. Above me and my Pokomam slave, the priests stood in their gold and silver raiment. They were the closest to the sun. They waited for Tecún Umán.

On the steps of the palaces, the noblemen stood with their en-tourage. Xtah's new husband, the nobleman Nine T'zi, waited on the steps of the Cawek palace. Nine T'zi was proud. He looked out at the crowds waiting for Tecún Umán and he was proud of his people. His was the face of confidence. Even from the pyramid I could see his sharp nose and fast eyes. He was covered with golden vestments.

I looked and I waited. I stood in that cold morning and thought of Xtah. I loved Xtah. She was K'iché, and she was married to Nine T'zi. K'iché must marry K'iché, and Kaqchikels must look on in pain.

She stood in the great doorway of the Cawek palace. She stood with three other wives of the nobles. She was pregnant. Nine T'zi was going to have an heir. I turned from her and looked at the crowds waiting for Tecún Umán.

Tecún Umán entered the city of K'umarcaaj. He came with a great many soldiers. He had brought with him warriors from all the tribes that paid homage to K'umarcaaj. He brought warriors from surrounding tribes. These men brought weapons of all kinds. Slings, bows and arrows, spears were held high as the soldiers marched into the city of K'umarcaaj. There were many thousands of them.

As they held their weapons up to the sky, the musicians played their drums and flutes. The conch sang from the steps of the temple. Tecún Umán was held high by his bearers. This was the captain who would protect the city. This was the captain who had military and spiritual power. He was dressed in long white and red feathers as he entered K'umarcaaj. He screeched as an eagle. The cry entered into my flesh and resided in my bones. He was magnificent, oh, my sons!

Tecún Umán was the manifestation of his eagle spirit. I remembered I had forgotten my own spirit. Who was I, a lowly rabbit, to fall in love with the wife of a K'iché nobleman? I remembered who I was. I was a small creature eagles could kill without thinking. All I could do was to write and to draw, to translate the world of the gods into the world of human beings. Could telling a story stop our destruction? Could anything?

They carried him to the steps of Tohil, they carried him to the steps of the temple. There he was greeted by the temple priests. They were led by Laughing Falcon. The music stopped.

"You are Tecún Umán," Laughing Falcon said. "You are a Nima Rajpop Achí. You are the grandson of an Ahop."

Priests walked down the steps of the temple and surrounded Tecún Umán. They chanted prayers at him. They swung jars of smoky incense.

Laughing Falcon continued chanting, "You are the spirit of an eagle. You are the one among us who can fly to the sky. You are our bridge to the gods. You are the great warrior who has vanquished enemies of K'umarcaaj, has vanquished enemies of the K'iché. You are now called upon to vanquish our enemies again. You are called upon to vanquish enemies who are gods. Only gods can vanquish gods. Are you able to accept this charge?"

Tecún Umán raised his long, feather-draped arms and screeched. This scream was not like any lowly bird. It was greater than a falcon. This was the screech of an eagle.

"Go and show yourself to the people."

The people carried him through the streets of K'umarcaaj. Every family group cheered the savior of K'umarcaaj. Lords and slaves, old and young, priests and musicians all waved and cried as the litter bearers brought him through the streets.

As the crowds left I saw Xtah turn from the plaza and walk into the palace. I walked to its wide steps. The guards stopped me with their spears.

EACH DAY, FOR SEVEN DAYS, TECÚN UMÁN came to the steps of the temple of Tohil. Each day Laughing Falcon chanted and prayed to him. Each day the people of K'umarcaaj gathered their spirits together in hope. Each day there were more sacrifices to Tohil.

The day Tecún Umán left the city was a day of magic. Priests and musicians and magicians covered the open squares. Music beat through the smoky incense as the crowds of K'iché circled the temples. Every god was called upon. Sacrifices were made to Tohil, Awilix, and K'ucumatz. There were eagle dances on each of the dance platforms. The ball games never stopped.

At each Big House, at each palace, mushrooms were given to the nobles and priests. There were sacred enemas, fasting, and blood letting. Thorny strands of rope were pulled through ears, tongues, and penises. The blood was caught by the priests and carried to the peak of the temples, then dripped onto sacred fire.

Long green quetzal feathers covered Tecún Umán. The litter bearers carried him to the base of the Tohil temple. He seemed to fly off the litter and light at the steps of the temple.

Laughing Falcon walked down the steps with all the other priests of Tohil. He stopped three steps above Tecún Umán, then placed a gold crown on Tecún Umán's head. Laughing Falcon placed a large emerald, glistening green in the sun on his chest. Tecún Umán did not bow before Laughing Falcon, but instead kept his eyes fastened on the peak of the temple. Another emerald was placed on his forehead, and another on his back. They were magnificent green mirrors.

Tecún Umán spread his wings and screeched. He walked, almost floated, up the steps of the temple. First he swept to the right, then the left. As he rose, he moved his wings like an eagle. The screech echoed throughout the city. The people danced and sang.

"Tecún Umán flies," cried one of the lords standing at the front of the Palace of the Caweks.

"He flies like an eagle," came another cry.

"He is an eagle."

"He is a great chief."

"He is a great animal spirit."

"He flies."

"Tecún Umán flies."

"TECÚN UMÁN IS DEAD,"YELLOW DEER SAID. He shook me awake. It was early morning of the ninth day after Tecún Umán had left. "Runners have returned to us. Your Kaqchikel joined with Tunatiuh. Together they have killed Tecún Umán. Tunatiuh is coming here, coming now to destroy K'umarcaaj. Belehé Qat, you will not be here to see our destruction."

Behind him stood the guard of the Caweks. Behind him stood five soldiers and Zorach. He was held captive by the guard. His eyes were wild.

"The apprentice priest must offer himself to Tohil."

They took us through the streets to the temple. My young Pokomam slave cried. Red fires burned on the steps leading up to the sacrifice alter. Again, I felt fear, my sons. But my greatest sadness was that my Kaqchikel people had joined the attack on my K'iché people.

Incantations were read, and incense was burned. We walked up the steps to the sacrifice altar. I tried to speak with Zorach. He had been fed the drink of the gods. He was delirious.

"Kiss me," he said to the younger of his Cawek guards. They restrained him.

Yellow Deer stood with the obsidian knife in his right hand. His tallness had led him to be bent over. His tooth was still missing.

"I am not who I seem," I said to him.

"None of us is," he said.

"I don't serve Tohil. I serve Awilix. I am of the moon, not the sun."

"You must be a woman, then."

"I am not a woman, but I am Kaqchikel. I cannot be sacrificed to the sun. I cannot be sacrificed to the day."

He held the obsidian and peered closely at me. I looked out at the city of K'umarcaaj. Orange and red torches burnt at all the temples. The glow reflected off the Big Houses and Palaces. I saw the paintings of Xibalba in the morning light.

An older priest came from the temple coverings. In my relief, I saw that it was Laughing Falcon.

"Hold the torch here, by their faces," he told Yellow Deer. He looked at my Pokomam slave. He nodded. He looked at Zorach. My cousin's eyes were wide and blank. The great bird priest laughed and shook his head.

Laughing Falcon turned to me, looking closely in the torch-light. He put his aged hands on my shoulders. He turned me around so that I faced the city morning. I felt his warm hands on my shoulders.

"This is the last time," he said. There was a tremendous kick to my rear. I fell and rolled down the steps of the temple of Tohil. At the bottom of the steps, I was bloody and hurt, but also laughing. Zorach crashed down and landed next to me.

My Pokomam slave did not follow.

THE PEOPLE OF K'UMARCAAJ GATHERED in the plaza underneath the temple of Tohil. That morning they gathered to talk and to understand. The red sun glowed, but we were covered in shadow.

"Tunatiuh has destroyed our nation," one K'iché said. Others joined in.

"He has killed Tecún Umán."

"Now there is no hope."

"We should never have left Tulan, we should never have left the place of the reeds."

"The gods are nearing the gates of K'umarcaaj."

Eight bloody K'iché warriors stood in the middle of the crowd.

Each cried. Each sang. Each told this story. This is the story of what happened to the K'iché savior:

"WE CARRIED OUR GREAT CAPTAIN, TECÚN UMÁN, on a litter into the fight. All around him were the feathered and beaded tribes of our land." The small K'iché warrior was speaking with sadness. He had a long red gash on his chest. He looked at me.

"All except the Kaqchikel."

He paused as the others in the crowd looked at me also.

"They were with Tunatiuh. All the lineages, the families, the priests, the musicians, the royalty, the slaves, the banner carriers, the magicians, the spokesmen, and the lords, all were there to drive out the unwelcome god.

"We gathered on a wide plane filled now with corn and green grasses. Hills rose straight up at one end of the flat valley. On the other side, tall volcanoes rose to the white clouds. The great white bulging clouds watched us gather. The bird that cleans the world floated above the plain and below the clouds. Wisps of smoke from the few houses of our people floated in the blue air. There were no Mam there. The vanquished Mam had retreated to Zaculeau after we defeated them a century ago. In the distance, close to the volcanoes, were the sacred temples of our second great city, Xela-juj.

"The Castilian invaders were on the left, fully armed and ready for battle. Their metal breast plates and spear tips reflected flashes of light from the sun. They stood in formation looking at their enemy, looking for Tecún Umán. Their monstrous deer stood at the ready, their heads covered with metal. Their dogs snarled. Their red and yellow flags waved above the green grass."

The fat warrior with one eye spoke next. "In front of the Spanish were the Tlacalans, the tribe that had sided against the Mexica, against the Aztecs. They were naked, dressed only in red and blue paint, carrying spears and carved clubs. They challenged us in the traditional manner.

"The strongest, most powerful, and most magical of our K'iché warriors returned the yelling threats from the Tlacalans. Our warriors dressed in the form of each clan—eagles, jaguars, scorpions, howling monkeys.

"Yells and cries echoed up the sides of the mountains. The Tlacalans and our warriors rushed toward each other, shouting, and swinging spears and clubs. The Castilians did not move, though their deer monsters whinnied and wanted to run forward. The battle was short. There was a gun shot from the Castilians. The Tlacalans stopped fighting. To the utter amazement of our warriors, the Tlacalans turned and fled. At first we did not follow. We watched in case it was a trick.

"The coward Tlacalans ran back toward the Castilians, through those lines, then toward the towering hills. Suddenly the Castilians turned their horses and cannon and flags away from us and joined the fleeing Tlacalans. We saw we had defeated the tribe who had beaten the Mexica. The white invaders had seen our ferocity. They had become frightened. In fear they ran.

"We cheered and set off in chase. Not only would we defeat the invaders, but we would also teach them a lesson so that they would never return. We ran after them.

"The Tlacalans ran toward the wall of hills. The Castilians were a short distance behind, horses, flags, cannon, everything, also running in full retreat. We had given up our single-line battle formation. We ran after the fleeing invaders.

"There is a small river, almost a stream, at the base of the hills. A man or a horse can easily ford it by wading through. We knew the stream. We knew the end would come for the Castilians there. They would be slowed by their deer monsters and equipment."

The short warrior took a breath, then spoke again. "Another

shot fired as the Tlacalans came to the stream. They stopped. We ran toward them, now gaining on the enemy. The Castilians stopped and turned. It happened quickly. We did not realize what happened. We continued to run at the Castilians. But they had turned and were running their deer monsters directly at us. We were out of breath, out of formation.

"The deer monsters ran through our warriors, trampling many. Castilian rifles decimated the rest, and the Castilian cannon destroyed our rear troops. We were wounded. We thought the battle over, but the Castilians war differently from us. Our wounded were speared through the chest or pushed toward the merciless Tlacalans.

"Tecún Umán walked out to confront the Castilians. He cried out to Tunatiuh, 'Why do you kill our wounded? Why do you kill us by the thousands? Is this the way you war? Fight me, fight just me.'

"Tunatiuh sat on his white deer monster. His spear was as blood red as his beard. His men parted the way as his deer monster walked to Tecún Umán. We pleaded with Tecún Umán not to fight Tunatiuh. A warrior chief, when his men have fought valiantly, has no choice.

"All was silent as Tecún Umán looked up at Tunatiuh on his deer monster. He pointed his silver spear to the ground, showing Tunatiuh that they would fight on the ground, facing each other as equals, as equal gods. Tunatiuh motioned to one of his men. The man handed him a long stick. Tunatiuh pointed the stick at our warrior god. The end of the stick exploded. A loud crack echoed through the valley of Olintepeque. Tecún Umán fell. He was dead. He died in the valley of Olintepeque.

"A Quetzal had flown above the war, above our heads. The Quetzal died the instant Tecún Umán died. The sacred green bird fell from the sky, fell onto the bloody body of Tecún Umán. The blood of Tecún Umán touched the bird. The Quetzal came back to life. As she flew away, the blood of Tecún Umán stayed on her breast. All the Quetzals I have seen returning to K'umarcaaj have the same red breasts. This was the magic of our dead warrior god, Tecún Umán.

"We stood and stared, we did not know what to do. We were butchered. They destroyed us with their fire bombs and exploding rocks. None of Tunatiuh's men perished. None died. The blood of our people flowed."

Another, taller, warrior spoke. "Our people ran. They had seen the destruction of Captain Tecún Umán. They had seen that his spells did not work on these gods. So they ran. Tunatiuh, seeing them run, attacked them again. He said they had to die also. Tunatiuh's men attacked and attacked, killing all except a few like us. He captured and tortured many.

"All he wanted, he said, was gold. The captured soldiers told him the gold was in K'umarcaaj. Tunatiuh released these captives. He gave them birds and eggs to eat so they would have the strength to come here, come to K'umarcaaj."

The short warrior ended the story. "They used us as messengers. The message they sent us to give to this sacred city is this— K'umarcaaj must accept the rule of Tunatiuh, his king, and the one true god, Jesus Christ."

6

WE WAITED FOR TUNATIUH AND HIS ENTRANCE into K'u-marcaaj. There were few preparations that had to be made. There was no need for sacrifices. There was no need for rituals. All we could do was to wait.

Oh, my sons! Tunatiuh sent his horsemen to guard the entrances of the city. K'umarcaaj was closed off and surrounded.

"He is planning to destroy us," Zorach said.

"He is afraid of K'umarcaaj," I said. "He is afraid he will be trapped within the walls of the city."

A messenger came from the Spanish. A Mexicu runner came up the causeway to the palace and was admitted to meet with the king and the nobles. Zorach and I saw him enter the city, and we saw him admitted into the palace by Nine T'zi.

That evening I was ordered to present myself at the palace. I thought again that this might be the time of sacrifice. Inside the green chambers, Nine T'zi spoke to me. He was a man of dignity.

This I could see in his still dark eyes when he spoke. He looked into my spirit. In that moment, I lost my jealousy. In that moment, I knew Xtah had found the right father for her child.

"You are Kaqchikel," he said. "You are of their royalty. We will never be able to prevent our destruction unless the Kaqchikel are united with us."

"It has been many years since I was at the courts of Iximché," I said.

"You are Kaqchikel. We followed the great river from the east as one people."

I nodded. He had both kind and warrior eyes. This was no Yellow Deer.

"Tunatiuh has camped outside of the city," he said. "He has sent us many gifts of feathers and jewels to make up for our losses. Tunatiuh wants us to meet with him at his council. We are to bring our nobles and our king, Three Quej. He wants to make an alliance with us. He promised all will be safe."

"Never in our two histories," I said, "has anyone insisted on meeting with a holy leader outside city walls."

"We do not have a choice," Nine T'zi answered. "Tonight we shall prepare a delegation. We will meet him in the morning. You will join us. It is now that we need your people."

The night in K'umarcaaj was cold and still. It could never be as cold as Iximché. The Kaqchikel home was much higher in the mountains. As I walked through the night, I thought of how close these people were to Tulan. In fact, we had all descended from Tulan, we were all their offshoot.

I walked to the causeway. The guard motioned me away with his spear. I turned and walked to the temple of Tohil.

Laughing Falcon.

He sat at the top steps of the temple. I walked up the stairs and sat next to him. He looked out over the city.

"What has happened?"

He did not look at me. "We had no prediction of this. The Mexicu talked about the return of gods. Their disaster made sense. Ours does not. We have looked at our calendar. We have chanted and prayed and experienced the stories. There was no indication that the gods would return. There was no idea of an escape from Xibalba."

We were silent. Below us the lords of K'umarcaaj were getting ready for the procession to Tunatiuh. A large orange moon colored the city.

"We have come from the east, and now we will join the moon in the west. We shall disappear like the moon. If they are gods, we shall all perish. If they are men, who knows?"

The thought that these creatures might be men had not occurred to me. "How could they be men?"

"How do we know they are gods? They might be the children of the men of wood. They might even have survived the black rain. Who knows?"

IN THE EARLY MORNING, WE LEFT TO MEET TUNATIUH. Leading the procession was Three Quej. He was carried on the royal litter by six holy men. His light-gray hair mixed freely with the green feathers that adorned him. He was followed by Nine T'zi and the other members of the council. Their adult children walked behind. I, and the other foreign dignitaries, followed. Behind us were the servants and slaves. The priests stood on the temples and watched us leave. Zorach stood by the skull rack.

There were no holy men or warriors with us. There were no musicians. The group was silent and unprotected. I could understand why there were no holy men—they had been disgraced by the defeat of Tecún Umán. But to bring Three Quej out of the city without war soldiers assumed a great trust in the word of these gods. Perhaps men.

Soon, after we left the causeway, we came to the K'iché town of Atalaya. The town people stood by the road, crying, and watched us pass. We came to the plain. The land was flat and covered with trees. In the distance I could see the men of Tunatiuh. He had brought many warriors with him.

As they approached, our procession stopped. The holy men did not lower the litter of Three Quej. He was held high to greet these gods. I stood on my toes to see Tunatiuh. Quickly, seemingly out of nowhere, screaming feathered Mexicu warriors ran at us, ran in full battle cry. They came directly at the litter of Three Quej. We ran to protect Three Quej. What else could we do?

The beasts, the monster deer, came. Each was huge and strong and appeared to be both beast and man. They ran at us with all the fury of Xibalba. The Mexicu warriors stopped their furious run and made a circle around us. Using their spears they threatened us if we tried to move. The deer monsters galloped around the circle. They were far more frightening than the warriors. All the Mexicu warriors could offer was death. The monsters offered an immediate journey to Xibalba. We relented.

They tied us. They yanked Three Quej off his litter and threw him to the ground. His green feathers and jewels were strewn on the ground. There they tied him as if he were an animal. The Mexicu were everywhere, tying and kicking and screaming at us. Around us rode the monster deer.

As I cursed the K'iché for not bringing their warriors with them, arrows began to fly through the air. The K'iché had planned on the possibility of betrayal. Their warriors were in the hills, in the ravines, behind the trees. They were everywhere at once. Several of the Mexicu fell. The men on the deer beasts ran after the warriors.

My hope quickly vanished. There were no more arrows. The

K'iché warriors retreated.

We marched toward the camp of Tunatiuh. Along the way there were K'iché attacks, then the K'iché warriors would disappear. As we walked through a small valley, the warriors rolled large boulders off the face of cliffs. One crushed a white god companion of Tunatiuh. I remembered a small mouse I had crushed as a boy in Iximché, his red intestines spread out from his belly. I smiled. Maybe these gods were really the sons of the wooden men. Maybe they had escaped the black rain. Next their beasts might attack them. Then their pots and pans.

We entered their camp. The faces of these gods were full of pride and security. They left us on the ground tied with rope. They beat the K'iché. They beat Nine T'zi. The Spanish grabbed at his long hair and hit him in the face and screamed at him. They did this because he would not look at them. Throughout the day we lay on the ground where they kicked and laughed at us.

As the sun turned orange, we were tied to poles.

This was the beginning of the trial. This was the examination of the lords of K'umarcaaj by the Spanish. This was the trial of Three Quej, the holy king of the K'iché. His most important aide, Xtah's husband, Nine T'zi, was tried. The lesser nobles and lords of K'umarcaaj stood in trial. There was terror in the faces of the royalty. This was my trial also.

It was then, oh, my sons! that I met Tunatiuh Avilantaro, I met Captain Pedro de Alvarado. I met the leader of the Spanish, the representative of their king and of Jesus Christ. Surrounded by his men, his gods, Tunatiuh read the charges. He read from a paper to the king and the nobles who were tied to poles under the trees. A short Mexicu woman walked next to him, translating everything he said.

"You men are Indians," Tunatiuh said. "You have ordered a war against Pedro de Alvarado, against His Grace Hernán Cortez, against the King, and against Jesus Christ." Tunatiuh had strange white skin and blue eyes. He twisted his red beard as his blue eyes looked everywhere at once. He was tall.

None of us knew who this Jesus Christ was. In their dignity, and in their terror, all the lords denied they had ordered any war on the Spanish.

"You have plotted to bring the Spanish into your city and during the night to burn us there," Tunatiuh said to the nobles, said to the king, said to me.

The lords of K'umarcaaj denied this.

"Where is the gold?" Tunatiuh paced in front of us. The ropes burned my wrists in my struggle with them. Tunatiuh yelled at us, and his men brought twigs and branches and leaves to the poles, brought them to our feet, lay them on the ground around our legs.

Tunatiuh screamed for gold at each pole. Each time the Mexicu woman translated. He walked from king to lord to noble to man and yelled for gold. I could not understand why the Spanish wanted glitter.

Tunatiuh's men lit a fire in front of us. They put long metal irons in the fire. Tunatiuh lifted out a smoky white tipped iron from the fire and walked over to Nine T'zi.

"Gold, you bastard Indian," Tunatiuh yelled. He drove the iron into the face of Nine T'zi, on the face of Xtah's husband.

I turned from Nine T'zi. I could not look into the eyes of this K'iché noble, of Xtah's husband, of Xtah's child's father. But I could not stop myself from smelling his burning flesh.

Nine T'zi said nothing. He did not cry out. He was the only K'iché who showed no terror. I felt great sorrow for Xtah.

Tunatiuh stood in front of me. He held the iron in his hand, and I saw blackened flesh smoking from it. I turned my face from him and looked at Nine T'zi. He had slumped down in his ropes. His eyes were closed, but he was breathing. The right side of his face including the eye was now curdled black and red flesh.

I looked back at Tunatiuh.

"Gold," he cried again, as he held the iron to my face.

There was fear in my heart, my sons. But there was also surprise. My surprise was that the awful smell of this god overcame the smell of Nine T'zi's flesh, overcame the smell of the iron, overcame the smell of my fear. His smell was that of the sick and unwashed. His was as an animal that never bathes, repugnant.

Tunatiuh looked down at my chest and smiled. Even his breath smelled of Xibalba.

He stank.

He looked down at my chest and saw the golden medallion of Hunahpú. Tunatiuh looked at the golden head and struck his hand through my robes, through my feathers, and grabbed the golden amulet. He yanked the golden head of Hunahpú from the silver chain that held it to my breast. The back of my neck stung from the tearing of Hunahpú from me. He let his hand rise and fall, seeming to appraise the gold's weight. I knew it to be heavy, heavy with courage and sacrifice.

"This is what I want," he said as he held our dancing god up in that horrible smoke.

There is a time, my sons, when safety counts for nothing, a time when hatred is more powerful than wisdom. This was that moment for me. There were no more Kaqchikel and no more K'iché, no more Mexicu. All that existed was my hate for Tunatiuh who burnt the face of Nine T'zi, who had taken what I had earned in Xibalba.

"You are not a god," I said to Tunatiuh in my first language, in Kaqchikel. "You are not even as high as a Pokomam slave. You have nothing in your mind. You have nothing in your heart. You are made of wood. You have no contact with the gods. You will be destroyed by your pots. You will be attacked by your pans. You will die from the black rain."

I did not believe what I had said, but this was the greatest insult I could think of to throw at a god, to say that a god was not even as high as human beings. I was ready then to give you up, my sons. I was ready not to have had you, oh, my sons!

Tunatiuh looked at me. With his blue eyes he looked at my mouth as the Mexica women tried to translate.

"You are not K'iché," he said. "Where are you from?"

"I am from Iximché."

I spoke K'iché so that Mexica woman whore could translate.

"Iximché? Is that Guatemala?"

"I am Belehé Qat, and the name of our city is Iximché," I said.

"Our friends from Mexico call it Guatemala," Tunatiuh said as he studied the dancing golden Hunahpú in his leathered covered hand. "We have sent messages to your people after our mutual victory over the K'iché. We have sent offerings. They do not respond."

"Yes, Tunatiuh," I said as my feelings for life began to overcome my hatred.

"You shall now be my messenger and emissary to Guatemala," he said.

"Yes, my lord," I said as a Spanish untied me. Oh, my sons! this was when I became someone other than I am. Can you blame me? Would you be here had I said who I was? Did I do this to live, to have you, to save my first people, our people?

"I would like you to stay and watch the trial of these infidels of K'umarcaaj. In this way you may see Spanish justice and then inform your people of our ways."

I bowed my head in agreement, I bowed my head in shame. Red from the fire reflected off his silver breast plate.

They were tortured. This was by fire and by iron. While they were being tortured, the Spanish screamed at them to tell where they had hid the gold.

All of the nobles, save one, kept their eyes wild, but said nothing as had been taught by the generations of people from Tulan. All cried silently except one. He screamed for mercy as the Spanish branded him.

"We planned to destroy you," he said in agony. "We deliberately made war on the king and Jesus Christ. We invited Tunatiuh into K'umarcaaj so that we might burn him."

He was set free.

The trial continued, and I felt a deep respect for the K'iché. Three Quej refused to cry out or even acknowledge Tunatiuh. He was the true king of K'umarcaaj. Nine T'zi was brought back by water then branded again. He did not cry out.

"You have no right," he said. They punished him all the more for his words.

And what did I do? This was nothing I could do.

I was a rabbit.

THERE WAS LITTLE LEFT OF THE LORDS OF K'UMARCAAJ. The torture was complete. The Spanish commanders took pieces of paper to the limp hands of the rulers, held a writing quill in their hands, and moved their hands on paper. They had signed what the Spanish called "confessions."

They burned our royalty. Tunatiuh held a torch to the sticks of wood around each noblemen. He lit the fires. As I smelled the burning flesh of Three Quej, the flesh of Nine T'zi, the flesh of the nobles of K'umarcaaj, Tunatiuh looked at me. In his blue eyes was the message: *You will do as I command, or your people will meet the same fate.*

All the eyes of the Spanish were the same as Tunatiuh's. Each was gratified with the infliction of suffering. Each wanted to continue the burning. I thought I would be burnt also. I did not care. I had seen Xtah's husband, the father of her child, being tortured and burnt. I had seen the destruction of the K'iché people. I could no longer feel fear, feel hate, feel anything.

"Burn the city!"

This was the cry of Tunatiuh. As the fire and smoke from the lords of K'umarcaaj rose into the black sky, the Spanish riding deer monsters rode off with burning torches in their hands.

Tunatiuh came over to me. All that could be heard was the crackling of the trees from the heat.

"Belehé Qat, their city is a strong and dangerous place. It is more like a robber's stronghold than a city. You are lucky you are not K'iché."

"Yes, Tunatiuh," I said. His Mexicu whore translated.

"Go back to your people in Guatemala. Tell them they are ordered by Tunatiuh to give up four thousand warriors. These warriors are to come to this place. They will be used to exterminate the remaining K'iché. If they do not come, I will know the Kaqchikel do not accept the rule of the crown. Leave at once."

This was on the day 4 Qat. On that day I left the golden head of Hunahpú in the stinking hands of Tunatiuh.

The heart of Tunatiuh was without compassion.

7

THIS IS HOW IXIMCHÉ WAS DESTROYED. This is that story. Here is the part about that destruction. This is the story of the preparation for the demolition of Iximché. I returned to Iximché accompanied by my retinue. Tunatiuh said I should have a retinue. This group was to include my cousin and friend Zorach, and eighteen warriors. I told Tunatiuh that I needed a K'iché noble. This was our custom, I said.

All the K'iché nobles were now dead or had fled to the forests. I told him, I said to Tunatiuh, that the greatest demonstration of Tunatiuh's power would be to send to the Kaqchikel at Iximché the wife of a nobleman. And even greater than that would be to send the pregnant wife of a dead nobleman.

This was a custom created by a rabbit's mind, not Kaqchikel history.

Xtah held her pregnant belly as we left the smoldering coals that had been K'umarcaaj. She held her child in her body as we traveled the roads from the K'iché. Xtah did not cry as we left. This was something she had to do, because, had she stayed, her child would have been killed by Tunatiuh. She left knowing that her husband was dead. She left knowing she was going to a people that had killed her father. Her love for me had become something other than love. Is gratitude love? I hoped, my sons, that this would become love.

She walked from the ruins of her people, but she knew that the Kaqchikel boy who had now become a man would protect her and save her and give her all he had. She knew that her K'iché child would be protected. She knew this because I told her this. She knew this because she could remember the play by the temple and the play by Tohil's Bath. She knew this because I loved her, loved your mother.

As we journeyed toward our city, to Iximché, many animals passed before us. Our joy changed to fear. Animals that have always had fear of man were not disturbed by us. They did not care that we were there. They were fleeing. All different types of animals. The small and the large. Many deer passed before us.

Late in that day, we came to the forests of Iximché. There were animals leaving the forest. We were frightened—not for ourselves, but for our city. As we entered the pine forests, the doves flew out. In great numbers they fled the forest. The beating of their wings drowned out the quiet of the day.

As we arrived at the causeway into Iximché, the forest was silent. The animals and the birds were no longer in the trees. The sounds that make a forest alive were gone. I feared for my people.

We entered the city without challenge. There were no guards at the obsidian doors. Our people were distracted. Zorach said that, if the Spanish were to attack the city now, she would collapse. He was right.

In great numbers the animals passed through the city of Iximché. Animals that belonged only in the forest fled through our city. Birds of many kinds flew past us, parrots, toucans, flew right in front of us.

In great numbers the animals of the forest passed. Above us we saw owls, parakeets, hummingbirds, and vultures. Below us all sorts of snakes slithered. They slithered and paid no attention to us. Down the streets of Iximché ran all sorts of frightened animals. There were weasels and coyotes. There were jaguars and dogs. And deer. I thought of all the bird and snake and deer dances I had learned. And here they were, all of them in front of me.

This was the return of One and Seven Death. This was the revolt of Xibalba. The Underworld had placed its chaos onto our people.

I was home, the living memory of my home. This earth was my grandfather's, my father's, mine. These buildings were of my people. This was a city of the earth. This was the city of the moon. There was no central temple to Tohil. The god of the sun was less here than at K'umarcaaj. I felt the power of the moon here. Warmth flooded my bones as I remembered that my people did not waste their time sacrificing hearts to the sun.

XTAH WAS KEPT IN THE HOUSE OF THE WOMEN to prepare for the birth of her son, of our son, of you. My grandmother, Queen Chuuyzut, took her to the place without men. My grandmother knew she needed to be away from us. She knew Xtah needed her time with women.

I did not know that. I wanted to be with her. I wanted to see if gratitude can change and grow when mixed with memory.

Zorach was reunited with my aunt and uncle, his parents. They rejoiced and were happy.

It was different in my family. There was great rejoicing also. But Zorach did not have a brother who had become him. My younger brother, Ahmak, had become my older brother. My sons, it was very simple. There had been no older brother while I was gone. There must be an older brother. I can't say that he wanted it, or that my parents wanted it, or that my grandparents wanted it. That was just the way it was. But how could he relinquish his place? He was not eager.

Each had their place. I had none. I watched my younger brother Ahmak sit in the hall of the dignitaries, sit next to my grandfather and father. I watched him take his place among the nobles. There he sat with his cape of dyed purple feathers.

He looked at me and grimaced. He stood in front of the elders. "We shall have war with the horrible K'ichés. War with the Tzutujil. War with the Pokomam. With the Chol. With the Kekchi. War with the pathetic Pipil. War with the men gods who have conquered K'umarcaaj." He moved his body under the violet robes as a young man courting a woman, bold and arrogant. His face was round and smooth. His face under his face was eager and ambitious.

I looked closely at him and saw the squalling child on our mother's lap.

"I have strategies for the defeat of each of our enemies," he boasted. He did not reveal the strategies.

He boasted and he planned and he carried on in front of my father and grandfather. He carried the mantle of authority and responsibility. He was in my place. But he also carried the burden of responsibility.

I did not understand how he could make plans for war without knowing our history and knowing what the gods wanted.

"This, the supposed Belehé Qat," he said, pointing at me, "brings back stories of the doom of K'umarcaaj. Destruction by a man who is a god but not a god. How do we know this is not a spy? How do we know that he has not converted to the ways of the K'iché? He has brought back a K'iché woman who is with child. Has he not become one of them?"

My father, the Ahop Achí Balam, and my grandfather, King Hunyg, listened quietly to his declarations and questions. In their wisdom, they frowned.

"We must discuss this," my grandfather said.

"We must attack this man god," my brother said. "We must move to bring together all the tribes of this land and attack him before he arrives in Iximché. We supported his attack on Tecún Umán. Now we should attack him before he enters our city and establishes dominion over us."

The conferring and conferencing began. Our noblemen were angry. Some yelled and swore they would be ready to fight any ancient god.

Our king, your grandfather, sat and listened. He did not look as if he was eager to go to war. He did not look as if he was certain of victory. He leaned over to the nobleman on his right and whispered. This nobleman left the great hall. Everyone else went on talking of the destruction of the old gods, of Quetzalcoatl.

The nobleman returned to the hall with four young boys. Each was painted blue with black feathers tied around their waists. Each had the appearance of magic on their face. They received their instructions, then left. I was told that, in the morning, they would attend to the sacred stone. There we would know the truth about the future. We were to meet there at daybreak.

THAT NIGHT, MY GRANDMOTHER SAT DOWN next to me as I wrote. This, my grandmother, was the wife of King Hunyg. She was respected by our entire city. When she walked through the plaza, all would watch her. Even the slaves would lift their eyes to notice her and love her. She was Queen Chuuyzut. She was large and almost fat, and all loved her because she loved all of us. Her long white hair was intertwined with blue and green ribbons. Her eyes reminded me of the dawn.

"What is all this, my lost one?"

"I am writing, grandmother."

"The priests do that."

"The K'iché taught me."

"They taught you to write?" She looked concerned.

"I was granted the spirit of the rabbit when I was in Xibalba."

She looked at me. Did she think that I had become K'iché?

"Our family is afraid you are a spy, Belehé Qat," she said. "They are afraid you have converted to the ways of the K'ichés, that you will tell of our military plans."

"I could never do that. This is my family. How could they think that?"

She held my hand and said, "You have changed. Belehé Qat has changed. The world has changed since you left. The night of your return, the people were frightened by the animals. Some are afraid you are a spirit that took over the body of my grandson."

"Grandmother."

"They are afraid that you are either a spy or a spirit. But your brother is afraid the most."

"He has everything. He has everything that should have been mine."

"He is afraid that you might be who you claim to be. Then what does he have?"

"What do I have now?"

"Your life."

"But what is my life if I am not in my rightful place?"

"You are so fast," my grandmother said. "You hop around, and no one can catch up to you. But to understand, you have to be still and let it come to you."

I wondered if she could see my rabbit spirit.

"When you were young," she said, "all you did was play. Do you remember? You and Zorach would play war with pine cones. When visiting dignitaries came, you'd dress up like the warriors and march around. Then you left. After you and Zorach were gone, there were two little spaces moving around the ball court. Empty spaces. We all cried and looked for you in the spaces. But you were not in those spaces."

I could not tell her, my sons, of Tohil's Bath. I could not tell her of Laughing Falcon. I could not tell her of Zorach's penis pottery in the temple. How could she understand the Snatch Bats of Xibalba? Truly I was Kaqchikel. Truly, also, I was K'iché.

"Grandmother, I would like to write our history, the history of the Kaqchikel, the history of the K'iché. Will you allow me to do this?"

She frowned at me. "This is not your place. You are the grandson of the king. You are destined to be a great warrior."

"Thank you, Grandmother. If this is my destiny, I will follow it. But I must fulfill my commitment to that which I learned in Xibalba." I looked down. I thought that no grandson of hers had ever talked to her in this way, no grandson had ever talked to a Kaqchikel grandmother in this way.

"You were born on the day Lamat. We celebrate your birth on the day of the rising Venus. Venus carries us to war. You were born on that day, the day Lamat."

"Thank you, grandmother. Lamat is also the day Tochtli. Tochtli is the rabbit."

"According to the people of Mexicu."

"Compared to the Spanish, we are all one people."

She looked at me and quietly thought.

"Itzam Na was the first priest and the inventor of writing," she said. "Itzam Na is the god of curing and healing. He became very old by sucking in all the vile miseries of our people. He tries to expunge this misery and heal the people by writing."

My grandmother sighed, then stood up. "He can never completely accomplish this, so he eats corn tamales," she said, shaking her head. "You will end up eating tamales, too."

THE NEXT MORNING EIGHT BLANK SCREEN-FOLD BOOKS lay by my mat. And a plate of tamales. I touched the materials, ate the tamales, then put on my clothes and joined the council.

The council of elders met in front of the gates of Iximché. Our king was carried on his liter by slaves. The rest of us gathered in a half circle around the four blue boys. They had prayed and purified themselves all night. That morning they carried bows and arrows. As the orange light of Tohil flickered around us, they raised their bows. When they were struck in the face by the light, they fired.

Their arrows flew through the morning to a huge round rock. The rock was perfectly black and smooth. Each arrow hit the stone. The boys used another arrow, and another and another, until there were no more arrows. Each boy walked over to the black stone. We followed and looked also. The black rock was still smooth and unharmed.

The boys turned to us and chanted. They sang to us the destruction of the Kaqchikel, the K'ichés. They sang of the end of the history of those who had traveled from Tulan. This would be the final defeat. The black stone was all that was not us, all that was of Quetzalcoatl, all that was of the Underworld, all that was not our people. In its blackness it was unharmed. There would be no more Iximché, no more K'umarcaaj.

The noblemen were still now. This was their inability to argue with the boys. My brother Ahmak looked at the stone and was silent. This prediction had never been given before. I looked into the carriage of our king. He also stared at the black rock.

The sun rose and the morning was silent.

"We have traveled from Tulan for this?" Ahmak asked as we quietly walked back to our city, Iximché. "This is what our journeys have led us to. This is what the gods have destined for us. To have traveled up the river Usumacinta, to have climbed the mountains, to have conquered the people of this land, only to be told that we now face total destruction. We need to prepare for war."

In that morning light, in that early light, as we walked back to the halls for more discussions, I saw your mother, my sons. She stood in front of the house of women and held her stomach, held you, our child.

Our kings and nobles decided that morning to ask Tunatiuh to wait. We asked the god man to wait. We sent representatives to him and told him that we could not send him warriors, but that we would like to greet him in Iximché. We would like to have him as our guest, here in this, our city. My brother smiled at the conclusion of the debates.

"If he is not a good guest to us," Ahmak smiled, "he will be a good guest for the lords of Xibalba."

THE PLAGUE BEGAN.

As we prepared for the arrival of Tunatiuh, the disease spread. First our people became ill of a cough, and they suffered from nosebleeds and illness of the bladder. It was truly terrible, the number of dead there were in that period. Little by little heavy shadows and black night enveloped our fathers and grandfathers and us also, oh my sons!, when the plague raged.

I wanted to see Xtah and her, our, son, but this was not allowed. The boy was born during the most poisonous time. He was named by his mother, he was named Cotuha. This was to honor his father's people. Xtah and her, our, son, Lord Cotuha, stayed away from all the people. She and the baby were in seclusion in the house of women. There she was safe, and there I could not see her face.

This was a different pain than the pain of the deaths. This was a pain I could not name, was not written about, was nevertheless real. The dead are the dead. This was something other than that. My sons, desire is hope, desire is fear.

The stench of the dead rose from the city. The people were confused, and we continued to take our baths and seek consultation in each other. More ambassadors arrived from Tunatiuh. He wanted to visit right away. We sent messages back to him that we were sick.

Fear spread through the city.

All I could do was write, write this. All I could do was to advise the sick to attend the baths.

Around me my family was dying. Around me the city of Iximché was dying. The smell of human decay began.

And then Ahmak became ill. He looked confused at the council. I went to see him. He had begun the sweats. I took him to the baths. There were many who lay sick in the steam and warm water. Ahmak felt more pain in the heat. I had never seen anyone get worse in the baths.

On the fourth day, his skin erupted. Within a day, the pus bumps covered his face and arms and legs. He had become my little brother again. When he was but a child Ahmak was shy and could cry. Here, now, he cried.

"There was no one to fill your place after you left," he said to me. "I was a child. They mourned you and expected me to be Belehé Qat. I could not be you."

The fear was still in his eyes.

"Eventually," he said, "I could not even remember who I had been. I was you. They were pleased. Then you returned. If you were back, was I supposed to return to who I had been? He was gone. Were there supposed to be two of us? That was not possible. Who was I supposed to be?"

The next day he was covered with pustules. He could barely see, and he could barely breathe. This was the day that I wondered if the jealousy I had felt aided his illness.

In the morning, he was nauseous and vomited. He rested, then bled from the nose. For a while he could not rest. He cried out that he was thirsty. His body ached, he said, and his heart beat as if he had run all the way from Xibalba.

This was when he should have died. But Ahmak did not die. I waited for him to die. He waited for himself to die. But he did not.

The priests came to him that morning. They brought him hot urine to drink. They washed his face with it. He lay on his mat and they washed his body with yellow ground chili. My heart hurt in Ahmak's pain. This writing does not extinguish that pain.

The priests came back every hour to wash his plague holes with incense and herbs. When the holes were no longer infected, they gave him juice from the herbs to drink. He rested, and I knew that he was not going to die.

As he slept, I looked at my lost brother Ahmak. He had changed. His face was covered with these holes. I could not recognize my brother who had cried in our mother's lap, who had swaggered about the council meetings. His face was not that of Ahmak. His face was hideous. Underneath that horrible face was the true face of Ahmak, smooth and strong. What face is under all the faces of the world?

I HAD TO RETURN TO XIBALBA. There I could understand that which I could not understand in Iximché.

I asked the priests of our family. They said that it would not be right for me to enter Xibalba. I had not been purified. I had not gone through the rites of entrance into the priesthood. I could not tell them that I had done those things at K'umarcaaj. I asked the priests of the other families. I asked the priests of the Keeper of the Dance Mat family. They all said no.

I went to my grandmother.

"Yes, go to Xibalba," she said. "Go there and seek some relief. I will tell the priests to aid you."

They consented. They had no choice. I went with them to the Temple of Awilix. They were not sure that she, Awilix, could protect me. In her temple I prayed and received the enema of consciousness. It was in her temple that I reentered Xibalba. It was in her temple that I reentered hell. From the temple halls I walked down through dark stairs, black tunnels, to the passageways to Xibalba.

I entered alone. There was no Laughing Falcon, no guide. I was alone, oh, my sons!

The snatch bats did not bother me this time. I looked for them, but they were not there. All the light had become yellow and white. The land was nauseous. I looked up to the clouds. They were red.

I came to the bank of the first river. Pus River was full and overflowing. The yellow and white of the river pulsated. Those were the colors reflected throughout Xibalba. I thought in fear that the contents of the river would emerge from the river and flood all the land. There would only be a pus swamp. Torrents of pus passed before me—the river overran the land.

I built a raft. From the trees around me, I took branches and found a way to cross Pus River.

I came to the second river. This one, to my astonishment, was fuller than the first river. The flow was dark, scabby crimson. Blood gushed down this river. The gushing stopped. The blood lay there and swirled back and forth. Then there was another tide of crimson.

I backed away from the bank as the blood overflowed onto the land. The blood spread back toward me, toward Pus River. I backed away. I was trapped between the two rivers.

I mounted my raft, and the two rivers converged. The yellow white pus flowed together with the crimson blood. Never in all of the sacred texts and drawings, never had it been written that Pus River could flow into Blood River. Pools of yellow and red and white flowed round my raft. Swirls and tides pushed and pulled it. I thought I would fall off from the dizziness.

Several times the liquid splashed on me. I immediately tried to wipe it away. Only tiny drops stayed.

My tiny raft turned and twisted, and, finally, crashed into a pointed black rock. In horror I fell from the raft into the pus and blood. I quickly climbed out of the river and ran up onto the land. I tried to brush the liquid off. Most of it fell away, but there were little red and yellow droplets that would not leave my brown skin.

"YOUR GRANDFATHER HAS THE PLAGUE." I looked up from my illness, I looked up in my recovery, and saw my aunt. I had never seen fear in her eyes before. Zorach looked down at me, too. He smiled and water came to his eyes. His face was smooth and round as it had always been.

Zorach and I had survived again.

In another day I was able to walk around. I felt my face. It was no longer smooth, but there were not the scars that Ahmak had. And I could still see my face under my face.

There was no happiness in my survival. All I could think about were the floods of Xibalba. This I had to tell my grandfather. This I was going to tell my father. But now my grandfather, the King Hunyg, was sick—he had the plague.

I went to him. He lay on his red royal mat while his wife, the Queen Chuuyzut, held his hand. He looked up at me and did not recognize me. He looked at her and did not recognize her. Then he fell back to sleep. I did not tell him about the rivers of Xibalba.

On the day 12 Camey, the King Hunyg, your great- grandfather, died. I stood with the royal family in front of the temple. The priests chanted and prayed. I looked around and saw there were few of us left. I saw that the servants and slaves had died also.

Two days later our father died, the Ahpop Achí Balam, your grandfather, oh, my sons! Our grandfathers and fathers died together.

I stood at the foot of the temple. Again there were prayers and chants. But the lords of Xibalba ignored the pleas. The floods were directly upon us now.

The number of deaths became such that we could not bury them all with services. Many were thrown into the drainage ditches of Iximché. There they rotted while the living cared for the dying.

The smell of Iximché was no longer that of the breeze, no longer of pine cones and hyacinth flowers. The smell was that of the dead. The stench was everywhere. The drainage ditches were full. The dead stayed with the living in their houses. Then all in that house would die. There would be no one to remove them.

During that time, we could tell which houses had died by the smell that came from it. It was the odor of decay, it was the odor of death. We would try to walk around the houses of death. Finally the living could no longer tolerate the silent voices of the dead. We began tearing down those houses. There were not enough of us to remove them. All we could do was to pull the house down on itself with the dead inside. This would diminish the stench of decay.

With the dead in fallen houses and the dead in the ditches, there came a time when there were more dead and sick than living. The city was dying from the plague and hunger. Animals roamed the streets of Iximché. They fed on the dead, they fed on the bodies lying in the streets of the city. Vultures rested on the rooftops after they had devoured the bodies of my family, after they had devoured the bodies of the children of Iximché. We were born to die!

Xtah and her child, our child, you, stayed in the house of the women. Xtah and you lived. I saw her in my heart every day, hoping she would see me, your father, in her heart.

8

THEY CAME RIDING ON THEIR MONSTERS. They came up the causeway, up through the mountains, up through the trees, they came to conquer our people. First were the fierce warriors of Mexicu. In front were the warriors who had helped bring down Tenotichlan. Behind them were the survivors of Tenotichlan. They were fierce in their incarnations of the jaguar, the eagle, the snake. We were crippled by the plague. They were in their greatest glory.

I stood beside my brother, the new king of Iximché, I stood by my brother, the Vakaki Ahmak. We watched as they marched toward our destruction.

"Traitors," my brother whispered.

"Defeated," I responded.

Behind the warriors came the Spanish. They rode up the causeway slowly. In front rode Tunatiuh, the Captain General Pedro de Alvarado. In my grief at the loss of my family through the

~74~

plague, I had forgotten my hate of this god man. As he passed through the obsidian gates of Iximché, I remembered the hate. I was reminded of the hate when I saw my amulet strung around his neck. Here was the golden Hunahpú I had earned in Xilbalba.

Behind the Spanish were the slaves. A representative slave of all the conquered cities walked there. Each was branded or scarred or in chains. This was the Spanish proof of power. In that group of slaves were also the priests of many tribes. They were humiliated in their helplessness. The last of the priest slaves had been stripped of his robes and his feathers. This was Laughing Falcon. He wore the tattered breeches of the conquered. A Spanish soldier carrying a wooden cross rode behind him.

Our people were afraid, as the K'iché had been. The women hid their faces, and the children ran behind their mothers' skirts. The lords stood on the steps of the temple and tried to greet them without shaking. I stood with the council. I stood with my brother.

"Clearly they are gods," Ahmak said as we watched them march by. "Look at their beards and light skin. The metal breast plates had to have been made in Xibalba. Their beasts are monstrous. I can barely look at them."

And so Iximché was no longer Iximché. Now she was Castilian, she was Spanish. Our city had been the result of the flight of the K'iché and the Kaqchikel from the sacred home of Tulan, had been the child, now daughter, of the rebellion of the Kaqchikel from the K'iché, had been the glory of the Kaqchikel.

Iximché changed on that day.

Tunatiuh was given the house of Tzupam to sleep in. This house had been completely redone to honor the killer of the K'ichés. There were murals and sculptures spread throughout the house. The workers and slaves had completed their project three days before they arrived. The Spanish lords entered the house with great pomp. Tunatiuh walked up the steps in a grand style. He brought with him his Tlacalan slaves. The King Vakaki Ahmak and I followed. The people of Iximché stood around this house and prayed.

Tunatiuh and his principal lords were given a banquet that evening. Our best musicians played for them. The food was the finest in the land. We gave them quail and deer, each resting in an orange or walnut sauce. The sacred corn drink was given to them in gourds. All their needs were met.

I sat as a member of council. I was also the bunny rabbit at Xibalba, watching and remembering and would write what I saw. I was both man and rabbit.

Tunatiuh's whore sat in the corner of the Banquet hall. She was of Mexicu. Surrounding her were her Tlacalan ladies-in-waiting. As they moved here and there, I could see her holding her baby, Tunatiuh's baby, to her breast. She was still and beautiful, a princess. She called the baby a Spanish name. Leonor.

Most of the council had thought that Tunatiuh was a fiery god from Xibalba who would strike down many people, then return to Xibalba where he belonged. As I looked at the baby Leonor, I knew he and his men would never leave. That is not the kind of thing gods or men do, conquer then leave. They have babies, and their babies become kings and queens. Maybe their babies would be overrun by merchants.

Our women would become their concubines. The children of the land would have the Spanish for fathers and our women for mothers. And who would the Kaqchikel men be? We would have no children, we would have no wives.

I felt only the snake's venom for Tunatiuh.

Our first night as the children of Tunatiuh was quiet and still. There was the winter chill, and as I walked back to our quarters, I thought that there would be frost on the ground in the morning. I could hear the strange sounds of the Spanish monsters in the distance.

In the morning, I was awakened by two frightened guards.

"Hurry, the council is meeting! Tunatiuh is upset with us."

I dressed and ran to the council hall. The others were just arriving also. Ahmak was already there. He looked as if he had had no sleep during the night.

Zorach's eyes were wide. "Is he attacking us? Is he going to devour the city?"

"I don't understand him," Ahmak said. "Tunatiuh awoke early, and ever since he has been running around accusing the guards of preparing an attack on him. We have done nothing but what he wants."

"Has there been any plots against him?" Zorach asked as he rubbed his face.

"None."

"What should we do?" Zorach asked.

"He is coming to us," Ahmak said. "He wants to talk with us. We need to formally greet him. Then we shall find out what our fate is."

As we began to get to our feet, Tunatiuh and three of his captains stormed through the entryway. His eyes were blue fire. His sword waved in his right hand in preparation for attack. His men were behind him.

"Why are you making war upon me?" he screamed at us, at the council. "Why do you sit here and plan your attacks on me? I have wanted to be your friend. This is no way to repay me." Here was the man who had set fire to Xtah's husband, your father.

Ahmak sat down, then motioned us to do likewise. Zorach remained on his feet but then finally sat down.

"I can make war on you," Tunatiuh said. "I can bring down my power and guns and destroy you. Why do you want to make war on me?" he screamed, and waved his sword at us.

Ahmak's voice became deeper than I had heard it before. "It is not so," he said. "We would not make war on you. In that way, many men would die. Have you not seen the gullies and ravines throughout the land? There are dead men in each one. The ravines are so full as to flow over with the dead of the people of this land. Believe me, Lord Tunatiuh, we would not go to war with you."

Tunatiuh's breathing slowed as our king, your uncle, spoke to him. He lowered his sword and said, "Is it true?"

"You are our leader now," Ahmak said. "We pay allegiance to you. Did we not send you thousands of soldiers when you were at war with the K'ichés? Have we not fed and cared for your people? We mean you no harm."

The eyes of Tunatiuh cooled, and he put his sword back into his holster. He sat down on the council mat. If he was a god, he had a right to do this. If he was a man, for that alone, he would have been killed.

"You are not enemies?" he asked us. He looked around at the council. As long as he was fighting someone, he would not be fighting us. I looked at Ahmak. He understood this.

"We have a great number of enemies, Lord Tunatiuh. I think they want to attack you. They have a great hate for you and your people. This, our spies have told us. Our spies have told us that, if you were to let your guard down, they would attack you and kill your deer monsters."

"Our horses! Who are these tribes? I will crush them."

"These enemies of you and these enemies of us are the Zutuhils, who live by the sacred lake of the volcano. The other enemies are kings of Panacat. These are evil men who do not believe in you. They are very powerful and I am afraid for your people, Lord Tunatiuh."

"Your people have been loyal to me," Tunatiuh said. "I will destroy your enemies. They will be exterminated, then your people and my people shall rule this land."

"Horses," I whispered to Zorach. "Their deer monsters are called 'horses.'"

WHEN TUNATIUH RETURNED TO IXIMCHÉ, he had destroyed our enemies. The Zutuhils and the kings of Panacat were exterminated. He rode back into the city with his slaves and warriors. To my shame, there was joy in the hearts of the people. He had now conquered the K'iché, the Zutuhils, and the kings of Panacat. Now we had no enemies.

"He has completely succeeded," Ahmak said as we sat in council. "The Kaqchikel nation is supreme. We are challenged by no one."

The other lords nodded in satisfaction. Zorach was looking at one of the younger men of the council. They were pleased. I was afraid.

"Tunatiuh wants to seal our agreements with him," Ahmak said. "He wants one of our daughters."

My uncle, the Dual King Cahi Ymox, did not hesitate. "I would like to offer my daughter to the Lord Tunatiuh. My family would be most pleased, and our lineage sanctified."

The council agreed. He leaned back and was very happy for himself and his people. How can a rabbit know what a royal council does not see? How can he tell them when all he is only a tiny rabbit?

That night, with drums and flute, the girl was given to Tunatiuh. I stood next to Xtah, your mother, during the ceremony. She was frightened by Tunatiuh. I let her stand close behind me. She peeked out once to say that she thought that Cahi Ymox's daughter was too young for this marriage. In that look was both fear and, I thought, the love from before.

Tunatiuh's woman, Leonor, and baby were not present.

The Kaqchikel nation slept well. There were no enemies left that needed to be defended against. Tunatiuh had married a daughter of one of the dual kings. For the first time in the ancient history of the Kaqchikel, there was peace.

I could not sleep. In a waking dream I saw the child bride of

Tunatiuh. I saw the smoky ruins of K'umarcaaj. I turned away from your mother, and our baby, arose, and took up my pens and paper.

That night I recorded the history of the entrance of the Spanish into our land. I wrote down the first rumors, then the warnings from Mexicu. I showed how the plague had destroyed us. I described the military prowess of Tunatiuh in the valley of Olintepeque, near Xelajuj, the place the Spanish call Quetzaltenango, some call Xela. I told of the trickery he used to burn the kings of K'umarcaaj. I wrote and drew his entrance into Iximché, the conquering of our enemies, and finally, this night of ceremony.

After I finished, I looked over it all, looked over this. I saw I had left out the four thousand warriors that we had sent to help Tunatiuh destroy the K'iché. I shook my head at our shame and my denial of it. It was morning when I finished. I gathered the papers together and went to the council.

"It is all trickery," I said to the council. "I have recorded the history. Look! He has tricked or destroyed every one of our peoples, our neighbors, our friends, our enemies. He will do the same to us."

CahiYmox was furious with me. He was small, and round, and he shook in fury. "Belehé Qat, you forget he has married my daughter. He is sealed into our family now. You cannot betray family."

"You cannot. I cannot. He can."

"He is a god," Ahmak said. "Gods do not disobey their own rules."

"Maybe he is a god, maybe not," I said, pointing to my papers. "I am not sure he is either god or man. He and his people may be wooden men, not yet human beings. They do not respect our customs, and they do not respect the calendar. They do not respect the gods."

"That is enough," Ahmak ordered.

I looked to Zorach for help. He returned the dazed look of a young man in love. There is nothing I can do, I thought.

The city rejoiced in the triumph of Tunatiuh. In their joy, they barely noticed when the widow of King Hunyg died. Your great-grandmother, my grandmother, Queen Chuuyzut, died in her sleep.

My aunt and I walked back from the death rituals together. My aunt, who is very old and now called Maria, cried.

"The world has changed again," she said. "The queen is gone."

I held her by the shoulder as we walked. She held my hand.

"There is emptiness where the queen was," she said. "There is emptiness where there should be the king and the Ahpop."

I wanted to console her. "We have the King Ahmak."

"He is a child," she said. "Soon there will be emptiness where the city is. At least your grandmother will have no need to change."

My aunt was closer to me than my own mother. She knew, as I knew, the end was near for Iximché. She knew and I knew, but no other. And I could say nothing. There was nothing to be said, only to be written.

I could write the truth, but who would listen?

IT BEGAN IN COUNCIL. Ahmak looked upset. At first, he did not want to tell us. But our way was that the kings would talk openly and fully with the council.

"He has asked for tribute."

"We are only to expect that," Cahi Ymox said. "This is what he should do as our supreme lord."

"Of course," Ahmak responded. "But Tunatiuh wants more than we can give him."

"We must meet his requests," Cahi Ymox said. I thought there was a gleam of avarice in his eyes.

"He has asked for our money," Ahmak said. The fear made the

holes on his face turn red. "He wants piles of our metals. He wants our pottery and statues. He wants our jewelry."

I looked at the necklace that lay on my brother's chest, the necklace my grandfather had worn. I looked at its ten gold jaguar masks. I looked at the thirty-eight gold beads holding the jaguars. This was now worn by Ahmak.

It should not be worn by Tunatiuh. Now, it would join my golden Hunahpú.

"He wants our crowns?" There was no happiness in Cahi Ymox. It had disappeared as fast as it had come.

"Our crowns?" Cahi Ymox asked. "These are the symbol of our bridge to the gods. The bridge to the other worlds. How can he ask that?"

"This is what he has demanded. He has not asked us."

There was silence in the council. Even dreamy Zorach was brought to attention.

"Tunatiuh wants all our gold and the gold of the tribes around us."

"He doesn't want cocoa beans?" Zorach asked incredulously.

"This is not what the Spanish use," Ahmak said. "They want jewelry, gold, crowns, and slaves."

"Must they brand the slaves?" one of the lesser lords on the council asked.

"That is their way," I said.

"We can't give him our crowns," Cahi Ymox said. "That would signal the end of our rule."

"And there would be no lineage to replace us," Ahmak said. "It would signal the end of the Kaqchikel."

They did not know what to do. I sat in that purple room and listened. I listened and saw the smoky ruins of K'umarcaaj. I saw the rise of Blood River.

"Here is the list of tribute Tunatiuh has demanded," Ahmak said.

"He wants this immediately."

The list was handed to each member. Each shook his head in despair.

"There is no way we can supply this," Cahi Ymox said. "In a year maybe, but not now."

"He wants it now."

"What is he doing? What is he building?" Zorach asked. "Those are very strange buildings that are rising from the plain."

Ahmak shook his head again. "Tunatiuh had decided that this, our city, will become his capital."

"He has not asked permission. We have not gone to the temple to ask permission. He has no right."

"He calls his new city Santiago de Los Caballos de Guatemala," Ahmak continued. "We are no longer in the city of Iximché. We now live in Guatemala. This is what the Mexica call our city. We live in the city of Santiago and the country of Guatemala."

"And where has Iximché gone?" I asked.

9

THE COUNCIL MET AGAIN ON THE THIRD DAY after Tunatiuh's demand. As we entered the sacred chambers, he was waiting for us. He was furious. His blue eyes were wild again. "Where is the gold?" he screamed at us. "You promised me gold and precious metals. I have been waiting patiently, and you have brought me nothing."

"We have to gather it together," Ahmak said.

"You have gold everywhere. Look at your crowns. Look at your jewelry."

"But we have very little in storage, and you have asked for a great sum," CahiYmox said. He seemed smaller than I knew him to be. "My great son in law, you must understand."

Tunatiuh pointed his white finger at CahiYmox. "I will destroy you. If you do not bring me all the money of the tribes, I will burn you, and I will hang you."

There was silence in the council room. CahiYmox looked as

if someone had hit him in the head. My sons, no one in history had ever talked to a Kaqchikel dual king in this manner.

"You must pay me twelve hundred pesos of gold," Tunatiuh said.

Ahmak spoke as Cahi Ymox sat, dazed. "Please, great Tunatiuh, please reduce the amount that we must pay you. We do not have that amount of gold. We will give you all that we have, but we do not have the amount you request."

Cahi Ymox was shaking. Zorach shook his head.

"Get the metal," Tunatiuh said. "Bring it within five days. You do not know what will happen to you if you do not bring it to me." He placed his hand on his chest. "I know my heart." He turned and walked away from us.

The council sat in silence. I looked at each member. I looked at their dress and jewelry. All wore gold nose rings and gold ear rings. Ahmak and Cahi Ymox wore gold crowns. There were gold necklaces and bracelets. These were worn to symbolize the relationship between these men and the gods. We had no great storage of gold and precious metals. Why would we? What was needed was worn. There was no need for any other.

"We have no choice," Ahmak said. He lifted his gold necklace over his head and lay it on the red mat at his feet.

"But that is not enough," Cahi Ymox said. "He wants more than we have."

"Then we must go into our towns and to our neighbors. There we can gather what is due."

And so the city began paying tribute to Tunatiuh. Each morning there would be a group from the council standing at the door of his house. Each morning they would hand over piles of gold and precious metals. The kings' warriors would go out in the day to gain metals from the surrounding territories.

The people in our city became confused. They had accepted Tunatiuh as of a higher rank than the kings. After all, they were gods, were they not? The paying of tribute was accepted as our due to our creators. But the people could not understand why the gods wanted the crowns of the kings. Did that mean the kings were unacceptable to the gods? But these kings had been elected according to all the rituals given through the ages. Could it mean that these Spanish were not true gods?

As the kings passed in the mornings to pay the tribute, some of the people did not bow. They simply looked away. Several even turned their backs on the kings. The seeds of rebellion had been planted in Iximché, oh, my sons! by the Spanish.

Each morning the tribute was paid. The precious metals from the people of Iximché was given to Tunatiuh. The gold of the kings was given to Tunatiuh. Half of the payment was handed over to the Spanish. We were frightened that we wouldn't be able to obtain the full payment. Our children looked for metals, our warriors raided surrounding towns.

And still, there was not enough.

BLOOD RIVER LAY WITHIN ITS BANKS, and the people looked over the edge into the river and saw that it was going to overrun its banks and flood out onto our people. Rumors ran around the city like crazed children. Some said the Spanish were going to eat us. Others said the Spanish had brought the plague that had killed many of us. Many blamed the kings for wrongs they themselves had committed.

But there were those in our city who knew where the ground was. They continued on. They went out to the fields so we could eat. They cooked. They raised their children. They went to the temple and prayed and fasted. It was almost as if they had not noticed that the Spanish had come. I looked at them with envy.

Zorach was like that. He had seen the horrors of the Spanish, he had been a witness to the negotiations to the downfall of Iximché, he had witnessed destruction. But he continued about his business. And his business at that time was as a young lord of the Baqahol lineage.

They would walk along the Spanish buildings and talk. They would visit with my wife, Xtah, and I, and talk about the configuration of the stars. Sometimes we would see them caressing just south of the ball court. They knew the Spanish were there, but they knew the ground of Iximché. They were happy, and Xtah and her baby, now our baby, were happy—worried for the future, but happy. But, at night, I could see Blood River overflow onto our love.

For most in the city, life had changed. There was fear and confusion. Out of this fear came a priest. I had seen him at some of the ceremonies. He had a following of the more angry and confused of Iximché. As the chaos and rebellion increased, so did his following.

Each night more and more people stood below him at the great temple of Awilix. Each night torches cast orange light on the murals of Awilix. Each night the people heard his sermons. The people had lost faith in their priests, who were replaced by this strange figure.

The council had once asked advice from the priests and occasionally accepted it. But since the rule of King Hunyg, this reliance on priests had lessened. Ahmak wanted to prove his own vitality. But with the arrival of the Spanish, they began to listen more closely, though still not taking the advice. The advice from your grandfather's priests and your great-grandfather's priests was lost in despair and confusion. The priests did not know what to do.

All the priests were confused except the dark priest who met the people on the steps of the temple. He had direction. Ahmak asked that Zorach and I attend one of his ceremonies.

The priest wore black and red vestments. Around and below

him were the many people of Iximché who were trying to understand the change in our lives. Many carried lit torches.

The priest raised his arms. "I am the lightning," he called out to
the people. "I will bring the fire. The Spanish have challenged our
royalty. They have acted with impunity."

Zorach whispered to me, "He wants us to fight the Spanish. We
would be wiped out. Is that what he wants?"

"I am the lightning. I am the fire," the priest chanted.

I heard the voice of the priest and, with amazement, I realized
I had heard the Falcon's cry. Laughing Falcon had changed again.

The council agreed to meet with the priest, with the transformed Laughing Falcon. Cahi Ymox was afraid he would stir the
people into rebellion against the council. Ahmak wanted to meet
him.

This new, but ancient, Laughing Falcon brought four of his
young priests with him. He began by paying all the respects
through rituals Cahi Ymox could have asked for. He showed respect
for the dual kings Cahi Ymox and Vakaki Ahmak.

"I am the lightning. I am the fire," he began. He eyes betrayed
no recognition of Zorach or me. "The Spanish are the evil shit of
the gods. They were not sent by the gods to us. They were expelled
by the gods. They had no home to go to, so they found our land.
The gods did not know what to do with them, and now they have
discovered us. They are not men. They are not gods. They are beings who have no right to be here. Have no right to be alive."

I looked around the council. Cahi Ymox, as usual, was afraid.
Ahmak listened with great intensity. Zorach looked to be listening
and not listening. He had a half smile on his face. I knew he was
thinking of the boy of Baquahol lineage.

"I am the lightning. I am the fire," Laughing Falcon said again.
"I will kill the Spaniards. By the fire they shall perish. When I strike
the drum, depart from this city. Let the lords go to the other side

of the river. This I will do on the day 7 Hunahpú."

"That is only two days from now," Ahmak said.

"On that day lightning will fall from the sky. My lightning will strike all those who are in the city. The city will burn. Fire will envelope all who have remained. You are warned." The dark priest, who had been Laughing Falcon, and his four men turned and left the council chambers.

"We cannot leave the city," I said to the council. "I know they have made unjust requests on us. They have taken all our money and gold. They have offended everyone of us. But Blood River flows near here. When this river overflows, there will be no way to prevent blood from covering all the land. The land will run forever red.

"If we leave the city, we shall have lost Iximché. We shall have lost the city of King Hunyg, the city of the Ahpop Achí Balam. We shall be in the countryside living as animals. Is it not our character determined by living in this city? Without our city, who are we?"

"What would Belehé Qat have us do?" Cahi Ymox was angry. "Sit here while they take our women? Take our money? Take our children?"

"They have already asked for five hundred of our children to clean their gold," one of the lords said.

Zorach finally looked like he was paying attention. "I agree with my cousin," he said. "If we follow this priest's directives, who is to say we shall ever enter Iximché again? The Spanish have been wicked, but we should not give them our city."

"Can a decision be made?" Ahmak asked. The council continued to argue.

"We shall meet again tonight," he said. "A decision will have to be made then."

As we left, Zorach shook his head. "There is no right answer here. Do we give ourselves over to our old K'iché priest who says he will rain fire on the Spanish? Or do we stay where we are in subservience?"

"If we do not decide tonight, my brother Ahmak will decide for us," I said.

"I think I'd rather take my chances on fire storms from the gods than animals and spirits in the hills."

"The people will follow the priest."

"Maybe the people are not afraid of snakes," Zorach said.

I laughed.

As the sun set, Xtah and I walked, hand in hand, out to where the Spanish were building their new city. It was a long walk, but I wanted to have a last look at the strange buildings before we decided the direction of the Kaqchikel. At first Xtah was afraid, but I told her it was not the way of the Spanish to grab a woman quietly walking with her bunny rabbit. Her smile created a smiling rabbit. She was in love again.

When we reached the halfway point between the Spanish settlement and Iximché, I stopped and looked back at our city. The temple Awilix had turned orange as the sun set. The green trees moved slightly in the twilight air. Even from that distance I could smell the incense from the dark priest's evening rituals.

Xtah said that the Spanish buildings looked strange. As we came to them, I agreed with her. They were unlike anything I had ever seen. It was hard to understand what we were looking at.

We heard the Spanish dogs yapping and growling. There was an image. It ran toward us. It was Zorach's young lord. He ran naked toward us. Two armored dogs chased him. He was smeared with blood as he ran past. He ran to Iximché. The dogs followed, growling and barking.

"Zorach," I cried. We ran toward where the young lord had come from. We ran toward the sounds other dogs. We ran through the trees as they became dark. We ran through that dark forest.

We came to the light of torches.

They were by the pond. They were standing in the clearing, the clearing that was reserved for young lovers. This had been Tohil's Bath for Zorach. This had been Tojil's Bath for the Kaqchikel. It had become the bath of blood.

The Spanish stood in a circle, holding their torches, yelling and laughing. One word they kept yelling. One word that I did not know. One word that gave them the right to slay. In the middle of the circle were dogs. Some wore metal plates, others had spiked collars. All were glistening in the torchlight, glistening red. All were tearing at a young naked body.

Zorach was torn open. A dog swung his intestines in the air.

I attacked the Spanish from behind. I grabbed one by the neck and tried to strangle him. I knocked his helmet off. Three of them pulled me off him and threw me to the ground. There they kicked me and called me the same name they were calling the dead body of Zorach. The dogs ran over and opened their mouths to show their teeth.

It was then your mother saved me and saved your births, oh, my sons.

"Belehé Qat," she cried. She threw herself on me and kissed me. She hugged me and kissed me and protected me from the boots of the Spanish and the dogs of the Spanish. They stopped kicking, then laughed at us. I stood up.

Your mother and I held each other as we left the forest. We held each other as we heard the sound of the dogs eating Zorach. We held each other as we walked back to Iximché. We did not look back.

Zorach's voice was gone from the council meeting that night. His voice had been like a flute to my drum. There was a space where he had been. There was no sound emanating from that space. My voice was as a drum without the flute, nothing to complement it.

"ZORACH'S DEATH TELLS US THAT THE PRIEST IS RIGHT. We must leave. We aren't leaving our city. It is no longer our city. It is their city. If they want it, let us give it to them. We will have told the Spanish we cannot be their slaves. We would rather live in the valleys with the animals, we would rather live in the mountains with the spirits, we would rather give up our history and our civilization than be their slaves."

In Zorach's memory, there was no dissent. We all worked together that night, our last night in Iximché. There was no distinction between the noble and the commoner, the prince and the slave. That was the night the Kaqchikel became one body, became one spirit.

The city was dark and the city was silent as we prepared to leave. Each of us put together only what we could carry. Each destroyed anything the Spanish might find valuable.

I gathered together all the papers and screen books and drawings I had made. I gathered together the papers of the K'iché, the Popol Vuh. I gathered together the annals of the Kaqchikel. I gathered them together and took them with us. Would we have a history if the Spanish destroyed us and destroyed our papers? Would we have existed?

On the day 7 Hunahpú, we abandoned Iximché, we abandoned our city.

10

THE FIRST NIGHT IN THE HILLS, IN THE FORESTS, there were dreams. K'umarcaaj was gone. Now Iximché was gone. There was no civilization. We lived among the beasts and spirits. It is no wonder that all the Kaqchikel dreamt.

As I fell asleep in the arms of my wife, your mother, I thought of Zorach. This was the time of mourning. I cried as she held me. I cried in his memory, and I wept at the loss of our city, our home.

In the dream I played with Zorach. His body was whole. In my dream I played with my brother Ahmak. His face was again his true face. It was as if he had never received the plague. There were no plague holes. His face was round and smooth.

The three of us played with pine cones around the ball court. We ran and yelled and pretended we were the rulers of Iximché. We laughed and giggled and were young.

My grandfather stood in front of us. King Hunyg had come back to life, and he stood before us, and we were terrified. He lifted us in his arms and carried us to the Awilix Temple. He carried us to the top of the temple. He held both of us in his lap and we looked down on our city. We were comforted, then delighted.

Down below us were our family and friends. Everywhere there was color: striped blues and greens and yellows, reflections from gold jewelry radiated around us, headdresses of green and red feathers that covered the square. All was motion, all the colors vibrated.

I felt warm in the lap of the king. I lay my head back onto his chest. The air made my skin tingle. There were no clouds in the sky, only blue, blue with one speck of green. The green was the Quetzal. She floated near us, then directly in front of the temple. We could see her long green feathers trailing behind her. Her wings were outstretched in a glide. Her breast was green, not red.

That morning I was cold and achy from the ground, but I awoke with the vision of the green Quetzal in my eyes and the song of the Quetzal in my ears.

The sky became blue as in the dream. There, in the hills of the spirits, we waited for the destruction of Iximché. We waited for the lightning that had been promised.

The sky remained blue.

WE MET AS COUNCIL. Under the trees, among the bushes, we met. It is impossible to explain how it felt to meet on the council mat under the sky. This had never happened before. At least not since our people fled Tulan and slept by the river Usumacinta.

"He will die now." Cahi Ymox was in tears. "He will die, and my daughter will die. I have given my daughter to the enemy, and I will be punished by her death."

Ahmak pointed to the sky. "Don't despair yet," he said. "There are no clouds. Lightning does not strike from blue."

"And if he is not destroyed by the priest's lightning, then he will destroy us."

"I don't think he will attack us," Ahmak said. "We have given him metal, more than he could possibly use. He has been satiated with gold. There can be no war in his heart."

The sky turned pink, then dark blue, then black, and there was no lightning. The people realized they had been tricked by the dark priest, by Laughing Falcon. He is wicked and he is evil, they shouted. Their anger was stirred by their fear of the revenge of Tunatiuh.

I convinced my brother that the priest was holy, the priest was sacred. Ahmak would not let the priest be destroyed by the people. He told them Tunatiuh was the enemy, not some mad priest.

Ahmak stood between the people and Laughing Falcon. He ordered the priest to leave the people, to enter into other parts of the forest, to never be with people again.

The priest was spared. He looked back at me as he walked away, banished. I bowed my head.

"Respect has not left all of our people. I am repaid," he said to me, smiled, and turned to stumble down the hill into darkness.

THAT MORNING THE SKY WAS BLUE AGAIN. Two of Tunatiuh's Mexica slaves found us in the hills. They found us and they brought a message from Tunatiuh. The council met again to decide the fate of the Kaqchikel.

"Tunatiuh has asked us to return," Ahmak said. Without the gold, the crown, and the feathers, sitting under the trees, Ahmak was still our king. When he stared at us with his black eyes, I saw King Hunyg.

There was confusion on the council. Some of the lords wanted us to return. Others said that a return would be a trap, and that we would all perish. We did not return to Iximché.

They were wooden men. If their pots and pans did not attack

them, then we would have to wait for the dark rain. But while we waited, we could try to kill them ourselves. The realization came to us all without words: We could not return to Iximché as long as the Spanish lived. Their bodies would be the doorway to our home.

But there was still the doubt—a nation of men could be killed. Could a nation of gods?

Tunatiuh sent us one last message. He wanted us to return to Iximché. He said he would no longer request gold from us. He needed us to attack the other tribes in the land. He wanted us to be the supreme rulers of all of the fields and forests. All we had to do was to accept His Majesty and Jesus Christ.

Our answer was the same the nobles at K'umarcaaj gave him: nothing. There was no answer for a man who claimed to be a god but was a man. There was no answer possible for a man with that kind of pride, the kind of pride that would make us all his slaves.

WARRIORS OF THE LINEAGE OF CAHI YMOX interrupted our council. The Spanish were moving toward us with all their horses, dogs, and Mexica warriors. This was on the day 4 Camey. Decisions were made quickly. All of our people would separate and disappear into the trees and bushes. There would be no Kaqchikel people who could be destroyed. Now there would be many of us. We were scattered under the trees and under the vines.

I took your mother and our son with me. We hid in the trees. We hid in the bushes. And still the Spanish and their dogs trailed us.

I hid our family. I hid them in the glens. I hid them in the caves and under the vines. They were hid from the Spanish. Even the dogs could not find us. The Spanish and their horses could not.

That night was long and dark and cold. In the morning, a green mist covered us. The birds' chirping was closer to us than when we lived in Iximché. We woke to the green mist and the singing of the birds.

We left the fog in the valley and climbed up the side of a mountain where there were caves. At the caves we stopped, and turned around, and looked out at the valley that had been Kaqchikel. Out of the green mist below us came the sounds of the crunching of rocks by the Spanish horses' hooves. I hurried the families into the caves, then crept out to look.

As they emerged from the fog, the sun lit up their silver helmets. I knew they were men. I knew they were not gods. But, in that instant, I could only see them as gods. In my confusion, I saw them as both gods and men.

Each helmet shone like fire. Their breast plates reflected the light, and they were men of fire, gods of the sun.

But they were men. I heard the man in the lead shout at the ones in back. His voice was gruff and angry, a voice of rage and fear. His voice reminded me of Tunatiuh's.

This group did not have dogs with them as they rose from the valley. I felt we would be safe if we were silent. I crept back into the cave. There was much fear in the faces of the people. I don't know if this was fear of the gods or fear of horrible men. Nevertheless it was fear.

The crunching of rocks was louder as they passed in front of the caves. It seemed to echo into our hearts. Then they passed.

They were gone.

WE STAYED IN THE CAVE THAT DAY AND THAT NIGHT. During the night I dreamt of Xibalba and Hunahpú. He had recovered his head and left Xibalba. The dancing god had returned. The wrathful gods of Xibalba screamed chaos and he danced, untouched.

In the morning I gathered my wife and our people together. I told them it was time to return to the mountains of our people.

We would cross the valley and follow the river until we came to the mountains. It would be as if we were deer, trotting and hiding in the forest. There was fear, but all knew that we could not live in a cave.

In silence we made the voyage. In silence we walked and looked for the Spanish. There were no Spanish. In silence we prayed. We were all in silence except your mother. She gently sang, she murmured an ancient song, and this song brought courage to our people.

On the mountain, the Kaqchikels returned. To the credit of our people, none had been lost to the Spanish. We had disappeared, and there had been no trail.

The council met as a war council. Ahmak took the lead in designing a strategy. There was no argument with his plan. We would never meet the Spanish on open land, never on a plain. The defeat of Tecún Umán was our guide. We would be like the tiniest animal in the forest. If Tunatiuh saw us, we would immediately disappear into the underbrush. We had found, my sons, that a direct fight with the Spanish would lead to our extermination.

Holes and pits were dug throughout the land. Everywhere the Spanish might travel, there were traps set. In each hole, there were seven long pointed stakes. All were painted with poison. The hole was covered with branches, leaves, and earth.

We would dig the holes, then quickly travel back to the mountains. We were truly like the tiny animals of the forest.

As we worked, I felt surprise in my heart for your mother. She had grown up in a lineage of royalty. There she had many slaves and servants. I loved her and saw the future of our lives, as we had children and grandchildren. She did not talk, except for an occasional song. But because of her lineage, I thought she would suffer much as we lived among the trees.

I was surprised as I watched her dig pits, sharpen stakes, and prepare the poison. This was not the Xtah I had seen being served so carefully. Here was a woman who fought for our people.

One of the young men on the council laughed and said she was acting as if she were a man. This young man was beaten by my wife's husband, your father, me, Belehé Qat—beaten until he cried. Your mother and the other women fought for your lives.

We met again as council. We sat under the trees in the morning. The women were cooking, and I thought of my wife, I thought of Xtah.

"We have prepared as thoroughly as possible," Ahmak said. "There is no further preparation possible." His face had gotten more angular since we fled Iximché. His eyes had become dark.

"It is not enough," Cahi Ymox said. Even with our lack of food, his face had become rounder. "We cannot defend ourselves against these gods. Somehow we must make peace with them."

"They will destroy us if we return home," I said. "If we fight, we have some chance. If they attack, we can leave and go to the east."

"Belehé Qat forgot the Rabinal," Cahi Ymox said. "The Rabinal are in the east. They will destroy us even more quickly than the Spanish. We must find a way to have peace, here, in our own land."

"We recognize you miss your daughter and fear for her," Ahmak said. "All of us on the council sympathize with you."

This was his way of reprimanding me for my callousness. At first I felt anger at him for a public rebuke. Then I accepted my blame. "We want no harm to come to your family," I said to Cahi Ymox.

Ahmak looked at me. His dark eyes were now sad. "We need allies," he said. "If we are to have war with the Spanish, we need to make alliances with our traditional enemies."

The council agreed.

"My brother, Belehé Qat," Ahmak said as he put his hand on

mine, "you can now speak the language of the Spanish. You speak the language of the K'iché. You understand the desperation of our people. You will go to the Rabinal, to the land of the Abyss of Carchá. There you will show them that our need is their need, our war is their war."

I nodded. "My wife and our son will have to stay here. However much the Rabinal dislike the Kaqchikel, they hate the K'iché. They would kill them both."

"She will be protected."

I heard shouts and looked up to see three women running toward us. They had dropped their cooking. Warriors ran down toward our defenses. As we rose, one of the guards came up to us and said that the Spanish were riding up the hill.

We joined the warriors and ran down to the pits. These holes had been dug at the end of a long, wide ravine. We stationed ourselves on each side, looking down. There was silence, then came the sound of horses. We were invisible, and we were silent. I looked through the vines.

Tunatiuh was in the front. This was their attack on us. This was to be their destruction of the Kaqchikel. As they passed below us, the morning sun lit up their helmets again.

They began to fall into the pits and trenches. Their horses were powerless in the face of poison stakes. They let out fierce cries and fought, but still they were impaled. The men who did not fall into the traps tried to turn their horses and escape back down the ravine.

The Kaqchikel warriors stood up and drew back their bows, and they let loose many, many of their arrows.

"Here is the gold you wanted, Children of the Sun!" was the cry of the Kaqchikel warriors. "Here is the gold you wanted, Children of Tunatiuh!"

The horses that had not fallen into the pits were struck by those arrows. The men who had survived the trenches were struck by them as well, and many died. They died in confusion by our arrows.

Below me was Tunatiuh. His red beard and my golden amulet radiated in the light of sun. The brightness of the rising star, Venus, Lamat, blistered away. The bunny ran in fear. The rabbit could not write, could not heal, could not fight. The rabbit left my body. In his absence was the light from the rising Venus, Lamat, war. The light radiated into my soul illuminating the god Hunahpú, the respectful and respected.

I, now the warrior, enlightened by Lamat, ran down the hill at the Spanish. Down the hill through the trees and vines I ran. It would be the time the tribes would win.

"Kill their horses!" I yelled as I ran. "They are not monsters."

I yelled it again and again. I screamed, "Kill their horses!"

In front of me lay a dead Kaqchikel warrior. He had been hit by one of the Spanish exploding sticks. He was destroyed, and there was blood everywhere. I picked up his spear and continued shouting.

From behind me I heard the war cries of Kaqchikel warriors. The writing bunny, the scribe, and the healer had been lost. There was only the raging warrior. Belehé Qat was now a vicious man who thought only of protecting his family and elders. A man with blood streaming down from his eyes.

And he screamed, "Kill their horses! Kill their horses!"

To get to the Spanish, I had to fight my brothers from Mexicu. But that did not matter, because this was the only way to get to Tunatiuh, to get to their horses.

The little bunny rabbit was gone and the man who had grown vicious teeth saw the horses. How fast can a man run?

As I approached the Spanish, I saw the man Tunatiuh. He was on a black horse, directing the soldiers. He pointed. He yelled.

He cried out orders. He was under the sun, but he was not the sun.

Blood and death were between the man Tunatiuh and me. But that was not enough to stop the enraged warrior. There is nothing that can stop a man who is protecting his people. So with spear held high, I, the man, I, the warrior, attacked.

His helmet and sword were bright silver. I came at him from the north, running, screaming.

"For Zorach, for Nine T'zi, for Three Quej, for my sons, for the tribes of Tulan."

Tunatiuh was giving directions from his horse to his men as I plunged the spear of the dead warrior into his leg, into his right knee.

He looked down at this warrior in horror as blood spurted from his pierced leg. He swung his sword at me but missed because he was a man and not a god. I yanked my spear from his leg as this man, not god, yelled in anguish.

As I drew back the Kaqchikel spear to kill Tunatiuh, Pedro de Alvarado, an explosion blew me to the ground. The horse bucked up into the air in fright. Pedro de Alvarado fell from his black horse and rolled down the ledge. This man, not a god, screamed in terror as he crashed through the grass and bushes. I saw the golden head of Hunahpú around his neck flash yellow as he rolled.

Alvarado's black horse turned around in confusion. Still an enraged warrior, I stood up and ran to the horse. As the Spanish were dying around me, I climbed onto the beast. There was no fear in me, there was nothing except a man's rage.

The horse bucked up into the air again and ran back down the ravine. I held onto the horse's black hair. I felt the Spanish power. The animal was strong and fast. I knew that if I could gain control of this animal, if we could master this animal, we would be as strong as the Spanish.

The horse's spirit and I became one, and we ran through the Mexica warriors, who screamed in horror. We ran through the Spanish legions, who screamed in fright. We ran past the Kaqchikel warriors, who screamed in pride.

But we ran past the battle, and I did not know how to tell the animal spirit that was enough. How do you tell a horse to stop?

With a sudden turn I flew off the animal. I did not let go of the animal. It was much more simple. It was just that I was in the air. Then I was lying in the bushes, looking up at the sky and listening to the horse galloping down the mountain.

Belehé Qat, the laughing warrior, walked back up the ravine. The battle was over. There were no more cries from the Spanish. They had retreated with their damaged Alvarado. There were few Kaqchikel deaths. I looked at the warriors. I looked at the royalty. We had fought as one. There was no division. All felt the truth. The Spanish were men and men could be defeated.

BUT THEIR DEFEAT HAD TO BE IN ALLIANCE WITH THE RABINAL. To defeat the Spanish, I had to give up Xtah, I had to give up you, oh, my sons! I had to give up the rabbit and the warrior. This had been ordered by the council. I was now to be man of negotiation, of discussion, and alliance creation. An ambassador. I left you to travel to the Highlands, to the Rabinal. I abandoned our people to save our people.

Book 11

BEATRIZ, THE UNFORTUNATE
1520 TO 1541

11

WE WILL BE MARTYRED FOR GOD. We shall enter heaven tonight." Margarita stood up. We had been kneeling at our beds. She twirled around three times. Her white cotton night skirt lifted, unveiling her black velvet slippers.

I was afraid to move.

"This will be our full and total commitment to God," she said. "There will be no question of singing with the angels. We will dance with the seraphim and cherubim."

I looked up at her. My sister was confident and beautiful in the orange flickering firelight. Her light eyebrows rested above her blushing white round face. I had not thought much about heaven; I was more worried about Mother's lashing tongue. And what were those things we were going to dance with?

"In this way, we will express our true love of Our Savior."

She knelt down next to me again.

"But will it hurt?"

"Yes, of course, silly. Our deaths will have no meaning unless we feel anguish," she said, laughing at me. "We will offer our agony up to Our Lord. We will join Him in everlasting joy and glory."

I wasn't taken with the idea.

"Across the square, past the cathedral, past La Giralda, is the bridge," she whispered. "Beyond the bridge are the murderous Moriscos. They *pretend* to be converted. They are not. They are still Moors."

I couldn't tell the difference between a Moor and the moon. I had no idea. Margarita wanted to meet Him, face to face. I wanted to run to the next room, yank our older brother, Eduardo, out of bed, and have him slap some sense into her.

"This will be an act of love for Christ and Crown."

I nodded.

We boldly strode, hand in hand, out of our home, covered in black shawls. We walked along narrow cobblestone streets. My mother had told me the Killers of Christ had lived here. Now they were gone. Who were they? Where did they go?

I preferred living on our finca in Úbeda. She had bullied my father into living in Seville, closer to the court. I missed the fields, the rolling green hills, the great billowing white clouds.

We didn't talk. It was very late, and the only sounds that could be heard were the dogs barking from the other side of the Guadalquivir. I couldn't pronounce the name of the river. Margarita had told me I couldn't because it was a left-over name from the vanquished Moors. *Wadi Al-Kabir*, great river. She knew every-thing.

It was a cool evening. The full moon created shadows. We must have been quite a sight for anyone who spotted us: a tall, full-bod-ied, smiling girl walking hand in hand with me, a thin child carrying a furrow, no, a trench, between dark eyebrows above terrified green eyes.

We walked by the cathedral.

Our huge cathedral, the Cathedral of Saint Mary of the Sea, was in constant construction. When we went to mass, I felt like the king's buffoon. I should have been telling jokes, doing summersaults, maybe petting the royal mastiff with my foot.

Margarita seemed to soar upwards in the great church. Rosy cheeked, it was as if she, angel-like, glided over the candles, the tomb of Christopher Columbus, even the altar, as the bells rang from La Giralda.

I would try very, very hard to soar until I smelled the incense. Then I would sneeze.

"How will they kill us?"

"They hate Christians. They will chop off our heads."

I sniffled back tears as we left the city walls.

"Don't be afraid, Beatriz," she leaned over and whispered. "When we die we will go straight onto the lap of Our Lord."

The fragrance of orange blossoms turned into the smell of sewage.

I stepped on slimy things on the slaves' mud path to the bridge.

Five great ships floated on the water. At dinner I had heard Father talking about the wealth these ships brought us from the Indies. Drunken singing floated from across the river.

After we walked between the two brick towers that stood as the entrance to the bridge, I stopped to look over the wire railing to the dark river below. It seemed to be calling our names. Under the bridge in the gray-blue moonlight, I counted nine anchored boats on which the bridge rested. Nine. I've always tried to calm myself by counting. Nine.

I turned back from the railing. "Will I be able to see through my eyes as my head falls?"

Margarita determinedly marched toward the other side of the bridge.

I followed, crying.

"This is the only way to totally give ourselves to God."

We walked off the bridge onto more mud.

"Triana!" Margarita cried triumphantly. She added, "Named after the Roman emperor Trajan. He was born near here." She knew Latin, she knew history, and she knew how to get both of us decapitated.

In the distance fires fluttered in front of wood huts. One of the dogs we had heard barking stopped, squatted, and relieved himself. We walked around the steaming pile and headed toward the huts of the murderous Moors.

A woman dressed in a long tan over-cloak, with a wide straw hat, holding a cane, stumbled out of the night. As she passed, she turned her head. Her face was completely black. I stepped back. I had never seen anything like that before. Determined, Margarita kept walking.

I ran to catch up with her. She stopped in front of another dark figure. He leaned over and grabbed her.

I said a thousand rosaries in the time it took the figure to pull Margarita back to me.

"My nieces," he said, "it is late."

In the darkness I saw Uncle Luis's white-bearded face. After a flood of relief, I wondered what he was doing on this side of the bridge.

"This is not a place for little girls," he said gruffly. I smelled rum.

He walked us to his home back on the civilized side of the river. I was happy; Margarita was not.

HE SAT US DOWN IN FRONT OF HIS FIREPLACE. A woman, with raven black hair pulled back with a dark blue scarf, carried three clay cups on a lacquer tray into the room. Her mouth widened into a warm smile. Her long silver earrings dangled beside tan cheeks that seemed to resemble my own color. Five strings of multicolored beads draped down to her red-lined black dress. She had penetrating black eyes and an angular, beautiful face.

She handed us cups of a warm dark frothy liquid. "Chocolate," she said.

"Chocolate," Margarita said, uttering each syllable slowly.

I had never tasted such a wondrous thing—spicy, tingling, thrilling.

"From the Indies," he said, smiling at my joy. "Dip these into the chocolate." He handed us a plate full of churros. "Shepard pastry dunked in the New World," he laughed.

I ate, drank, and dipped as Margarita told him our story. He had been *there*. The woman was quiet, sitting, nodding, warmly watching us as he spoke. Mysterious. These Indies must be heaven on Earth, I thought. Another kind of heaven. Without loss of one's head. A chocolate heaven.

"It is time to return, my children," he said.

I smelled spicy sweet cloves on her breath as the woman hugged us goodbye.

Uncle Luis's hand was warm and leathery as he walked us home. Margarita cried in her failure. I was delighted. My mind was full of wonder about that strange, beautiful woman. And I was doubly delighted by the dancing taste on my tongue.

12

THE LIGHT FELL ONTO HIS MEDALLION, then reflected beams up into my eyes, blinding me. The gold was from the pagan kings of Guatemala, an emblem of their barbarous god. Our people, Christians, refined a portion of the precious metal into a splendid coin medallion stamped with the profile of our homely King. Around the top of the coin was inscribed: *Plus Ultra.* Always further.

The savages thought this man, Captain-General Pedro de Alvarado, was the sun god. I sat by the fountain, facing my captain, aide to Cortez, ruler of all the Americas south of Mexico. He told me stories of fierce battles with Indian warriors, of the royal cities of Iximché and Utatlán, of the Indian god brothers Xbalanque and Hunahpú, a hell they call Xibalba, of the promise of cities of gold.

There was nothing in my head except moist memories of Margarita. I listened and smiled. That is all I could bring to him. She had told him of the latest gossip, intrigues of the court. She had asked how to pronounce the strange Indian words. I was afraid to open my mouth for fear of an overflow of cackling crickets.

"This new world of yours seems more a story of soul than geography and power," I said, attempting wisdom.

Father smiled at us from his upstairs window. His white hair fell onto his elegant skin. Until that moment I thought Father was a man of the sun. A man of the court. He looked with awe at this conquistador with the pink skin and red beard. Father nodded and turned away.

My captain had changed since he married Margarita. His brow was wrinkled, his hair receded, older; now he walked into our home with a limp. I thought his right leg lame. The greatest difference was in his eyes. I remembered soft gazes before. Now his blue eyes flew around the courtyard. I wondered if he saw savages peeking out from behind our new purple bougainvillea.

I wanted to reassure him I was not one of the savages. I reached over and touched his hand. It was cold. His eyes became still as he looked at me.

Mother shook her head—no, no, no. She sat opposite us, watching. Her twitching face and trembling dark lips protruded from a black veil. She hated him. She could not forgive him.

For all her concern about the badly educated, she herself did not care for manners.

"You see only a future of red silken robes, gold, sacred music. You forget the death of your sister," she said to me.

I could not imagine why he courted me. Margarita had been beautiful. She carried her full frame steadily through the world. My thin young body could be blown across the fields from an angel wing's gush. She had been charming and witty. I was not. But Lucía said my eyes were like bright butterfly wings.

"Beatriz," my conquistador said, turning his attention to me and away from mother, "I carried your name in my heart. Everywhere

I went, I thought only of you."

"I was but a child when you last saw me," I said, looking down at our shadows on the white cobblestone patio.

"You will join your sister," Mother said. "Look at him. His family is no better than savages. His Castilian is soured with a base Extremaduran accent. The gold he has amassed will never right that. He is from a family of scrounging beggars."

My suitors, the boys, wore their doublets to the chin with stiff collars. The harsh material scratched their necks as they begged me for the favor of a glance. My captain did not have to beg. His doublet was cut in the smooth regal style. My heart's blood flowed with his exploits. His violet silk cloak rested over his square shoulders.

"God has granted me a special vision," he said, touching his red beard, winking at me with his blue eyes. "With this vision I can see the evil contemplations of the Indians of Mexico and Guatemala. I destroyed them. And with this self- same vision, I could see the beauty in the little girl. I could see the woman in the child. I could see you as you are now." His melodic voice mixed with the sounds of the fountain. He had ignored my mother.

"Gold can not transform the man inside the doublet," Mother said, now crying for effect. "Symbols betray."

I had worked hard to present myself to my captain: long black hair braided with blue and yellow ribbons, gold earrings with red centers, a dark-blue silver-striped jacket tied together at the sleeves by crimson clasps, a bright blue skirt sprinkled with silver half moons, and finally, gold embossed sandals tied with crimson leather.

I looked up. "But you were courting my sister then."

"The vision I had of you was fleeting." His voice and the fountain became one, became song. "In a moment you were gone. I went on to the New World. I faced death. Almighty God chose to let me live, live to see you as a woman, to see your full beauty."

Mother rose to cry real tears.

I turned to her. "You give the gift of fear."

"He does not mention your sister. His gift will be another loss for me."

He stood with the air of dignity, as was expected, and nodded to me and to Mother. My heart flew to him as I watched the damage of the Conquest in his broken stride as he walked to the doorway.

"No one is worthy to court the child of a grieving mother," Mother said.

"Then why did you let him come here today?"

"Your father gives the gift of ridiculous hope." Her voice was separate from the fountain. It grated like a broken wagon wheel on rocky cobblestone.

"What more does he have to do to prove himself?" I heard my voice rise. I tried in vain to keep control. "Hasn't he been through enough? It was not only your daughter who died. She was not only my sister. She was also Margarita, wife of Pedro de Alvarado."

The youngest is always the most protected. Perhaps this protection added to my passionate advocacy for him.

"All the Galicians who have gone to the Indies have been infected with some sort of evil. They bring back disease, plagues. The conquerors of the New World are turning our world savage."

"You hate him."

"You betray your sister," she said, staring at me.

"I loved Margarita. I pray to her every morning and every night. But now, he will make me Queen of the Americas."

"You are a child, barely fifteen. You are forbidden to see him again. Forbidden."

"What do you want of me, Mother? Here I will marry and become supervisor of servants. Or I'll enter the convent. There are no other choices for me."

Mother's face was red. "There is no respect. You will do what is right."

"How could you understand my feelings? You are old."

"Wicked."

With that one word, Mother made the birds and their songs scatter like cattle in a lightening storm. I was a silly little girl. She stalked out of the courtyard.

I imagined Margarita. I was jealous. Her full beauty, her straight white teeth, the dignity and power of her walk. I was a thin thing with dark hair and a baby face. Her light hair fell to her shoulders. My black hair and tan flesh were base.

Poor dead Margarita. Killed by some disease at some swampy port six days after they landed. Vera Cruz. Was this the homily of The True Cross? Had she suffered? Had she become afraid? Our brother, Eduardo, had waited for her in New Spain, waited in vain.

When I was a child and was confused, I would go to the cathedral. I would pray for guidance from Our Lady. As I grew older, I retreated to Father's books. I walked to his sanctuary, sat in a corner, and remembered the chocolate and churros. I had not drunk that foamy dark drink since the night of the bridge. Uncle Luis never brought any more back from his travels.

I wondered if my captain had drank that heavenly beverage. To avoid falling into despair, I picked up my favorite book. As I read of The Knight of the Green Sword's pain, his yearning for his lost Oriana, I heard my father.

"You and your sister are just alike," Father said. He had quietly crept up from behind to startle me. He loved to tease. He still referred to Margarita in the present tense. "You read such garbage. I'd like to take those books on romance and chivalry and throw them in the fireplace."

"They're harmless, Father."

"I don't understand how you two can be so virtuous and holy and at the same time waste hours reading that nonsense," he laughed. "And I thought at least you would have better things to do."

He could always make me laugh and cry at the same time. We walked out of the library arm in arm.

"Mother—"

"Your Mother litany needs to be addressed to another," he said kindly.

Upstairs, in my bedroom, I knelt and prayed for guidance. Neither Our Lady nor Margarita answered.

WILLIAM VLACH

13

SHE WON'T LET ME SEE HIM. He will leave for the New World next week. I will become old and die alone." We waited while my mother and father spoke with my great uncle, Francisco de los Cobos y Molina, secretary to Charles V. They were in the royal residence, the Alcazar, across the cobbled stones from the cathedral. Lucía and I stood in the cool shadow of the cathedral's bell tower, La Giralda.

Lucía's face saddened. She was like a younger sister, though she was only a simple handmaiden. Her shoulders were slight, and she tugged on her skirt when she became afraid. Her eyes were round, and the brown color deepened to gold when the light changed. La Giralda's bells tolled. Lucía looked up as she pulled on her brown skirt.

"Just bells," I said.

"I heard the devil built that," she said, looking down. A horse-drawn carriage tumbled by.

"The Moors. It was a minaret. They called their followers to service from there. Do not be afraid. They are gone. The crown rebuilt it after we reclaimed these, our lands. The archbishop blessed it over a hundred years ago." I had tried to pick up Margarita's educated mantle.

Her eyes darted to the strange writing on the great iron doors of the cathedral.

I grew impatient. "They are gone, Lucía. You will see. Our people, Christians, will replace heathen temples with monuments like La Giralda throughout the New World. I can imagine one standing in front of a great bay with a grand city behind it. The bells will toll across the Americas. I must be there. They argued about it last night. My mother is merciless."

Lucía's brown eyes filled with tears. She reached over and held my hand. The families leaving Mass swirled along the street in front of us. They opened way for a man slowly walking by, his head covered with a brown sackcloth, wearing only a gray apron. Blood ran from his back as he lashed himself with a short leather whip. Lucía looked from my face to him, then pulled at her skirt. Blood scared Lucía.

"I do not want to become like her," I said. "I suppose God has given us no choice. You get old and wrong. But dear Lord, do not let me become like that."

"I will pray for you," Lucía said, blessing herself.

I grew tired waiting for them. We joined the people on the street for the short walk back to our home. Everyone had dressed in their finest and darkest clothes, deep blue silk, crimson gowns, gold and silver ornamentations, for Holy Thursday.

"I think she is like this because her mother destroyed her dreams," I whispered to Lucía. We were the same height. "I wonder what she wanted when she was my age. Power? Love?"

We walked through the crowded streets, arm in arm.

"I think of him all the time. My every moment is devoted to my captain."

Three young dandies strutted by. Each gave the manly Spanish look, direct eye contact, shoulders back, puffed chest. Each received in return Beatriz's blessing, a look the other way.

"I do not want to turn into Mother."

Lucía nodded, sneaking a look at the boastful boys.

"All she thinks about is herself."

The people in front of us gave way, this time for a mule. Lucía and I stepped aside. Atop the mule was a woman wearing a tall red-and-white dunce cap. Her hands were tied, a stupid grin spread across her face. Her husband held the reins with one hand and hit her with a stick with the other. The people in the streets laughed and pointed.

"Easter Week has become a circus," I said. "Let me tell you about last night. Dreams prophesy, don't they?"

Wondrous wide leaves. Sparkling crystal drops of water rest on top of each dark green leaf. Somewhere nearby is my captain and his men. Through the leaves and trees I hear the ethereal song of a bird. I walk off through the white mists to look for her.

The foliage breaks open, and a green bird flies up, frightening me. It is exactly as my captain described. The feathers are greener than the forest. Emerald. A magnificent long tail follows her as she flies. She disappears into the high blue sky. How could she have sung that odd song and be so incredibly beautiful?

I come to a small lake. In a cove protected by trees and green leaves, I take off my clothes, slide into the water, the cool blue green water. I swim deep with a school of orange-striped fish. My body becomes longer. I breath in the water. My body turns blue; my skin tingles. I have elongated.

Lucía looked at me with strange dark eyes, embarrassed. I disentangled myself from her and quickly walked on to our house.

I WAITED FOR MY NEXT SUITOR BY THE FOUNTAIN. Mother lined up these wastrels like a row of rotten eggs for me to step on. I would have preferred to kick the first, then let that one smash into the next, creating a line of crashing shells and splashing yolks. In the babbling of the fountain I imagined my captain telling incredible stories of the Conquest and the Indies. After a while I couldn't hear his voice, so I sat and watched the birds chase each other through the trees.

Young Diego sat down in my captain's chair. His green velvet cap was ornamented with a huge red plume.

"You are lovely," he said, struggling to look directly into my eyes. "Your gown of crimson and gold symbolizes the incredible beauty of your soul."

"Diego," I said, "this is not fitting on the Thursday before Good Friday."

"Love exists beyond time," he said, knowing he had been reprimanded.

"You are considerate and wealthy," I said looking directly into his gray eyes. "You would take care of me. You would be a splendid father. But you would be perfect for my mother, not for me."

"I will go to Africa. I will fight the Moors." His voice was low and sweet, but the faster he spoke, the more it lost its depth. "In the east, the Turks must be destroyed for what they have done to Constantinople. All this must be done, not for personal wealth, like some do, but for the Crown."

"You would do this, and you will do that," I mimicked him.

He looked as if I had just struck him across the face.

"My love for you is brighter than the stars, brighter than the sun." He was trying again. "My love for you has the depth of an old woman holding her grandchildren." He was on one knee now. "My love for you is the hope of the newest baby. My love for you is the happiness of the sinner who meets the Virgin Mary in heaven."

"Your love for me!" I exploded as I stood up. "Your love for me. . .your love for me. . . . Have you ever asked yourself if I have any love for *you*?"

"But," he sputtered, "I exalt in your beauty and glory."

"There is no hope for *us*," I hissed.

If Diego's love for me was the hope of the newborn, his face became that of a mother who delivers stillborn. He stood and hurried to the gate.

"Lucía," I called out.

She ran to me. "The men here act like bulls with no horns."

Lucía forgot her place and smiled.

"We will take a walk. It is time we visited Uncle Luis."

"But, Madam—" fear spread across her face— "he has been excommunicated."

"Lucía, Uncle Luis is old. He sits in front of his house all day drinking sherry manzanilla."

"What would happen if your family should find out you've seen him?" Lucía's eyes welled up as she pulled on her skirt and her blouse.

As Lucía and I entered Uncle Luis' neighborhood of small houses and dried-up flowers, I heard crying and wailing. Three women dressed in long, flowing black robes came toward us. Each was counting Hail Marys on olive wood rosary beads.

Lucía held my sleeve tightly as they walked by. "Why do they grieve so?" she asked.

"There is always death," I said.

Uncle Luis was sitting in front of his door. He rocked back and forth, whispering a silent song. His long gray hair twisted and turned, then fell onto his gnarled face. In that instant I saw his two faces—the returned conquistador who had saved us from a beheading, and this remnant of a soldier.

I hugged him, then told him of my needs and fears. My captain was to leave in seven days.

"You are a child of fifteen," he said as if that had anything to do with it. His eyes were soft, defeated. I involuntarily smelled chocolate.

"I came to you for help, and you give me the words of your younger sister, my mother. I thought you would understand."

"I too have doubts about this man. I remember his overwhelming ambition in the war in Tenochtitlan. The city was twice the population of Seville. I thought I was dreaming when I looked at its towers and pyramids. But Alvarado was more interested in blood than conversion and conquest."

Uncle Luis looked down in memory.

"But he loved Margarita, Uncle." He stood up, and we walked through the doorway of his small house. He seemed to have gotten shorter and rounder as I had gotten taller. I waved for Lucía to wait outside. The rain was light.

Uncle Luis shook his head as I closed the door. "Who knows what is true anymore?" he sighed. "Our land has been betrayed. Everything costs too much. No one knows what has value anymore. The King pleads with the German Houses for more Conquest money. Then there are more wars to protect the loans."

"The King and my captain are not gold grubbers."

"The King must repay the vast loans from the House of Fugger in Germany. If he cannot, there will be bankruptcy and disaster."

"This has nothing to do with my captain."

"There are rumors," Uncle Luis said, looking down again, "that he has another family." I knew he knew far more than he said.

"You do not conquer the Americas for Christ if you are a sinner."

Uncle Luis sadly shook his head.

I raised my voice and said, "You don't know. How could you possibly know?"

"Child," he said softly, "child, you are still young. Your captain is closer to my age than yours. He is fifty-two years old. You are a child, a child."

"You must have forgotten your Jewess, old man," I said in a rage. The gruff features of his face melted into loss and loneliness. I smelled rum. Shame poured over my soul.

"I miss her," he said, his gaze now inward. "It has been years. I see her, taste her, taste her like the morning dew. They needed to purify the land. They didn't know she was already perfect."

UNCLE LUIS, LUCÍA, AND I WALKED through the night to our house. The memory of his lost woman had brought him to my side. I was afire with hope. He entered the patio to speak with my mother, his younger sister. As he left my side, I noticed the scar running along the left side of his face. I did not remember that from the night of our abandoned martyrdom.

I waited in my father's library as they argued. My uncle was the oldest in the family. That gave him sufficient power, I thought. But he had betrayed her by sailing to the Indies, by living with an unconverted Hebrew, by not acquiescing to the Tribunal of the Holy Office of the Inquisition, by being excommunicated.

As he left, he passed the doorway to the library.

"Time, my child," he said, shook his scarred face, and walked away.

14

OUR CUSTOM ON GOOD FRIDAY MORNING is to fast and pray before attending the Stations of the Cross at the cathedral. Father and I knelt together in front of the central fireplace, where we quietly prayed the rosary.

Mother walked in and interrupted us with a cruel smile. "We found out from my uncle yesterday. Your captain is having more troubles in Court. They have taken away his Captain Generalcy of Guatemala."

"How can they do this after all he has done for the Church?" I asked as I stood up. Father looked down at his Jerusalem-wood rosary, blessed by the Pope. "He has brought pagan souls to Jesus Christ. He has brought the Crown great new lands for Spain. They must be jealous."

Mother laughed at me.

I stalked from the room in a rage. I ran to my father's library to cry and read. I just stared at the floor.

Antonio entered the room. He did not see me. He glanced around, then turned quickly over to the books. I wondered, Would my father have allowed a servant, a converted Moor, a Morisco, to read his books? I didn't know he could read. My father had broken many laws by teaching Margarita and me to read. But a Moor, a Morisco?

He picked out a small black book at the end of the highest shelf. I thought he was going to steal it. He opened it and read.

Antonio was a dark man. I thought he must have been handsome when he was young. Now wrinkles covered his arms and face. He was older than my father. His twisted right arm dangled in space while he held the book with his left. The arm had been ruined during his conversion.

He must have believed in his pagan god as strongly as I believed in Jesus, Mary, and Joseph. If Mother had known these thoughts, she would have shoved me into a convent. He closed the small book, then held it to his chest. It was almost as if he were receiving warmth from it. His eyes closed. His passion. I could not guess what book of my father's could give him so much joy.

Antonio opened his eyes. We found ourselves looking at each other. His black eyes widened in fear. The book fell from his hand. He picked it up, returned it to the shelf, pretending he had been dusting.

"What is that?"

His face went stiff.

"Nothing. Nothing at all."

"Bring it here, Antonio. Bring it here now."

"Yes, Madam."

He walked over to me carrying the book with his good left arm. He handed it to me, then turned to leave.

"Wait," I said. I opened the book as he stood by the door. The first five pages were in Arabic, the rest in Spanish.

Curiosity overcame me.

I looked at the cover. *Al-Muqaddimah*. I had no idea what that could mean. The author was Ibn Khaldun. How could my father have allowed this? I read on.

It was a book of science and philosophy. I glanced though chapters. I did not know they could think so clearly. The Arab writer described Aristotle as "The First Teacher." A strange name, not Christian.

As I read I become nervous. Could I be excommunicated for reading this? There was nothing that could help me. I looked closely. The writer condemned the black arts. I thought, Does he condemn them because of their power? The Moors were a mysterious people.

Perhaps here was a power capable of bringing my captain and myself together. No matter what the expense, moral or spiritual, I would use anything to bring him back. I asked Antonio about the book.

"I don't know anything about that, Madam," he replied.

"Antonio, you are a Morisco. You must know about what this writer condemns."

"I am a Christian now. I do not know anything about the black sciences."

"Do you know anyone who knows about these things?"

"I am a Christian. I have nothing to do with this."

I looked into his face. His eyes were dark, but no darker than those of many Spaniards. His thin face was wrinkled and tired. He seemed almost to be pleading with me. I realized he had no choice.

"Just the other day I heard of a *converso* who was accused of stabbing a consecrated host. Blood ran from it. They say he had been using it for evil magic. I don't know what the Dominican Inquisitors did with him."

Fear flooded Antonio's face. "Madam, would I not be as vulnerable as he if I joined you with a sorcerer?"

"At least you would not be accused of doing something you had not done."

The matter was settled. I tried to douse the painful flames blistering my conscience. Maybe a month in the fires. Maybe a year. Maybe eternity. Nevertheless, I would have my way.

I WALKED UPSTAIRS TO CHANGE FOR CHURCH. Mother stood in front of me at the top of the stairs, happily holding several sheets of paper.

"You doubted me," she snapped at me. Her teeth protruded from her face in a wicked smile. "These are the charges drawn up against your captain by the Audiencia of Mexico." She threw the sheets at me. "And this is the man you wish to spend your life with. Even your patron, my brother, your Uncle Luis, can do nothing now."

I left them scattered on the stairs and ran to my room.

I marched around my bed, calling my mother names. I banged my head against the wall.

I remembered her yelling at me to not drop the canister of flowers I had brought her for Easter when I was seven. I could not concentrate, and I dropped them. She yelled and whipped Antonio and Lucía. She told me I could never read because I was an idiot. She screamed at my father that he should scold me in church, that he let me get away with sacrilege. I remembered at night how I would walk through the courtyard to feel the cold on the bottom of my naked feet as a way to feel something other than shame and rage. I counted the squares on the flooring.

My captain had been through far worse. This is my test, I realized. I returned to the stairway and gathered up the sheets of paper. In my room I put them in order and read.

The first two charges were that my captain had robbed and

burned Indian villages. The third charge was that he had not paid the Royal taxes, that he had received large quantities of gold, jade, and cacao and had not shared them with his companions or the Crown; that he had massacred four hundred Aztec nobles who were innocently dancing and celebrating; that, because of this slaughter, war had broken out, and two hundred Spaniards had died and four hundred thousand Indians been killed.

I read about the land my captain would take me to.

> *And the further charge is made against said Pedro de Alvarado that, coming to Guatemala by command of Hernán Cortez, the people of these provinces warred with him and afterwards came to make peace, and the said Pedro de Alvarado seized the Kings and Lords and told them that they should give him gold, then burned them without any other reason or cause whatsoever.*

I stopped reading. They obviously did not know this man. They had gone too far. It was impossible my Spaniard, or any Spaniard, could commit acts of barbarism in the name of God. The Spanish conquered in the name of God, not gold.

"HOW DO YOU KNOW THIS WOMAN, THIS CARMELA?" I asked Antonio as we crossed the same bridge Margarita and I had crossed years before.

"When I was a child we lived next to her," he said. "We were very poor, and she offered to help my mother. I was her servant."

"And in that the way did you find out she practiced the dark arts?"

"She practiced every art. There was nothing she couldn't do."

"She hid her magic?" I asked as I heard the bells ringing from the cathedral. The sun was directly overhead. This was the hour Christ had been placed on the cross. The bridge was about the same as it had been that night. Now, there were ten magnificent floating ships in the river. They came and went, bringing riches and taking back hungry men and priests. Few women. I remembered waving good-bye to Margarita from here. I looked down and saw, tattered, the blue ribbon I had tied onto the bridge for her. I halted Antonio's hurried pace. I untied the ribbon and let it float down to the water. I attached a small metal lock to the wire railing. On the lock was written my love for my captain. I turned the key and threw it into the Guadalquivir.

"Not exactly," Antonio answered as we began to walk again. "It just seemed to be one of the dozens of things she did to make a living. She was a seamstress. She made perfume. She brought together young lovers."

"Does she use magic to solve problems that otherwise cannot be solved?"

"Yes. But I don't believe in that."

"It doesn't matter what you believe," I said, saddened at myself the second I said it. I excused myself: I was desperate.

We entered the impoverished Triana, then followed rocky streets to an old stone shed.

A shapeless old woman, covered with a dirty brown sack, opened the door. She shook her head in recognition. Her ancient brown skin was covered with splotches of yellow and red.

"Antonio, I loved you as a child, and you left me, you betrayed me," she said. She reluctantly opened the splintered door to us. The room was small and dark. I was disgusted by the smell of rotting things.

"I taught you all that I know. Where did you learn how to change fear into hope, garbage into money, hate into love? Wasn't all that from me?"

Was this is the Moor who was going to chop our heads off? I asked no one in particular. Not likely.

Old Antonio looked down. "Yes, Mother." Her head was covered with short white hair and seemed larger than it ought to have been for her short, squat body. White and brown moles covered her face like measles. A single black mole emerged from between her eyes.

"And now you stand there wanting a favor from me. You've gone off and become a servant to the wealthy, and here you are, wanting a favor. I cannot eat from the plate of old times. This old mouth can not survive on nostalgia."

"Mother Carmela," I said. "We did not come here to take advantage of you. If there is payment that you want, I will gladly provide that."

She threw a pathetic glance at me, then turned back to Antonio. "But it is my destiny, no matter what you have done to me, to love you. I have been treated like this by all whom I have helped. Everyone. Why did I suppose that you would be any different? Aren't all surrogate mothers blind to the deficiencies of their children? You must be able to see that, because I am sitting here talking to you instead of throwing you out with the garbage."

It looked like the garbage resided inside that miserable hovel.

Carmela picked up a glass of yellowed sherry from the table in front of her. A dead fly was floating in it. How could someone like this help me? I began to count rosary beads in my hand.

"No matter what happens to me, no matter what my children and lovers do to me, I can still see," she growled. She looked down at the fly, then drank it, too. "I can penetrate their thoughts. I can still peer into the roots of things. You know that. Or have you forgotten my skills, too?"

"Yes, Mother. I know you can do that." Antonio stood across from her in front of the table. I felt his fear of her. You do not fear something you do not believe is real. A tall black candle separated them. "That is why I have brought this good lady to your attention.

She has a problem you could help solve."

She turned her evil gaze on me. For a moment I was nauseous. But then I thought, I will do this for him, I will do this to gain my brave captain.

"A young woman dressed in finery. What could you possibly want with an old hag like me? There is nothing I could possibly do for the likes of you." She spat, and flies flew from the filth.

"If Carmela will consent," I said to Antonio, "I will tell her of a situation, a problem, that perhaps she *could* solve." I loved my captain, but I would not beg for help from this old heathen.

"Antonio, you've brought me such a fine lady. So young and so beautiful. She dresses in such finery. This must explain why she talks to you when she wants to talk to me. But that is sufficient. What is an old lady like myself to expect? I am beneath the glances of such a woman." The plaintive voice was betrayed by the anger in her eyes.

"A problem has arisen, Mother. You could help," Antonio said.

"It must feel wonderful to call me Mother again. I am poor and weak, and anybody can call me anything they want. Even ungrateful sons." She scratched at a mole on her arm. It bled. She turned from us to light another black candle.

"This woman is horrid," I whispered to Antonio. "Why did you think you could get her to help me? She despises you."

"Let me try again." Antonio rounded the table and stopped next to her. He began talking to her in a whisper. I could not understand what he was saying. It was not Spanish.

I blushed. This was what I had become. I consort with the devil's minions.

I looked at the books scattered about. I tried to count them.

"I will help you, Antonio. But I am embarrassed by what you have become. I did not raise you to become a lackey to the Christians." She turned her wrinkled old face to me. "Antonio has told me of your dilemma. For his sake I will help in any way that I can. I am old and do not practice this sort of thing anymore, but this frail old body and spirit will do the best that they can." Her smile was hideous.

"What can you do?" I asked her, genuinely frightened she could read my mind.

"Here." She pointed to a chair. "Sit down. Sit down. You sit down, and we shall get to know one another." Her tone was oddly sisterly.

My pride was broken. Righteousness had fled. I wanted my captain back. In my humility, I cried. I actually cried in front of this disgusting hag.

"Don't you worry," she said. "I can use spells and charms. There are things in these books that could change the world, if it were written that I would be allowed to do that. Sadly, it is not written. But I do have great powers. There are magical formulas that can help you, in this your hour of need."

I detected a note of sarcasm in her last words. She went on as if there were not. Antonio slowly shook his head. He did not believe in her powers. I didn't care.

"I can keep away the evil eye. There is nothing to it. I can stop the noise that one hears in the ear. It is simple. I can make people urinate when they don't want to or can't. It is easy. I can save the grape fields from drought, I can stop the fever and plague, I can break fever and bring snakes into the land. I can do this and much more. But you must tell me the truth. You must leave nothing out. If you tell me only half of the truth, not only will you not receive your request, your problem will become intractable. One of my lovely young clients turned into a hare because she left out a small detail. You must tell me everything."

I did. God help me, I did. I told her everything.

She asked me about my dreams. I motioned for Antonio to

leave us alone. In my shame and anxiety, I told her of the dream of the emerald bird and my swim in the water. She looked at me for a long time. She laughed. I wanted to kill her.

"My lady is quite passionate," she said.

"Now you must help me," I demanded

She shook her head, smiling. "Underneath all this torment is the desire of a young woman. There are great tides in you. The captain is the beach your waves strike. When the ocean is in torment, the sands on the beach rearrange to fit the desires of the waves."

"I request your aid, Mother."

She sighed. "If you insist. Nobody takes my simple advice. Everyone wants an amulet. Today is Good Friday. That will work. It is not a favorable day, but it should work. Yesterday I would have told you to go home. Wednesday is the day the Pharaoh sank into the sea. Last night was a full moon. That is also favorable to you. Some days are lucky, some are unlucky, and some start good and end badly."

"You must help me, Mother."

"You are *being* helped. Here, draw these designs. You will need them. You will boil three eggs. Remove the shells and write these inscriptions on each. Eat them. They will cool you."

I wrote down the symbols: lines emanating from circles with lines, swirling spirals that seemed to lift from the page.

"I want you to write this with your fingers on an empty glass." She drew lines that became circles that became spirals that became the cross that became a crescent moon.

"After you have done this, pour water into the glass and drink it. By drinking this charm, you will be safe for what follows." I copied the inscriptions. I wanted to throw up.

"Now here is the part that will bring your captain back. You must perform this task exactly as I outline it for you. But I don't think you *can* do this. We should stop now. I have asked you to do too much already."

"We must continue, Mother."

"You must do exactly as I tell you."

"I will, Mother."

"Take the skin of a black cat and the fat of a white chicken, mix them, and rub your eyes with them. This will allow you to see methods to bring your captain back, God willing."

"Is this what I need to do?"

"Partially. After you have done this, take the heart of the black cat and wrap it in the skin of a wolf. Cook it until it is tender. Feed it to your mother. Your captain will be returned to you." Her left eye began to twitch.

I thought: I will be damned to eternal fires. But I will have my man.

15

I RETURNED HOME IN TIME FOR SHERRY WITH THE LADIES. Traditionally, after Good Friday services my friends would meet at our house. We would refresh ourselves. He had suffered on the cross from noon to three p.m. After three, we could have *fino* sherry and a taste of green olives, salted almonds, and various cheeses.

I hoped none of them noticed I had not been at the cathedral.

I sat as Lucía served us. The four girls smoothed their dark gowns with light, dainty hands. They talked and puffed themselves up with gossip.

"And Diego, have you heard what has happened to Diego?" Eugenia put her glass on the table and looked at me.

"No, what has happened to Diego?" I asked, looking at the painting of the Crucifixion on the wall above her head. A dagger had entered His chest, and blood had spurted out.

"He has sworn he will become a priest."

The others covered their mouths with napkins and laughed.

"I felt something in my heart for this boy once," I said. "But now it is time for Diego to grow up and mature and to see other girls. Perhaps you, Eugenia."

"And you, Beatriz," she responded. "This must be a very difficult time for you. First, losing Diego and then this old man, some sort of sailor I understand, keeps trying to take up all of your time."

"This man, this sailor as you call him, is the savior of the Indies. He is the conqueror of more of the world than you can imagine," I said, feeling the blood rush to my face.

They laughed openly at my indignation.

In a rage, I pushed over the walnut table. Fine glass *copitas* flew through the air, crashing to the floor. I stood up. "This man has saved the Crown by bringing the King vast amounts of gold. This man I will marry. I do not care what my mother says, you say, or the Crown. Or the Church. I will marry him."

I stalked out of the front room, leaving them paralyzed in their chairs.

"Lucía!"

She boiled the three eggs. There was no complaint. I began with the easiest of the tasks. She brought me the cooked eggs. I removed the shells and sat them on the table. Steam rose from the small white eggs.

I stared at them. Lucía stared at me. On each I inscribed the symbols Carmela had given to me. I did not look at Lucía, but I could hear her gasp. After I ate the first one, I looked at her. She blessed herself over and over again.

I wondered: eternal fires for love?

I ate the last egg then told her to bring me an empty glass and a pitcher of water. She looked frightened. She returned as I had directed her. With a shaking finger, I inscribed the pagan symbols on the glass. I poured water into it and drank. I thought Lucía was going to faint.

She refused the next task.

She cried. She begged. "This will be my damnation. My children will be born of the devil. I will do anything you ask except consort with the devil. This is the devil's work."

"Lucía, stop it."

She shook with fear. "I do not want to spend eternity in hell. I will be damned, and my children will be damned, and my children's children will be damned."

"Your soul will not be lost," I said.

She grasped at her skirt. She pleaded. "I will sit in burning embers for the rest of the days of the world and all the days after. I've not even had children yet."

"The hell with your children!" I screamed. I knew the Lord would forgive her, not me. It would be me who would burn, not her. "You will do this for me. You will do this for me now. I don't care about you or your damned children. This must be done, and it must be done immediately. I wish it, and the good Lord wishes it. Remember who you are. Now do it."

Trembling, she brought me the skin of a black cat and the fat of a white chicken. And, yes, before I went to bed, I rubbed my eyes with them. Lucía whimpered.

I knew I would go to hell. That would save Lucía. The good Lord would accept me in exchange for her.

THE NEXT MORNING, THE SATURDAY BEFORE EASTER SUNDAY, I told Lucía to go to the tanners. She knew she had no choice. She brought back the heart of a black cat and the skin of a wolf. She said the tanner suspected her of witchcraft.

I was impatient but held my tongue. I touched her hair and gently caressed her face. "Lucía, I promise, you will come to no harm."

I thought of the times when we were children, before I could understand she was our servant. She had been my best friend. I remembered the two of us running around the fountain, giggling, throwing pink flower petals into the water.

She muffled her tears. She cooked the heart in the skin until it was tender.

In the heat of the afternoon I peeked around the corner as Lucía told my mother that this was a delicacy prepared especially for her. Her hand shook as she placed it on my mother's plate. My mother ate and complimented Lucía.

Lucía returned to the kitchen crying. Mother did not notice.

I saw no outward effects on my mother. As she left the table, she waved a bony finger at me, insisting I never think of that disreputable captain again. After her nap, Mother sat in the patio and prayed the rosary, white bony fingers grasping the black olive pits beads. Lucía turned to me, smiling.

"She has not died."

Lucía could see no difference in her. I had not wanted her to die. But a tiny illness would not have bothered me.

I could see the difference. She was talk. She was air. Here was an old woman chattering endlessly. Where had the substance gone? I looked at her and felt pity for her empty life. Carmela's magic had worked.

Mother had not changed.

I had. I could see.

BY LATE AFTERNOON, HOLY SATURDAY, I was standing in a long room in the royal Alcazar. This was the exact room from which our queen had sent Christopher Columbus on his fabulous journey. I ran my fingers along a long, cool mahogany table. Warmth from the great stone fireplace calmed my face. My great-uncle Francisco de los Cobos y Molina, secretary to the crown, had loved to tease me when I was a child. "Why are you so small and I so tall?" he'd say looking down at me, eyes twinkling.

As he entered the great hall I saw, again, he was taller than any man in our family.

He stood across from me, resting his sensitive light hands on the long table. I swore, if he was not my great-uncle, I would have fallen in love with him. My grandfather's brother reminded me of my father. This father with wisdom and power.

In the painting behind him, the Virgin Mary looked down at me, smiling. The grateful Indians of the New World surrounded her.

I gulped down another breath before beginning my petition to him. I was free from my mother now. I could speak my own mind.

"Wait, my child," he said, coming around the table, and took my hand. "Let's walk in the gardens. It is a beautiful afternoon, don't you think?"

He guided me from his office in the house of trade out to the hunting courtyard. At first I was overwhelmed. I began counting the large rectangles embedded in the flat brick-and-limestone plaza floor. I became disgusted by my fear. I forced myself to look up at the ancient walls and arches.

"You can say whatever you want about the Moors," he said, "but they knew how to build a beautiful wall."

I looked carefully at my great-uncle. From any other this would have been sacrilege. He walked with pain and steadied himself with his carved wood cane. He had earned the right to give them honor after killing so many of them.

"Here, take my hand," he said. "It is dark in the passageways." The hand was warm. At first, I thought it was a ruse to steady him. He steadied me.

We passed into the ancient building. A dark arched passageway opened into a bright-flowered patio. A long rectangular pool emerged from the surrounding garden. Strange designs in blue and red covered the walls. A strange peacefulness settled my soul.

"This is the Maiden's Patio. You know the story."

I looked down, embarrassed. The Moors had demanded a hundred Christian virgins every year as tribute.

"Don't worry," he said with a smile. "They are gone now. Don't believe the stories."

"Right through here," he said, leading into another passageway. We emerged into a vast garden with an overwhelming fragrance of orange blossoms. The Royal Alcazar was a labyrinth.

He held my hand tighter as I almost fainted from the sweet smells.

"Few have seen this. Here, I want to show you something," he said with a smile in his aged, twinkling eyes.

We passed alongside bubbling fountains beneath tall palms planted by the Moors. They were so ancient I thought the trees themselves must have forgotten who planted them. He stopped in front of a small building.

"This is the pavilion of Charles, king of a finally united Spain," he said. "After everything, I still don't know whether to call him Carlos or Charles. He loves his first tongue, French. He tells me Paris is not a city, but a universe. His Spanish is barely understandable. You know what I heard him say the other day? 'I speak Spanish to God, Italian to women, French to men, and German to my horse.'"

My great-uncle laughed.

"We have reconstructed this for him from the *qubba* of the Muslims. That was their oratory, their chapel. Every afternoon, our King leaves the royal alcazar to come here, to relax from the diligence of office. Come in."

Five arches seemed to hold the small building in place. Moorish tile covered every square inch. Orange lanterns lit our way to the royal armchair. My skin tingled. Embedded in the tile, repeated endlessly, were the words *Plus Ultra*.

"That was his idea," My uncle said. "It is everywhere."

He was dressed simply. Black velvet cap, subtlety embossed with gold and silver, a thin white collar with a black flowing robe below. The only jewelry he wore was a gold-and-silver medallion hanging from his neck. A deep red ruby radiated from its center. Twelve perfect pearls surrounded the medallion.

After a few minutes, my uncle saw I was recovering. He held my hand again.

"My dear," he began kindly. "I think you must miss Úbeda. Even after all I have seen and done, I still miss her."

He looked down. "And Margarita. There are so many losses in life. This is why I support the great artists. Their images carry on through eternity." He shook his head, musing. "Titian will allow every generation to see, and understand, our king. Unless another storm sinks our ships carrying great paintings and sculpture. The world lost a grand Titian to Neptune." He shook his head, then looked at me.

"Your parents spoke to me of this, uh, situation." He said "situation" slowly, deliberately. "I understand your mother's fears."

My heart died.

"Look at me," he said. His fingers guided my face to him. "Some of this is hard to say. Especially to a young girl. You need to know what the world offers as you enter into this marriage."

I thought he must have felt my heart jump through my face. He put his hand down. Could it be true? It would be allowed?

"Old Spain is dying," he said. "We have rid the country of seven hundred years of Muslim occupation. Our king and queen have exiled the Jews and Moors, even if converted. Ships arrive every week from the New World. Everyone thinks it is a new era."

He paused. "Look at the mazes on the walls in the palace, in this chapel," he continued. "Imagine that wall is Spain. You cannot have a vibrant nation if you untie the binds that hold her together. Follow a line, any line, in the *azulejos*, the ceramic tiling."

He pointed to the brilliantly colored tiled walls. "Spot a ceramic ribbon, a *cinta*. Put your finger on it and follow it, wherever it goes."

I did. But I really wanted to celebrate and sing and dance. The wall felt cold as my finger touched it. With my finger, I followed a green ribbon downward. "See. It goes over a different-colored thread, travels down, goes under, turns right, goes over, goes above, turns left, travels down to the baseboard. Imagine pulling that green thread out of the ceramic fabric. The whole thing would unravel. By the banishments, this is what we have done to Spain. Old Spain is no longer stable, no longer viable. She will collapse unless New Spain regenerates her."

I started to argue.

He waved me off. "The Jews and Moors are gone. Who will clean for us? Who will bring the horses? The new ones, with their foot stomping music, are migrating into Triana from Jerez. Where did they come from? Who are they, anyway? I think they will bring disease and pilfering. We need to be replenished. Luckily, that Italian, with his crazy ideas, came along at the right time. The way for Spain to survive is to rebirth herself through the Americas. You can be a part of that. We need the Indies. Our Indies."

It had never occurred to me that I could help the Crown.

"We will still owe the House of Fugger, the Germans. There will be no other way to repay them than from the Indies. No other way." He shook his head.

And yet again I was being told of our national debt. "But this great crusade is for God, not gold," I stammered.

He smiled.

I tried to understand. His was the message of my mother.

He saw my despair. "You have my blessings," my great-uncle sighed. "There will be no problem, I will speak to your mother. I will petition our King, Charles, to allow this marriage. The King will have to request dispensation from the Pope, but I'm sure that will be given."

I said, beginning a litany of gratitude, "My great-uncle—"

"In fact," he interrupted, "Charles looks quite highly on your beau. Perhaps with a little talk, His Majesty could sign a decree restoring the Captain-Generalcy in Guatemala and void the sentence passed by the Audiencia."

I wanted to kiss his white-goateed face.

"Beatriz, you have always been my favorite great-niece. Perhaps it is the fire inside you. Look at the garden. Do you remember this maze, child? I took you here when your family moved here from Úbeda. You were very young. You got lost and frightened. I heard your crying and found you. When you go to the Indies, if you become lost, I cannot save you. It will not be a game."

"You *have* saved me. I don't know how I can thank you."

"I could do no less for you. Though now that I think of it, perhaps Charles would be willing to nullify all future charges against Alvarado."

I tried to hide my tears by looking away. My wonderful great-uncle honored my pride by not noticing. "Stay here for a bit. Enjoy the garden light."

With this last gift, he rose, took up his cane, and slowly departed the ancient chapel into the gardens. I called after him, "God bless you, my uncle."

I rested my head against the tiled Moorish wall. The incredible beauty of the garden seemed to seep into the chapel. Every sensation was acute. The light carried orange-blossom fragrance mixed with the finest herbs. Through the arch a peacock spread his brilliant tail to greet me, to congratulate me, to confirm.

I stared at him. There is beauty here, I thought. What will be the beauty of the new world? Will that fantastic green bird of my dreams welcome me?

I left the pavilion by the entrance to the garden labyrinth. I had been very small when I got lost.

The gardens were like a symphony. Doves called deep and throaty—*who-whoo-who, who-whoo-who*. Swallows dashed overhead in singular twisting motions. Nine green yakking birds flew above. Green parrots from the new world.

I tasted chocolate memory.

I stopped in front of the Mount Parnassus fountain. It had seemed completely huge when I was a child. Not all that tall now. The fern-covered mountain, now hill, rose out of a pale blue pond. Greek god heads sprouting water looked out at the labyrinthine gardens. Heathen gods, cruel. But lovely. I counted twenty-seven. A white dove landed on top of Zeus's head. Wisdom. These were signs.

Two small tunnels had been carved into the base of the sculpture covered mountain. I leaned over. Inside the tunnels were water-sprouting nymphs. I was thrilled with the hidden joy. *Plus Ultra*. Without looking for them I wouldn't have seen. Without looking. . . .

In my bliss I lost my balance and fell into the cold blue water.

MOTHER AND FATHER STOOD IN THE CHILLY TWILIGHT in front of the open door to our house. In the failing light, they did not notice the wetness of my dress and hair.

"They have been consorting with the devil," Mother cried. "My daughter is killed in the New World by a man who wants our wealth. My youngest daughter wants to marry the murderer. And now my servants have been dealing in witchcraft."

Father looked at his fine leather boots.

"Mother?"

"After you went for your walk, Lucía came to me with a horror story of witchcraft and betrayal." She lowered her voice. She had realized the neighbors could hear her. "They've tried to poison me. Antonio is a part of the conspiracy. Lucía attempted to implicate you in this. She came to me because she was frightened for your soul."

I smelled incense.

"Leave by the back alley," Mother ordered the dark-robed priest who emerged from the door. He ignored her as he walked by, chanting the rosary. Three monks of the Tribunal of the Holy Office of the Inquisition followed him.

"Please," Lucía cried, looking at me as she appeared too from the house. A monk held each arm. The cry echoed into my heart. But fear froze my body. My God, where was my courage?

Antonio walked straight, head up. One of the monks held onto his crippled arm. He looked at me with his great dark eyes. The look entered into my bones, chilling me far more than my wet hair. At the end of the procession, a monk swung a silver canister of burning incense.

"I don't understand them," Mother said in both sadness and disgust. The procession turned from our street and disappeared. "They were loyal. We have been kind. What more could they have wanted from us?"

She saw that I was shaking and crying. She reached out and held me in her arms.

"Don't be afraid," she said gently, patting my hair. She pulled her hand back and looked at me quizzically.

I said nothing. What could I say? Despicable cowardice. I had won my captain, won dominion over my life, and lost that very thing I received when I was baptized.

16

N HIS RED VESTMENTS, BISHOP MARROQUIN smiled at us, then turned back to the altar and raised the golden chalice to the heavens. The altar bell rang. The other penitents bowed their heads. I continued to look. The two of us knelt directly in front of the altar.

Purple light from the high stained-glass windows streamed onto the cup. The gold chalice transformed the light into yellow and sent it flickering around the altar. The light hit the altar's silver and glass, then bounced rainbow colors back into our eyes.

After Communion, Bishop Marroquin carefully poured Holy Water into the chalice, drank from it, and dried it with a small white cloth given him by the tiny Indian altar boy. Against ritual, he turned to us holding the cup. My captain held my hand.

"This, my daughter," the bishop said, looking down to us, to me, "is a gift from your husband, Don Pedro de Alvarado Y Contreras, to honor the third anniversary of your marriage."

He nodded to my captain, then handed me the chalice. My captain smiled. I carefully held it. Inscribed onto the gold were the words *Beatriz, the Fortunate.*

"From a medallion to a chalice for my love," my captain whispered. He had taken off his great gold coin ornament when I told him I would finally bear him a child. I had wondered why, and what he had done with it. More gold had been added, and the Plus Ultra medallion had been transformed into a symbol of his love for me.

I held the chalice in my right hand, then carefully placed it on the wood floor next to me. I threw my arms around his broad shoulders and kissed his red beard. The choir sang "Lumen Ad Relationem."

He laughed.

"My daughter," the bishop warmly said.

I reached for the chalice and held it up. The bishop made the sign of the cross. "I bless this golden chalice in the name of the Father, Son and Holy Spirit." I knew what the church-going colonists were thinking—The chalice is lovely, and the woman holding it is beautiful.

My veiled dark hair was combed into a swirl on top of my head, which made me look older. My face had matured, and I had lost the plump little-girl cheeks. I was a woman now, far more beautiful than Margarita could ever have been.

I gasped as I realized my sin of pride. I held the chalice tightly.

"I pray that your journey will be safe and you will bring many souls to the arms of Christ," the bishop said to my captain.

OUTSIDE, ON THE STEPS, IN THE BRIGHT SPRING LIGHT, I held up the chalice for all to see. We heard the choir singing the "Gloria" from inside the cathedral. The Indians who had surrounded the front of the church cheered. Many fell to their knees and blessed themselves. Four of my Indian ladies-in-waiting cried. Beyond the throngs of Indians were the new Spanish buildings, then the silent green volcano.

The festivities began. There was dancing, and the Indian horn music echoed off the mountains. This was his good-bye celebration. The Indians were happy. Their clothes were sewn with every color of the rainbow. But their clothes could not hide their ugly scars, and almost every face was pockmarked.

"May I carry that for you?" one of my Indian maidens asked, looking at the gold chalice. With her dark eyes and smooth skin, she was the most beautiful of her people. I had asked her heathen name on her first day with me. Her tongue clicked when she spoke it. It sounded like "Exshtah." I had the priest write it in Christian—*Xtah*. I immediately christened her "Lucía." She would be my Indian Lucía. I could find forgiveness in my care for her. Perhaps not.

"No, Lucía," I said. "This is for Christians."

She nodded in understanding.

Many Indians gathered around us. In each face was the reason he had returned to this land. He was their god. Many eyes were cast down in fear. Even though he stumbled from his limp, he was the incarnation of dignity and power.

As we led the procession of conquerors and colonists through the town, I looked down the streets and alleyways. Crowds of Indians happily ran toward us. When we entered the town square, I noticed one narrow empty alley. I looked away from the thing hanging from a tree.

At the square, in front of our palace, we stopped. My captain stood in the center of the square. He touched his magnificent red beard. Throngs of Spanish and Indians cheered. He had returned a hero and was now leaving a hero. Many struggled to get a glimpse of me, his young wife, who was with child. The cathedral bells rang, and white birds flew through the cool Guatemalan air.

In front of the flagpole and under the flag of the crown, my captain ceremoniously said good-bye to the leaders of Guatemala.

First in line was the Dominican, Father Bartolomé de Las Casas. His fat assistant, Brother Domingo, stood behind him with his silly sloppy-dog smile. I could not stand his stupidity. Behind them were the other black-and-white-robed Dominicans.

My captain, in a gesture of forgiveness, put his hand out to shake that of the renegade priest's. To the dismay of all, Father Bartolomé turned away, toward that small alley.

I could barely hear my captain's whisper: "You will pay, Priest."

Next was the treasurer, Luis Castellanos. My captain embraced him.

"We will miss your great husband, Doña Beatriz," Castellanos said to me. I had never liked the way this man looked at me, eyes furtively glancing at my bodice. His voice sounded like a pigeon's. "But we shall carry on the affairs of the state in his name with his spirit."

"And my other surprise," my captain said, touching his beard and winking at me. "Your brother has left his post in Mexico, so that he could stay with you while I am away."

Eduardo made no move to embrace me and barely looked at me. He nodded. "I am fortunate to be here for you in this your hour of need." There were dents and scratches in his metal helmet. He looked exactly like mother would have looked had she been born a conquistador.

"And this is my wife, your sister-in-law, Leonor."

Her black eyes seared into my soul. She nodded and smiled at me. She seemed to be saying, *You do not need to accept me. You need to ask for my acceptance of you.*

Her full white-and-green dress was as fine as any I had seen in Seville. Her blue eyes and long, wavy red hair sent icy trembles down my back. She turned and spoke to her husband, my brother, then touched her red hair and gently twisted it. She had the high cheekbones and dark skin of the Indians. I looked over at my captain as he touched and gently twisted his red beard in the same fashion.

Leonor.

Those were his eyes, not the shape of them, but the color of them. There were his teeth. The cheekbones were not of him. They were of the heathens, high and bony. The skin was not of him. But the rest was. She was small and beautiful and almost my age.

I asked, Who is she?

My body and my soul traveled in two separate directions. I trembled. I did not want to show weakness in front of my sister-in-law. My step-daughter! I desperately looked for something to count.

I fell and gave up this world. The courtyard floor rushed up to me.

"YOU HAD A FIT, A CONVULSION," MY CAPTAIN SAID. "You were not of this world for three days."

I woke to the birds playing outside of my window. I smelled chocolate. I looked back at my delayed and concerned husband.

"The entire city has prayed for you during those days. All the affairs of work have stopped as the people, Indians and Spaniards alike, have prayed. You received the Last Rites."

My captain rose toward the open window, where he raised a white handkerchief and waved.

In minutes, the bells of the cathedral rang out. My captain looked relieved.

"I was worried."

I wanted nothing to do with him.

"You still look pale. I will put off my journey for a week."

I turned my back on him. The man did not exist. He was but

a pain brought to torture me. All I could think about, though, was how could I have married this creature, this pretentious man, who had killed off my sister and fathered a half-breed who married my own brother.

I glanced from my bed to my mother's wood cabinet. It had come from her mother, and her mother's mother, back to, I thought as a child, the Roman Empire. She had not let my sister take it to the New World. But she had given it to me. After four months, it had arrived. Nothing broken. I had placed Francisco de los Cobos y Molina's golden crucifix on top of it. I awoke each morning with the image of my uncle's love for me and my lost sister. I could feel the warmth of his hand in mine as I struggled through the cold Guatemalan nights.

The crucifix was gone. The medallion had been of insufficient quantity to make the chalice. There was nothing sacred to this pernicious creature.

IN THE PALE LIGHT OF THE MOON, I watched him get ready for bed. He was always gentle with me. This was his love for me. I was celestial, his angel. He quickly fell asleep. After his breathing slowed, I carefully unbuttoned his night shirt.

Red hair sprouted here and there from his pale flesh. A long scar ascended up from his chest, along his neck into his red beard. I had glanced at it before and imagined him heroic because of it. Now, it was only a symbol of error.

Another. A long red gash fell from his shoulder past his breast onto his stomach. His stomach was rounded with lines of age and gashes.

His thighs were covered with scratches and scars. I knew he was proud of each. Who had done this to him? He had been a farmer in Cuba.

"Would I have loved a farmer?" I whispered. "Would I even

have looked at you?"

I ran my finger, then my fingernail, along the scar that ran down his thigh. I imagined small dark Indians jabbing and scratching and slashing him. I pressed down into the lumpy mess that had been his right knee.

His right hand lurched up to grasp my throat. I choked.

"I NEED MORE SERVANTS," I TOLD MY CAPTAIN AT BREAKFAST.

"Twenty handmaidens. I would have thought you had enough," he said calmly.

I pointed to Lucía and her seven assistants standing along the wall. "Do you think this is enough for me? You have hundreds of soldiers."

My captain laughed. "Of course. Whatever you would like, my love."

That afternoon, he brought a group of twenty-five Indians, both male and female, to the palace dining room. They gathered in a group under the entry way. His gift.

In the middle stood an Indian male who, unlike the others, did not look down when I looked at him. I accepted the group with a nod to my husband. He shook his head and walked away.

"What is your name?" I asked the one in the middle.

"I am Francisco Hernández Arana Xajilá. I was born Belehé Qat, son of the Ahop Achí Balam," he said. There was something familiar in his bearing, something I had seen in the other Francisco, my great uncle Francisco. Something of my servant Antonio's dignity. He looked past me, with surprise, to the Indian ladies-in-waiting.

He was dressed in typical Indian clothing—black pants, a black jacket with curled red designs that reminded me of the Moors, and a small black cap. I looked at the Indian women. There were no expressions on their faces, except Lucía's. She had tears in her eyes.

I placed Francisco in charge of the rest. For some strange reason, I trusted him. The other Indians did exactly as he told them.

TWO DAYS LATER, FRANCISCO, THE FORMER BELEHÉ QAT, brought me a cup of chocolate as I sat in the courtyard.

"Where is your family?" I asked.

He was older than me, but not as old as my captain. His brown face was smooth, with few pox marks.

"Scattered in villages and in forests." He spoke in clear Spanish.

"But your people are all over this city." I was surprised to find him handsome. "Many of the Kaqchikel live in the mountains. There," he said, pointing past the dead volcano. "Others live by the holy lake, Atitlán." Lucía stood to my right. I glanced up from my chocolate and saw them gazing at each other.

NIGHT. I WALKED BY THE OPEN DOOR OF OUR HOUSE CHAPEL. Francisco sat on a wooden bench under the candles, reading strange fold-out pages. There were strange designs and writing. Indian books, I guessed. I stood in the doorway, watched, and thought of Antonio.

"I MUST RETURN TO SPAIN," I TOLD MY CAPTAIN.

"You are homesick."

"I grow bigger every day," I said. "Sometimes he moves in me. I despair much of the time. I need my mother during this time. She is not here. There are only old Indian women who offer to help. I think they are witches. What am I to do?"

"You are acting childish."

"If childish means I am now with child, yes, I am acting childish."

"Leonor would like to stay with you."

"I hate her. How can I accept help from this half-breed daughter of your Indian wife?"

"My Indian wife has been dead for seven years."

"And didn't you marry Margarita eight years ago?"

His hand shot forward to my throat. He held it there. This time he was fully awake. He looked down to my belly, then let go. I took in a whoosh of air as he stalked out of my room. I picked up my golden chalice from the wood stand by the window and threw it at the wall. As it completed its roll on the floor I saw a dent on one side.

Another earthquake shook the walls. I sat down next to the wall and held the chalice to my heart.

I began this journal that night: I was a child when I was a child. I thought I was a woman. Simply, I was a simple girl.

17

A LETTER ARRIVED FROM MY MOTHER. I could almost see her bony finger pointing at me and her crying out, "I warned you. Look at how you have ruined your life."

At first I refused to read it. The letter lay on the table by my bed. I could not bear her admonishment.

I opened it. Perhaps with an overabundance of pain, pain might lessen.

I read the sweetest letter imaginable. She was glorious. Every letter, every line of ink, every breath that had touched that paper, was Spain. She was marvelous. There were no recriminations. I was careful none of my tears touched the paper.

She knew my heart. She knew my soul. How could I have been rude to her? She knew me better than I knew myself. She told me to find a confessor, a confessor I could trust. God has sent this trial. He wants me to accept this trial and continue my life in His light.

"Mother, Mother," I wrote back to her, "I miss you. I was

wrong. Somehow this miserable man made me a drunkard of love. I was inebriated with him. You were the sober one."

AT DINNER MY CAPTAIN AND EDUARDO discussed the Dominican, Father Bartolomé.

"He's been appointed Protector of the Indians," Eduardo said, his mouth full of chewed beef. "He sends letters to the court all the time. They actually listen to his ravings."

Leonor ate little. She smiled at me. I looked at the two small silver angels hanging from the white wall above her head.

"The court will change its mind once they see what a fool he is," my captain said.

"He is more self-appointed than court mandated."

"In Cuba, he owned slaves. Now he is holy and sanctimonious."

"He should be driven from the land," Eduardo said, throwing red wine into a mouth still full with beef.

"No, he can't be," my captain said. "He is protected by the King."

He will be my confessor.

LATE THAT NIGHT, I LOOKED FOR FRANCISCO. He was in the chapel again, sitting on the wooden bench, reading in the candlelight. Lucía sat on the bench next to him. They both rose when I came through the entryway.

At his feet were white pages, an ink cup, and a quill.

"What are you doing?" I demanded, pointing to the papers.

"The Dominicans taught me how to translate the Christian bible into our language. I am translating our bible into your language."

"*Our* bible? You have heaven and hell and an Indian Jesus Christ?"

He looked at me and smiled. "A little different."

"Do you know how to find the Dominicans' house?" I asked.

ON MY THIRD VISIT TO THE MONASTERY, Father Bartolomé consented to hear my confession. During the first two meetings he had complained about my husband.

"Do you own slaves, my daughter?" Father Bartolomé had asked. He was bald, tall, stooped over. The light of the candle lengthened his nose, giving him a frightening countenance.

"Everything I possess is not mine. I possess nothing. My husband owns everything."

"My daughter, if you do not own slaves, I can hear your confession. I cannot hear confessions of those who own slaves. That is the devil's work."

Now he was different, quite different, softened. He said not a word as I told him of my life. The orange light lit his face.

"You are new to a foreign land," he said. "You are young. Your obligation is to your husband. He is the work Our Savior has given you."

"But Father, I am with child," I pleaded. "I do not want my child to be born in this land that killed my sister."

"My daughter, it does not matter what land you are in. Follow the Holy Family's example. As they fled the cruelty of Herod and found strength in each other, so too must you."

"But, Father, I am pregnant. My mother is across the ocean. My husband is planning on conquering new lands. There is no one that I can call friend in this land. Father, I want to go home."

"My daughter, this is a woman's sacrifice."

"Father, I hate this land. Father, I hate this man."

"My daughter, there are obligations we must keep. It does not matter how we feel about those whom we are obligated to."

"Father, I heard a rumbling last night," I rushed on without taking a breath. "It was very late, and there was no one awake. I was asleep in my bed, and there was silence. I heard a low noise that seemed to come from the deepest part of the earth. It got louder.

I heard the rumbling, then I felt the rumbling. It was like it came from my very bones. I rose out of bed and could see that the room was swaying.

"Father, I am so frightened. My husband, the great captain general, rose from the bed and looked at me, looked at my white nightgown, and did not console me, did not protect me, did not offer aid. Father, my husband rose during the night, heard the rumbling, saw my terror, and took me. I thought husbands were supposed to protect their wives like mothers protect their children. I am his chattel."

The Dominican nodded in understanding. He closed his eyes, then said, "Daughter, dry your eyes. This is the way the world is. He sees you as the Spanish see the Indians. You have an obligation to him as a wife, but you also have an obligation to God. Both obligations must be fulfilled. There is no choice in this matter. To meet your obligation to your husband, you must allow him to be a man. To meet your obligation to the Lord, you must find ways for the Indians to be released from their slavery."

"Father, what about my own slavery?" My pain began to turn to anger. "I am having his child. What if she is a girl? Does that mean I am sending another slave into his world?"

"Daughter, your obligations are to the Lord and to your husband."

"And what of my obligation to myself, to my unborn child?"

"Daughter, your highest obligation is to the Lord. Next is your obligation to your husband. Your obligation to the Lord is that you must find a way for this man to release the Indians."

"Father, you would save these savages and leave me in subjugation."

ON MY CAPTAIN'S LAST MORNING IN OUR CITY, he killed Indians. From my bedroom window I counted eighteen Indian bodies hanging from trees in the plaza.

I was afraid for Francisco. If he had not been killed, I knew where he would be. His books and papers lay at his feet. My poor bent golden chalice sat on the chapel altar behind him.

"They have killed us. The Captain General Alvarado has hanged Vakaki Ahmak and Cahi Ymox, our kings."

For the first time I thought, They may not be savages. There was water in his eyes. They feel as we feel. They have hearts as we have hearts.

"Before your husband has left, he has hanged our leaders, our brothers, our friends. My brother. They have been in jail for fourteen years. What more can he extract from us?"

I thought of Lucía and Antonio walking off to the Inquisition. I shook my head and, again, in my shame, could not find anything to say.

I TOOK MY PLACE AT THE PUBLIC SQUARE in the same line that greeted me after our third anniversary mass. I was at the head, followed by Bishop Marroquin, the Dominicans, Castellanos, and finally Eduardo and Leonor. The eighteen Indians had been cut down and tossed into a ravine.

The conquistadors marched in front of us with my captain at the lead. The Captain General Alvarado dismounted, took off his helmet, and limped over to me. The rest of his men sat on their horses at attention. Their silver-peaked helmets pointed to the empty blue sky.

He leaned down to kiss me. The captain's red hair looked more like blood than beard. In front of all, I turned my face from him. He stood still.

"I am grievously sorry to be leaving you," he said, loud enough for those in line to hear him. "These are the King's and Our Lord's orders I follow."

"I am a piece of meat you left unfinished at the dinner table," I hissed.

"Now that the Indian traitors are gone, you will be safe. The Treasurer Castellanos will be in charge of the city. Your brother and Leonor will assist you."

"Your baby and I will not be here when you return."

The captain walked down the line. He shook hands with the bishop. The Dominicans turned and walked away. Castellanos wiped tears away from his eyes. Eduardo saluted, and Leonor curtsied.

The captain, no longer my captain, Pedro de Alvarado, mounted his horse, saluted me, and with his conquistadors, rode through the earthen city streets to the green mountains beyond.

Though I never wanted to see him again, it did occur to me that I might never see him again.

"There will be a special dinner at our house tonight," Leonor said after the last horse had trotted out of sight. "I have brought entertainers and musicians from Mexico to entertain you."

Eduardo's cool gray eyes followed the dust of the last horseman.

"Your musicians would serve you better," I said calmly, "if they were magicians and could transport you back to the mud hut you came from." I turned from Eduardo and Leonor and returned to our palace accompanied by Lucía and my handmaidens. They were too afraid even to look at me on the walk back.

"Go inside and do something useful," I yelled at them after I stopped in front of our palace. "Go eat a tortilla."

In my rage and despair, I marched around to the back of our great house, to the side that faced the volcano. I stopped to look up at the great green mountain. There was a path that led to the volcano. I walked along the path. After one turn through the trees, I saw an Indian on his knees, swinging a canister of coals. Francisco rose quickly.

"What are you doing?" I asked.

"Praying."

"That's why God gave us churches." I pointed to the cathedral.

"I pray in the church to your god. Here I pray here to Hunahpú." He nodded toward the volcano.

At that moment, again, he reminded me of my lost Morisco, Antonio.

"Hunahpú?"

"His spirit lives in the lake on top of the volcano."

"He should have been around this morning," I said, "to have saved your people." As I turned back I thought, He should have been around when I fell in love with that red-haired madman.

NIGHT, AND THE RUMBLINGS BEGAN AGAIN. I lay in bed, and the baby moved. I could not breathe. It was like a great weight placed on my chest. I could not push my chest upward to bring in any air.

I wondered what fear would do to my baby. Would he be stillborn? That would be the final gift from my husband.

I had daydreamed for years what our firstborn would look like: red curls, flashing blue eyes, wide shoulders, pale skin. The son of the great conqueror. He would continue the great captain general's legacy. I would raise him to be strong and willful. The girls would swoon, and cowards would hide.

As the earthquake continued, I knew I wanted a girl.

In the morning, there was a gray overcast. Behind the vines and red flowers there were cracks in the walls.

HE WROTE TO HER FIRST. He showed his greater love for her than his love for me. At dinner, at the idiot Castellanos's house, she showed off the letter. Everyone touched it and read it.

"I thank the Lord everyday for this great man," she said.

"Do your people also thank the Lord for your father, their conqueror?" I asked calmly. There was a moment of silence in this ridiculous dark creature's red hair and blue eyes.

"My people are grateful for this great man because all Christians celebrate the conquest of souls," she replied in a lecturing manner, then acted again like a silly little girl, chatting endlessly about another woman's gown.

FINALLY, HE SENT ME A LETTER. It had been a full week since Leonor had received hers. My humiliation was complete. I was second in his estimation.

I did not open it but held it in my right hand. There was nothing in the letter that could right this. He had absolutely disgraced me. I imagined tearing the letter into shreds, then burning the remnants.

I dried my tears and opened it.

I sat in the patio next to the fountain, as I had in Spain. Above me was the green volcano. The sky had turned pink. Dark birds flocked to the trees.

It was a letter of a man who detailed his ship's supplies. A man whose vainglorious plans rendered me irrelevant.

Rendered irrelevant by an Indian child; rendered irrelevant by a husband who had left me. I, who was to be queen of the New World, had less station than a child.

Another month went by, and my handmaidens began to marry, one at a time, the handsome captains and lieutenants the captain general had left behind. They had taken on great lands and become *encomenderos*.

I cried at each wedding.

She walked through the streets as if she were the queen of the land. She called out to Castellanos, "Wonderful morning, isn't it?" She waved to the clerics. She smiled and laughed with everyone except the Indians, whom she ignored.

I remembered the widows of Spain. Their husbands were killed in various wars or during the conquest. They wore black and their lives were over. I have become a widow with a breathing husband.

Leonor asked about me every time she saw me, "How are you? Any word from your great husband? I pray daily for his safe return."

"I am well, thank you," I said coldly. "He will write soon."

She nodded and continued on.

My handmaidens began to turn to her. She provided them with favors from her husband, my brother. They attested they loved her and would do anything for her. I thought, when my husband, the true Captain General returned, there would be changes. Even though he had written her before me, he could not allow my place to be usurped by this Indian impostor.

CASTELLANOS LOVED BEING THE TEMPORARY CAPTAIN GENERAL. Indians were beaten in the streets. Hangings began again. Small colonial ranches were taken and given to the Castellanos family. He thought he himself was the sun god. I did the best I could to deflate his self-importance when he brought me mail.

"This letter," he squawked as he handed me a letter as I sat in my courtyard, "has your husband's seal."

I leisurely took the envelope and wondered if she had received the same letter.

Castellanos casually tried to look over my shoulder.

"I need to rest now," I said as I fanned myself with the letter. He left with his lower lip hanging from his mouth.

I looked at the dense and correct lettering of my husband. He had written from Mexico. The viceroy of New Spain had proposed that the captain general join him in the search for the Seven Cities of Cibola. They had worked out a contract to share in the wealth of the Seven Cities as well as the wealth of the Spice Islands.

As I read the captain general's description of the Seven Cities, I heard his voice; I heard his tones and rhythms as I had heard them long ago sitting by the fountain. Here was a rich voice, full of feeling and excitement and imagination. I remembered the excitement I had felt for him.

I also heard my mother's voice: *Silly girl. Marry someone responsible. Someone you can trust.*

The Seven Cities, he wrote, are reported to be more fantastic and rich than anything heard of before, anything recorded in history. *The monk Marcos de Niza has described them in exact detail. They lie north above the Gulf of California. This,* my captain general wrote, *is the first hint of the actuality of El Dorado.*

El Dorado.

I read on for a glimmer of detail, then held the letter to my breast.

The line of Spanish conquistadors slowly descends from the mountains. They march toward the seven cities. He leads as they cross a wide waterless desert. Suddenly in the distance, he sees flashes of reflected light, golden light.

A city.

As he and his troops march closer, they see it is several cities, each with towers, glowing in the light. They march forward; his men want to rush ahead in excitement. He orders them to calm themselves.

As they march into the first city, natives rush out to greet them. They wear magnificent cloaks of colors and feathers and jewels. My captain general is welcomed with baskets of fruit, baskets of green feathers, and baskets of jewels, jewels of every color and hue.

They continue the march through the city. The Indians fall to their knees in worship. They recognize the red cross of the Order of

Santiago and pray. They accept him immediately as their leader and shepherd of Christianity.

The Spanish troops stop in the center of the city. He looks down for a moment. The children are playing with gold. He looks up at the towers. They are made of gold. This is the first of the Seven Cities of Cibola.

The chief humbly escorts the Spanish into his ancient palace. The steps are made of gold. The tall and wide door is made of gold. The doorknob is made of gold. Inside, the sweet odors of incense surround them. They become accustomed to the twilight-like light and then see that the grand hall is covered with magnificent weavings. He looks closer and sees that woven into each quilt are diamonds.

"Stop this, you silly little child!" Memories of Mother's voice burst into me like thunder. I was a fool.

18

AS MY TIME DREW NEAR I FOUND MYSELF in church, praying. I looked at the cross. Leonor knelt next to me. I imagined my baby playing and rested my arm on my enlarged womb.

At the end of morning mass the rumbling below the church brought me back to Guatemala. I looked at Leonor. Her calm and placid face was terrorized. There was a certain joy in my heart for this.

The swaying of the cathedral stopped. Bishop Marroquin turned to us, his parishioners, stretched his arms out as if he were on the crucifix and said, "God's will be done."

I could hear Leonor breathing, trying to control her panic. She was truly frightened. I reached over and touched her arm.

As we walked down the aisle I tucked her shaking arm under mine. She looked as if I had pulled her from the grave.

From the bottom of the cathedral steps the Indians watched us. Their eyes were focused in continual amazement. There was strange movement on the steps this morning. People spoke quickly, secretively, without glancing at me. I looked up and saw a green bird with long emerald tail feathers fly up into the church tower.

IN THE AFTERNOON, I SAT BY MY FOUNTAIN in my little garden in our courtyard and felt the captain general's baby touching my insides, laughing, playing, tickling me.

Francisco walked quietly over to me.

"Will you receive the bishop?"

"Send him in."

Bishop Marroquin stood before me. He looked down at his hands, then further down to his shoes. His clothes were newly arrived from Spain. Here was a rich bishop.

"We have received a letter from the North," he said.

"Does Castellanos have an overabundance of Indians to hang and is therefore too busy to deliver my mail?"

"The letter comes from the Viceroy Mendoza. The letter is dated July fifth. It has taken almost two months for us to hear of God's will."

"Father, I am with child. Please tell me the contents of the letter before my baby is born."

"Doña Beatriz, your husband is dead. He was killed in a war with the savages."

THE WIDOW BEATRIZ. At first I rejected the bishop's declaration. I thought whoever this Viceroy Mendoza was, he must be mistaken. Then I thought: How could anyone mistake the Captain General Pedro de Alvarado?

He was dead.

I felt my baby crying as I read and reread the letter. My baby was to be born without a father. The baby would have no father. The Americas have lost their father. Whatever kind of father, nevertheless, Father.

"I've requested the Captain General Castellanos to proclaim that the city has entered into a state mourning," the bishop said.

"Acting."

"Doña?"

"The acting captain general."

"Yes, Doña. The Acting Captain General Castellanos has proclaimed a state of mourning."

I did not understand why, after all the years of crying, I felt no tears.

"How was he killed?"

"It is in the letter, my lady," the bishop answered. "Your husband and his men attacked savages. A horse on the ridge above him stumbled and fell."

"Fell on him?" After all the wars and conquering, he had died a fool.

"Where is this place?"

"On the mountains near Guadalajara, in Jalisco. The Indians there are brutal. We can arrange your return to Spain. It should be after the baby is born. But immediately afterwards, you can return to your family."

"Spain? It is gone for me and will never return. I do not want it back now. I am the widow Doña Beatriz. Of Guatemala. Of the Americas."

The bishop's eyes widened.

"Francisco," I called as I stood. "Thank you," I said to the bishop, "Please leave me to my grief now."

"Of course."

"Francisco," I called again.

Francisco knew. He had the slightest smile. I did not care. I did not care if he had killed the captain himself.

"The letter says he was killed in Muchitiltic. What is this place?"

"It means black lands. All black."

Muchitiltic. I was no longer the child Beatriz, the younger sister of Margarita, the wife of the captain general, the daughter of my mother, the niece of the secretary to the Crown. No. I was the widow Doña Beatriz.

"Paint the palace black. Everything. All black in the name of the place of his death."

Francisco did not flinch. "There is a black spring at the foot of the volcano."

HE GATHERED TOGETHER THE INDIAN SLAVES. Before they left to retrieve the oil for painting, he returned to me. I sat in the chapel, holding my dented gold chalice.

Your husband's daughter is here," Francisco said. I had asked him never to refer to her by her given name.

"Leonor. I will see her."

THE INDIANS AND THE CONQUERORS AND THE PRIESTS all thought the black was my grief. They were wrong. The black was the emergence of the true Beatriz.

The Black Beatriz.

There was a moment while I waited. Time. Before, everything was urgent. To have the captain, to travel to the New World, to stop Leonor. Now time had become my servant.

"Doña Leonor." I rose from the wooden bench to greet her.

She looked up at me from her black dress. She was shocked. I had never called her Doña; I had never given her that respect.

I opened my arms to her. We embraced. She began to cry, to sob in my arms.

"What will become of us? He was all we had," she sobbed.

"There is your husband, my brother, Eduardo," I said.

"He is not of the gods."

I held her dark face and caressed her long red hair. She was a child. How could I have been frightened of her? I could see as I saw after the charms of Triana.

"You are his daughter. You are my sister-in-law," I said. "You are my step-daughter. We are family. I will protect you."

She cried into my arms. I held her as I had wanted to hold my lost Seville Lucía.

By morning the outside walls were black. By the next evening, the inside walls were black. But that was not enough. I had them paint the roofs black. That was not enough. I had them paint the stones of the courtyards. Even that was not enough.

BISHOP MARROQUIN AND THE ACTING Captain General Castellanos looked at the black walls and black cobblestone. At first they stammered and seemed confused. I sat by the fountain. Fountains always refreshed me, reinvigorated me, brought me peace. Fountains were a gift of the Moors, my uncle had told me. As they spoke, I wished there was a way to turn the water in the fountain black.

"Doña Beatriz, we have great respect for your grief, especially at this hour," Castellanos said. "But we also must tell you that many residents of this city are upset with you. Even the Indians are chanting at their volcano. We share your grief, but this is too much."

The acting captain general was a boring man. His voice was that of the *castrati* and his soul the same.

"Be silent, you! How dare you come into his house and challenge the grief of his widow."

The bishop tried to console me. "We understand your grief. We respect this pain. God Almighty is merciful. He could have sent an even greater disaster. There are many things that He could have done to us."

I screamed at these paltry reflections of true men. I ordered at them to leave, leave immediately, leave the house of the captain general. "There could be no greater catastrophe than the loss of the captain general."

The shock and dismay spread over their faces. One does not question the will of God. I had.

Francisco lurked in the background. He stood at attention the way we had taught Indian slaves. His face was impassive. Yet when I said that there could be no greater catastrophe, his eyes had become like the morning sun. Not a muscle in his face moved, yet his eyes were on fire.

They were shocked. I had no use for any of them. They were now afraid of me. Even the Bishop did not attempt to correct me.

"This is September 8, 1541," I said as a teacher would say to an ignorant child. "This is the day, this is the time, that all history in the Americas will change."

Shock and confusion covered their faces.

"You will name the widow Doña Beatriz as governor and captain general. You will name her as this, and you will accept her in this capacity. This is an order. You have no choice."

They were as children when the mother says, "You have done wrong. Go to your room."

"The church will see this as a sacrilege," the Bishop said.

"Your minds are small, and your bodies are weak," I said calmly, rubbing my stomach. "I am with child, and my body is vibrant with the correctness of what I have proclaimed."

"But Doña Beatriz," Castellanos sputtered, "there are no legal arrangements which could allow such an event."

"You, a minor official, were planning to become the new captain general, to take my husband's place. But your body, your mind, your spirit, are weak."

They stood in silence. They stood exactly as I pictured they would. The captain general would have had an answer instantly. They had no answers.

"Leave me to my grief," I said, waving them away.

They paid their respects to me and quietly filed out of the palace. This was the way of poultry. They would walk over to the council chamber. They would talk, discuss, belabor, ponder, and argue. Out of confusion and fear they would agree with me. I had only to wait in my black garden for their return.

The gentle sounds of water dropping from the fountain caught my attention.

"Francisco," I called out. He came immediately.

"Have them pour what is left of the dye into the fountain."

Again, his face did not twitch or waver. Again, his eyes were ablaze.

"You do not approve?" He looked down to the black cobblestone. "Francisco?"

"It is not my place to approve or disapprove."

"But you disapprove."

He looked at me. He could not control his eyes. His soul could not be controlled.

"We Kaqchikel have never understood the Spanish."

"What was he to you?"

He hesitated, then smiled. "My people called him Tunatiuh, the sun. We thought he was a god. I think he was made from the trees. He was wood."

Wood? I had no idea what he was talking about. I wondered if this Indian had a soul. If he didn't, he was like me.

Francisco had them bring black oil for the fountain. Black water bubbled from the fountain in memory of the Captain General, Tunatiuh. I had long sheets of black cotton attached from our great ceiling. I walked through the halls of the palace, holding his baby in my womb. I was covered in black. The Indians had sewn me long sweeping robes of black. This was the true Beatriz, the black soulless Beatriz.

IT WAS OVER. They had met in the council chambers throughout the night. With baggy eyes and glittering clothes, they stood at attention in the great hall of my palace. Some acted as if it were their own idea.

Castellanos was the first to chirp. He smiled. His kind eyes twinkled with good will. He acted happy, and he lied.

I stood before them in my black robes. Leonor stood beside me. She was also dressed in black. Eduardo stood next to her, and they held hands. Great black curtains fluttered in the breeze from the doorway.

"Doña Beatriz has been elected captain general of the land," Castellanos announced in his high voice. He smiled as if he was doing me a favor.

He spoke to the great glory of my husband and the glory that was mine. *Castrato* or not, this was still a man to challenge my position.

"I accept the charge that has been given to me in the name of my great husband," I said to the celebrants. "I would like to thank the officials of this savage land for their bestowing this title on me." I tried thus to make my peace with these small people. "I will carry out my duties and serve His Majesty as if I were Pedro de Alvarado."

I repeated the oath of loyalty to the king.

Castellanos held the council book before me.

The bishop handed me a quill. "This signifies your title, Doña Beatriz."

I waited while I thought. They became impatient. They had to wait. Then I signed. *Doña Beatriz, The Unfortunate.*

The bishop shook his head. He did not approve. He must have thought it too dramatic.

I looked back at my signature. It was not correct. A lie. There was no more Doña Beatriz. I crossed out part of the signature.

Now it read, simply, justly, *The Unfortunate.*

The bishop and Castellanos frowned, then remembered their positions. They both solemnly applauded.

I turned to them and said three words.

"No more hangings."

NIGHTFALL. A great storm besieged Guatemala. I knelt and prayed in my small chapel. Though I could not see the damage, I knew it was washing the black oil from the palace walls.

In a flash of lightning, I saw Francisco and Lucía in the doorway. In that blinding flash they became my Antonio and the first Lucía.

"Will you return to your people?"

"Some of our family are here, servants and slaves to your people." I nodded. I had thought they were going to thank me.

"Our son, Cotuha, is a servant for the Castellanos family," Lucía said. She was small, weathered by these storms, but she carried more stature than the bishop. I wondered how my servants could have a grown son within seven months of meeting. A servant with an Indian name: Cotuha. They must have known each other before. The mysteries of Guatemala. Someday, I thought, I must ask them.

Francisco handed me two packets of papers, crude Indian pages with drawings and writing. He motioned for me to save the first packet. The pages were wrapped in leather strings. Clearly they meant something to him. The front page referred to his sons. I put them in my cabinet.

With urgency, he pointed to the second packet. These were drawings. They were clear. In the first panel, men gathered around, talking. In the second, they rushed here, rushed to this, my palace. In the third, they entered this building and surrounded me. In the next they took me away to the capital's jail. In the last, there was a ceremony declaring a new captain general.

Castellanos! The Indian had drawn Spanish treachery. Indian loyalty.

I listened to the rain pouring down the outside walls.

"You're from their royalty, aren't you?"

He looked at me.

"And so are you, Lucía."

Their gaze did not waver.

"Francisco, bring Eduardo here. Tell him to bring his guard, also." My fury felt like the wind and rain falling from the black sky. They departed together like some kind of tiny, brilliantly colored king and queen. I rose and turned to the altar. At the center was my poor dented golden chalice. I held it to the candlelight. In the bowl of the chalice, I saw my shimmering, determined face. I was more like Margarita now than myself. The night rain fell, the earth rumbled. The earth turned into sea waves. The great earthquake had begun.

I held the chalice to my breast. I felt my baby kick as I trembled and the walls shook. This was to be my chocolate and churros heaven; it had become my hell.

In that moment I picked up this journal. I wrote out of loss of my dream. I wrote so that my child would one day understand. On this night of torrential rain and earthquakes, I write this. I will keep this journal safe in the top drawer of the cabinet. After the storm and the earthquakes subside, I will retrieve it and send it to my family in Seville.

THIS IS MY REQUEST FOR FORGIVENESS from my unborn daughter's grandmother.

Book III

Under Heaven, Above Earth
1536 to 1541

19

WHEN I CAME TO THE NEW WORLD, I thought I would convert every savage in the land. There was my sin of pride. It was washed away by the flood of reality. By the time I die, I will be lucky to have converted thirty-eight. Maybe forty.

Naked Indian girls and women played on the sandy banks of the ocean when our ship landed. I felt my heart beat. I thought I would faint. I blessed myself and considered looking away. I did not.

We went ashore. I carried all the things I was expected to. I lugged and dragged everything imaginable. This was the New World. And I saw none of it. Sounds of birds, trees blowing in the humid breeze, but my eyes and ears were elsewhere.

I glanced over my shoulder when no one was looking. The naked savages were gone. Returning to the ship to pick up more baggage, I quickly walked over to the railing where I had seen them.

I stood, shameless, with my hands on the rail, looking out to the beach. I worried one of the sailors might guess what I was looking for. But the worry did not dissuade me from standing there, looking, yearning.

I knew they would not return yet I still stood there. As I looked out toward the white sandy beach I tried to imagine exactly how they looked, each one. My mind could bring back the details, the running, laughing, the slender shoulders and round breasts. I thought I would never leave the railings.

"Brother Domingo, we still have a lot to do." It was the crackling voice of The Saint.

I quickly returned to the unloading. Could he see my face was blazing? Why is it the Good Lord has given us no control over blushing? I think it is to shame us into acting correctly. It didn't work on me, and I will spend that much more time roasting.

The Saint will go to heaven faster than a pigeon takes flight. He is a saint. I am not a saint. I never intended to be a saint. I am a man. I try to be a holy man, but there are impossibilities to that task.

For me. Not him.

"Brother, we still have a lot to do."

I stood looking for the naked savages in my mind, and he needed to unload a smelly ship.

He nagged at me. He yelled at me. He insisted, cajoled, blamed, then insisted again. What was I to do? He reminded me the Good Lord is watching and we shall be judged.

WITH THE SOLDIERS, WE BEAT BACK the jungle and headed north to Guatemala. The land cooled as we ascended into the mountains. At a pass we stopped to look down at the city. This great capital of the New World looked like a mound of ant hills. Oh, well, I thought, we are high in the mountains. Perhaps when we are closer,

I will see her Spanish glory.

The Saint did not complain.

As we descended from the pass, I fell. One of the horses kicked me. The fall seemed to last an eternity. I fell and fell. To my shame I wanted to live.

Lord, let me live, I cried.

Who was I to ask the Lord to live? The Lord decides with infinite wisdom. I was ashamed that, the moment before I met Him, I was telling Him what to do.

The rest of the way down I yelled. Yelling at myself to shut up. Yelling for the Lord to forgive me. Yelling to be yelling.

I landed on a mess of branches. Captain Alvarado and his soldiers made their way down to me, then stopped underneath the tree.

"How ridiculous you are, Brother Domingo," Captain Alvarado said, scratching his red beard, looking up at me.

"It was not my intention."

"Lead us not into intention, Brother." He and his lieutenant began shaking the tree.

"Captain," I babbled, then fell again. I crashed into the bushes below the tree. I lay on my back. My right leg pointed to the heavens, and my left leg pointed to the other place. There was an arm to the east and another arm to the west. Twigs and branches poked and prodded at me underneath my robes.

It was God's eternity before Captain Alvarado reached me. Then I heard him laughing. I was unable to move.

"Captain, I am pleased that you find humor in all of God's wonders, but would you please help me out of this."

He laughed and pointed to my midsection. I heard the soldiers gathering around us, laughing. I, with much strain, pulled my head up and looked to where he pointed. I had landed on an evil branch that narrowly had missed my buttocks. It was covered by my white robes and black cloak, but nevertheless pointed skyward from between my legs.

Again I heard Captain Alvarado's voice. "Brother, I thought you were a man of the faith, not the flesh."

I knew this man was sent by You to be a thorn in my side. If You suffered as greatly as You did, could I not suffer through one insufferable soldier? Of course I could. I offered up my humiliation and pain to You and to Your Mother.

But he did irk me.

Indian slaves gathered around as the soldiers moved and twisted my brush-embroiled body. The women looked down and giggled. The men pointed and laughed. It was a great honor to have been the catalyst for the Old World and the New World to unite in a single gushing laugh.

As I made my way to my feet, I looked at the Indians who had gathered to watch the spectacle. The men wore long pants, white background, and red stripes. Around their waists were wide red and blue ribbons.

The women wore long red skirts, red with blue and purple and green stripes descending down to their naked feet. Blue and green ribbons held up their hair.

And above their waists they wore brown flesh.

WITHIN A MONTH THE SAINT had me translating the bible into some strange Indian language. I sat in the monastery of the city. I wondered how that mess of mud huts and shabby wood could be called a city. It was cold and damp. It drizzled all the time, and I could feel pain every time I moved my shoulder. At night, I did not have to move to feel pain.

Every day he yelled at me and told me what an awful monk I was. I could not translate the bible into his precious Indian languages.

"How can we ever convert them if they do not have the Holy Bible in their own language?"

Where is it written that God wants them converted anyway? Maybe we ought to leave them alone.

He showed me some of his defenses of them. He defended their slaughter of human beings.

"This is their custom," he said. "They believe in certain kinds of gods that not only permit such behavior, but demand it. How are we to judge that which is all they know?"

I think he would change his mind if they ever took him to the top of one of those ugly rocks and tried to reach in and grab his heart. No, no, please take my heart, rip my intestines out, that is fine with me because that is all you know.

What kind of human being rips the heart out of another human being?

I heard the drizzle outside my room. It was cold. My arm hurt. My shoulder hurt.

The Saint, Father Bartolomé de Las Casas, was happy while I was miserable. This dour, critical, caustic saint flew through the doors of the church to announce a deal he had worked out with that maniac, Captain General Alvarado. Instead of the soldiers entering the north and butchering the Indians, as is their custom, he would send us and we would peacefully convert them.

I was overjoyed. I entertained celestial bliss. My prayers were answered: I would be a martyr to the conversion of the Indians. My place in heaven assured. They would place my poor pain-wracked body on a heathen alter and gouge through my chest to rip my heart out.

Thank you, dear Saint, but why don't you go instead?

"This is the chance the Lord has given us," The Saint cried. "I've beseeched the Crown for years to convert the Indians by the cross rather than the sword."

Ah! Such a holy man, a saint. He can do no wrong. And Father Bartolomé, how did it turn out when you demanded African slaves be sent to Cuba so that the poor Taino would not be destroyed? Dear Father, weren't both destroyed? That was a mistake. Yes, of course, a mistake. I understand.

This would be his penance. Hordes of white- and black-robed Dominican missionaries would troop into the north and convert the Rabinal. Not a mistake?

"Father, aren't these the very same Rabinal the soldiers have avoided because of their violence?" Fear had overcome my natural cowardly ways. "Avoided for almost twenty years."

"Yes, they are the same, but the difference is that we shall bring them love instead of hate. We shall bring the world of God, not the sword of greed."

I saw my corpulent body dragged up to an ugly rock, placed on its back, sung to in a heathen language, then stripped and gouged. A monk of God.

I would have rather been a cook or a cow.

WE STUDIED EVEN HARDER. We never prayed; we rarely ate. All we did was study. He brought in old men to teach us the languages of the Rabinal. I looked over at my brother friar, Brother Luis. He was tall, thin, and earnest. The tall ones are always like that. He listened, learned, and applied his knowledge to translating the bible into their languages.

"Luis," I whispered. He tried to ignore me.

"Luis," I whispered louder.

"What now, Brother Domingo?"

"What is the name of this language he is forcing down our throats?"

"There are two: Kekchi and Pokomam."

"If it is so important we learn these, why does he not learn them?"

"Shh, not so loud." Luis could see I was getting upset. "He does not learn them because he is learning K'iché and Kaqchikel."

"He does not learn those languages easily," I said. "He can not learn new language because he is so busy berating us. 'You have not learned the new languages fast enough.' You cannot eat and puke at the same time."

Brother Luis turned and would not look at me anymore.

Madness. The soldiers butchered the Indians. And we, as God's soldiers, try to convert them. Everybody will go to hell. We will. They will. There must be a special hall in hell reserved for everybody involved in this ridiculous affair: soldiers, Indians, friars, everybody.

Luis continued his work. I was beneath contempt. We'll see how he feels as they drag him up the rocks and gouge his chest and rip his heart out, I thought. He might think back just before he dies, he might think back and say to himself, "Brother Domingo had warned us. Oh, dear Lord, why did we not take Brother Domingo's advice?"

Probably not. That would be nice. I would be glad if the Good Lord would at least hear somebody sing my praises. But I don't think so. Most likely Brother Luis will, as they prepare to crack his chest open, pray his great thank you to the Good Lord and to Father Bartolomé, The Saint, for providing him with an unhindered route to heaven.

He might even look over at the rock next to his and feel a moment of pity for the fat friar who is screaming his bloody head off. But he won't have time to send up a prayer for me; he would only have time to thank everybody for getting butchered. He won't even be able to hear the fat friar screaming that it was his goddamn fault we got there in the first place.

What an ending that will be to my career as a friar. This is not what my father wanted. No, not at all. I was to be a great warrior. Conquer the Moors. Destroy the defilers of Constantinople. Save fair Christian maidens. Conquer lands for our great Spanish empire. Luckily, my eldest brother took care of that. Of course, he did lose half his face fighting off the Turks.

Who in God's name ever thought it a good idea fighting Turks? Give them what they want, and cheat it back from them. The whole race of them are so goddamned stupid you could cheat their mothers away from them.

My brother came home with half a face, and my father then searched through his list of children for another sacrificial lamb for the Crown. Why were we so lucky to have a father whose beliefs were so passionate?

My next brother headed off to attack the heathens. He came back straightaway without an arm. We sat around the house and looked at this young man, who was the handsomest of us all. He had the ladies from all the surrounding towns a-flutter. He could have had anyone of them. He was to be the lover brother. Their fans would flitter. Instead, he sat at home and looked at where his arm had been. And no one came to visit.

Father returned to his list of sacrificial sons. By this time, my mother was beginning to get worried. She had not an infinite supply of sons. The arsenal was finite. The next brother went, and she began to talk to me of The Calling. The third brother did not return. Now I had one brother with half a face gone, another brother with an arm gone, and another brother who was completely gone. I began to see the sagacity of my mother's belief that my soul had been Called.

My next-older brother left. I read the bible. To tell God's awful truth, I had never so much as picked up the book until José left. He was one year older than me. We were five sons. I was the youngest. The youngest is not supposed to worry about war and death. The youngest is supposed to lie around the house and give his parents something to worry about so they don't notice they're getting wrinkles.

José was my friend, not just my brother. He and I would sneak across the courtyard to watch our cousins change clothes. He and I would run from them laughing as they threw pots and pans at us. José was the light-skinned brother. He had bright blue eyes, and he enjoyed mischief even more than I did. My father would try to beat respect into him, but José's eyes were bright blue. He came back blind.

There were great white clouds floating high over our heads as we walked out of the house that morning. My mother insisted I had The Calling and was going to become a priest now, this morning. At the door my father yelled at us. He raised his fist and screamed, "You are ruining our family. Sons are supposed to fight for God and Crown. What the hell is the matter with you? Don't you know that? You are turning your last whole son into a *maricón*."

She whirled around, her black skirts twirled. She screamed at him and shook her fist. "Better a faggot than dead."

Everyone in our village heard this. Thank you, my mother. That's just what I wanted everybody to hear as I was going off to become a monk.

She grabbed me by the hand. We walked off to the church. The men in our village glared at us; my friends laughed and sniggered, and the girls waved good-bye. Especially Marta. Marta, I think, cried.

Marta had great sad dark eyes. Beautiful sad eyes. Her voice was like her eyes, sad and haunting. She and I had a few moments here and there before her mother, my mother, or an aunt would grab us.

Marta.

There's one thing about the monkhood that is really stupid: the vow of chastity. I mean, I don't understand it even with the sisters. Sure, they have married God. But they are human like us. Sometimes God is not present on lonely nights. But I did not marry God. Not at all. I am unmarried. So what am I supposed to do?

No, it is not that stupid. No. What is really stupid is trying to convert a bunch of savages who want to crush your chest and eat your heart. Now that is really stupid.

20

I QUIETLY CURSED BROTHER LUIS, then walked out to the court-yard. Red and purple flowers blossomed everywhere. I felt life surge within me. I felt alive, then deadened by the glory. How could I be so lonely in a country full of passion and beauty?

Cloud shadows covered the flowers; the red turned deep and dark. I looked up. Heavy dark clouds passed above. Again, the rains. I could see them begin on the green mountains. And an earthquake. Again. I spread my legs so I would not fall. This is supposed to be land, not sea.

The Indian servants came into the courtyard. I tried to breathe slower; they should not see my panic. I watched them. First, they began with their crazy language. They chatted with each other, that's the only way I can put it. Chatted. Maybe chattered, like someone threw cow dung against a wall, and the dribbling off that wall is the sound of their language. *Click, cluck, dribble.*

They looked at the ground, at the sky, then at the volcanoes surrounding us. They did this a few times, then they laughed and went inside again. In their minds, I am just another priest who was not particularly afraid. How could they see my fear? I did not move. I was petrified. As soon as they left, the quick breathing began again. This time, it was all the fear that had been hidden while the Indians were in front of me. The price I pay to be a Spaniard.

And I could not stop the rapid shallow breathing. I began to pray to the Blessed Virgin Mary. I am a monk, am I not? The panic slowed; then the Good Lord had a gift for me: another earthquake. My tender psyche was not equipped for this one.

The next thing I heard was the sound of dung rolling down monastery walls. I opened my eyes, and there were the Indians staring at me. And speaking their gibberish as usual. I lay on the ground.

Underneath me the earth was still. The panic was gone. I found myself thinking of earth and heaven and hell. The difference between those saints who studied shit rolling down walls and myself was that they believed, dreamed, and hoped for an afterlife. This life was merely a preparation, a testing time for the glory later. Whatever happens to the body is irrelevant. That which is real is later.

This big old body of mine was never convinced. The foods I taste, the sweat from the fear, the laughs, and the gas passing are real. My sad failure.

And then I wondered if the Indians could tell I had wet myself.

THE SAINT'S BOOKS ARRIVED. We stopped all our research and studies of Indian dribble. All we did was carry pounds of books. They never ceased. Piles, mounds, loads, books everywhere. We had to rearrange our rooms; brothers and priests lost their sleeping quarters to his books. The Saint thought books were more important than men.

I had never seen him so happy. By day he walked around, trying to talk to the savages. By night, he read. He did not spend much time studying their languages. This was our work. Why is it that saints make the lowly do their work? If he wants to convert these heathens so badly, why did he not learn all their languages?

Why am I so lucky?

We had to pray more. Four hours a day was not enough. It had to be six hours a day. And somehow in the day we were to prepare our food, take care of our rooms and halls, translate Indian dribble, and occasionally go to the bathroom.

And what should we pray for? Of course, for the Indians' salvation. They were being treated harshly, destroyed, crippled, used for Spaniard's lust. We prayed for them and for eternal strength to fight for them.

This went on for twelve days. There was something seriously wrong in all of it. Some of the monks took to flagellating themselves to bring on the consciousness of the Indians, to find measures to save them. The last four nights of the twelve I awoke during the night to the cries of monks beating themselves.

No sleep, and no time to prepare food. Little time to eat what little food there was. I could not go on after the twelfth day. I met The Saint as he was leaving chapel in the long dark hallway. The torch on the wall made his narrow face twitch in dark orange.

"Father, I must talk with you." He was bent over, holding his bible as if it were a small baby. He looked up at me. "Yes?"

"Father," I said. "I am sorry to disturb you. There is a problem. We, God's servants, are struggling to do what is right. But we are praying so much for guidance and the deliverance of the Indians that there does not seem to be time to eat. For His humble servants to perform the necessary tasks, we must have nurturance to continue." I was sweating like a pig. He scared me.

"Yes, Brother, I understand," he said. He looked up and down my body, then walked away.

On the thirteenth day, The Saint ordered us to commence a fast. He said corpulent monks do not save Indians.

Skinny monks do?

I did not ask for favors from him again.

My stomach ached, and my mind hurt. My hatred for Indians grew venomous. During the day, all I could think about was food. At night, I had nightmares. Each nightmare was more vivid than the last. Indian maidens, girls, dancing naked on the white beaches. Running into the white surf giggling. They were happy and they were free. And they were naked. Every morning I awoke with incredible physical sensations. I cursed the Indians. My torture had to stop.

"Alfredo," I said to one of our Indian servants. The Saint would have referred to him as a K'iché or a Kaqchikel. Kakkapoo for all I cared. Whatever he was, he could bring me food if I could talk him into it. "Alfredo, you know we are engaging in a fast."

"Yes, Brother." I never understood why these people could not look you in the eyes. I assumed they were hiding something.

"Alfredo, I am preparing a special offering to Our Most Holy Lord. I need some cooked meat for this. But it is a special sacrifice. Even Father Bartolomé should not know of this."

"Yes, Brother." Brother? That would mean we had the same mother. I'm not sure my father would have approved.

"Could you bring that to me tonight? It will be like a sacrifice. You understand about sacrifices, don't you?"

He looked down in shame.

"You will do this for me? I will say extra prayers for you in the chapel tomorrow."

"Yes, Brother."

That night, while I could hear priests and monks battering

themselves with whips, I ate. It was not the best meal I have ever eaten, but it was filling. At the end I thought it would give me that much more energy to pray for the Indians, especially Alfredo. I hid the chicken bones under my bed. I could bury them in the garden in the morning.

As usual we woke before the animals. We walked in the dark to the chapel to pray. We walked in silence. In the chapel we knelt for silent prayer. The birds were not even chirping yet. In the silence I heard rumblings. At first my fear told me there would be another earthquake. Perhaps the volcano would finish us all. Then I realized that the rumblings were me.

I was panic stricken. Could the others hear? I placed my arms over my belly, and the rumblings grew louder. Was it my imagination, or were the other brothers looking at me? And snickering. The rumblings grew lower and quieter. I released my arms from my stomach. I began to breathe again. I tried to return to prayer and contemplation. The others returned to their thoughts.

There was silence, then an enormous eruption. It sounded like cannons were bashing the walls of the chapel. Crashing and echoing resounded around us. And again it was me. How I hated Alfredo in that instant. What had he done to those chickens? Where had he bought those pieces of shit?

Every eye was on me. How can a fasting priest pass gas with such a resounding explosion? This was the question each asked. And each answered: He has broken the fast.

But of course that was not the worst of it. The joys of Guatemala are relentless. We returned to our rooms. We were to sit in individual meditation. I gathered up the bones and hid them in my robes. I hurried out of my room and headed to the gardens to bury them.

I crossed through the patio. I was again stricken. Only this time, in God's grace, I was not attacked with gas. This time it was excruciating pain. It was in my stomach. It attacked, kicked, and dealt me a blow as I had never received. I stopped by the fountain. I could not continue. The retching, vomiting, and diarrhea began. By the time my brothers and the priests found me, I was a complete mess.

They dragged me from my catastrophe. I knew they would find the chicken bones, but I did not care. I hoped only for death. I could take the embarrassment, but not the pain. Let me die, Oh, my God, I prayed. Could cracking open one's chest and ripping out one's heart be more painful?

I lay in bed dreaming and seeing visions. The pain was relentless. It was as if I had eaten a snake that had crawled around my innards and was biting me. Then, I would wretch. Chicken remnants flew out of me. They crashed against the wall. Another round smashed against one of the priests. Exhausted, I fell into an hallucinatory stupor. I saw Marta dancing on that white beach. She smiled and waved to me. Naked, we ran through the surf.

The pain began again.

As I came out of it, I knew the brothers and priests hated me and laughed at me. I did not care. Everything hurt too much for me to worry about them. Besides, I was busy plotting revenge on Alfredo. His heart would be gouged out. A spear through his eye. Tied to a tree, thousands of red insects would eat at his flesh. He would be starved and then fed tiny morsels of cow dung.

"Alfredo," I said to him three days later.

"Yes, Brother." He was holding a cup of herbal brew.

"That chicken you brought me the other day?"

"Yes?" Now he looked proud.

"Tell me about that chicken."

"Oh, yes, Brother. It was a special chicken. It was roasted in the same way that we used to roast chicken for our priests. It was roasted and basted in herbs and holy oils. It was prepared in the special way for these holiest of persons. I hoped you liked it."

"Yes, Alfredo. It was a very special chicken."

"Thank you, Brother."

I almost did not have the heart to trip him as he left. As he turned to leave, I pushed a small wooden stool in front of his feet. That was the least I could give him for the great gift of the diseased chicken.

He stepped over the stool and left.

21

THE SAINT HAD ME LEARNING THEIR LANGUAGES, again, as soon as I recovered. He wanted the bible translated before we left for the mountains to be sacrificed.

Lord knows, I tried. But what can you make of a language that determines male and female by the prefix, by *a* and *al*. So I write *Awan* for *Juan* and *Alway* for *Juana*. They do everything backwards.

Their plurals make even less sense: *-ab* and *-aib*. The word for man is *achí*. For men it is *achaib*. *Mam* is old man, *maib* is old men. I could not remember all the details. I am not a man of little things. My size is large and my thinking is large. *Ixox* means woman, *wixoquil* means my wife.

I have had no feeling for languages. I did not want to get killed by the Moors or the Turks, but here I will be sacrificed, or poisoned, or my mind will become deranged with a weird language. *Wa'ic* is to eat, and *wa'im* is meal.

I desperately needed to *wa'ic* a good *wa'im*.

These are simple people. They act simple. They look simple. But why is their language so complicated? Instead of a smooth flowing of musical sounds, they do tongue snaps, Germanic coughs, and lip pops.

They do not differentiate between the words *believe* and *obey*. They mingle together like two streams becoming one river. If I believe, I obey. This is their world. Mine is different. I believe. I try to obey. I told this to The Saint. I wanted him to understand.

"See that book on the table?"

"Yes, Father."

"Pick it up."

I picked it up.

"Did you try to pick it up?"

"I picked it up."

"You see, my son, you cannot *try* to do anything at all. You either do or you do not."

"Thank you, Father."

No wonder The Saint and the Indians get along so well. Neither are human beings. He gave us different sections of the bible to translate. I sat in my cubicle and looked at the bible. I looked away, then back at the holy book. I had struggled through that book in the university in Salamanca. I struggle through it every day of my life. But to translate it into a language I did not understand was impossible. I let my head fall onto the book. I moaned in frustration.

I began. It felt like a woman must feel when she is trying to give birth to a mule. There were impossible passages. I could not translate our beautiful language into that gibberish.

I accomplished what I could. There were sections in my translation that were not from the Holy Spirit's voice. Sometimes when I got stopped, I would perform the simple task of translating a paragraph from Brother Domingo's voice.

All were teaching paragraphs, though.

If a woman's goat wonders away, the family should follow and return the goat. How could the Good Lord disagree with that sentiment? I grant it is not a great parable. But I know how to translate the word *goat*. May the Good Lord forgive me, but it is a good thought.

As soon as I finished my section, The Saint told us that the translation would not be necessary. At least not for a few years. He had found a more effective way of conversion. We were to translate bible songs.

How can one be angry at a saint? They are blessed by the Holies. Their name will be passed through the generations. Each pope will whisper his name in gratitude for prayers answered. The soul of The Saint will sit at the right hand of God. He will rest in heaven for his sanctimoniousness, while I will boil in hell for parable substitution.

THE SAINT BROUGHT US FOUR INDIAN MERCHANTS. We translated songs for these four to sing to the savages of the north. The four were Christian; they had chosen conversion over hanging, then fallen in love with the teachings.

Father Bartolomé was pleased with them. They were willing to go into the Land of War, the place of the Rabinal, a place that even Cortez skirted, to sing Christian songs to the Indians there. I watched as he talked with these Christians. The Saint was so happy it looked like he had already died and been declared a saint.

Soon enough, Father, soon enough.

His eyes became wide and shiny. "You are the answer to our prayers," he said. He was overjoyed. That night I sat next to them at our meal, what little there was of it. Our meals had become like the Indians'. We ate tortillas and beans. If they could eat this slop, God willed we should also. Or at least Father Bartolomé's version of God's vision.

We ate tortillas and beans, and conversed in our language. Every once in a while, The Saint would look over at these four and smile. "Oh, my children. I thank the Good Lord for sending you to us. You are kind and childlike. You are like unspoiled land that easily produces worthless weeds and thorns. After plowing and cultivation, you will yield useful and wholesome fruits."

I engaged in some dialogue with these children of God. I wondered if The Saint knew that their conception of God and the heavenly hierarchy was bit different than our own.

The Trinity is three separate gods. The Father was angry with the Son, so He sent Him to Earth to be sacrificed. Saint James is the brother of Jesus Christ. And Alvarado, Tunatiuh, is stronger than any of them; after all, he beat back the devil Moors. Hence, Alvarado is the top God, with Jesus Christ acting as his underling.

They sat eating tortillas, with ridiculous grins on their faces, explaining this to me. I shook my head and tried to eat the black beans. How could I? The beans looked the same going into my body as they looked coming out.

Mary is the Temptress. She schemes and creates false worlds. A Dangerous Lady. Magical. Strange. The Indians shook their heads in wonderment at Her power.

"What is hell?" I asked.

They were ready for that. All nodded in preparation to expound on hell.

"That is the place Down There," the tallest of the four said. "That is the Land of the Underground, Xilbalba. There are many powerful spirits there. We can see them at times."

The others nodded again, mouths full of beans, faces full of horror.

"If you do not keep your room clean, they will sneak into through the corners. If you walk along the road and forget what you are doing they will attack you and kill you."

The smallest and darkest one tossed in his experiences: "My cousin was with his wife during the wrong time. He had been a servant at the *encomienda* and had missed her. But when he returned to her, it was the wrong time. For a year afterward, their goats were born with three legs."

Again, the four nodded in agreement.

"How is it that you became Christians?" I asked.

Again, the short one spoke. He seemed to be their leader. "We travel throughout the land, far from our people. We buy and sell housewares. When we arrived at Iximché, we found the city had been decimated. There was an old woman who told us what had happened. She told us of the priests. We thought these priests must be very powerful. We found the priests and the Spanish, then Jesucristo."

"Jesucristo?"

All four looked down in reverence.

"Tell me about Jesucristo," I said.

"Jesucristo is very upset now," the short one began. The others nodded their heads. "Jesucristo says, 'My children do not pay attention to me anymore. I have given them so much, but they ignore me. They eat corn. They have plenty of beans, tomatoes, rice, chili. They have all of that. My children do not offer me candles. They do not offer me food to eat. I don't get anything from them anymore. I am hungry.'"

This was a Jesus Christ I had never heard of before. I glanced over my shoulder to see if The Saint was listening. He was looking at the four, benevolently smiling. He understood nothing.

"He took the corn, he took all people's corn and hid it," the small dark one continued. "He hid it in a rocky cliff. No one could find the corn. In the land of the Kaqchikels, in the land of the K'ichés, in all the land, there was no corn."

It was as if they were one person separated into four small dark men.

"Then came the ant. The birds said they were going to eat the ants because they were hungry. The ant said, 'No, you will not eat us, because we are going to do you a favor. You are going to have corn again. Tomorrow, at daybreak.'

"'How are you going to do this?' the birds asked.

"The ant said, 'All you have to do is to crawl between the rocks and bring out the corn, kernel by kernel.'

"Out came the food. All the food we eat today, we have because of those ants. We have rice and these beans and hot peppers and chilies, all because of that ant."

The other three Indians nodded in smiling agreement.

"That was that. Because of the ant we are now alive. Without the ant we would have starved. For this we must thank the ants. If they come into our gardens and our homes and our fields, it's not right to set fire to them, to burn them, to stamp on them in anger. They are not to blame. They just want something to eat.

"It is much better to simply place a candle out there, to burn incense, to say a prayer. They will go away. All they wanted was some tiny bits of food. This is what Jesucristo commanded us to do. Because of them, we can eat today. Therefore, we must ask for help from the ants. It's no fault of theirs that they destroy plants."

These were the people whom Bartolomé, The Saint, wanted us to convert. Convert to what? This bizarre brand of Christianity? My brother Inquisition monks would have had a party.

WE TAUGHT THEM HOW TO SING. We created ballads for them. Each ballad was in part the history of Christianity and in part a seduction into Christianity. There were four of us in this task. The Saint thought four would be fitting, as there were four Indians. The teachers were Brothers Rodrigo, Pedro, Luis, and, of course, Brother Me. Each had a different voice and each beautiful in its own right.

But our voices were no match for the Indians'. They could sing like no human had ever heard before. Their voices were like cats being trampled by horses. Like witches giving forth babies. Like boats grinding against their moorings. Like the devil returned to earth to bring the groans of hell with him. Goats farting.

Hearing our complaints, The Saint reminded us that the idea was not aesthetic beauty, but the beauty of conversion to the One True Faith. The Good Lord wanted their souls, and when they sang flat, in heaven, their pitch is heard as perfect.

"This is as it should be," Brother Luis said. "These people are in great need for us to teach them the truth. If they can not sing in our manner, they should sing in their own."

Clearly, The Saint had a convert within his own camp. Brother Luis had become vicious in his righteousness.

"But their own is unintelligible," I said. "They cannot sing. Their version of the holy stories is distorted by animal gods. They cannot think. A few months ago they were sacrificing humans to rock gods. He thinks we can, with a few Christian songs, bring them into civilization. Maybe for a few months, but then we shall all have our hearts ripped from our chests."

Brother Luis had no use for me. "Their languages are beautiful. Did you not feel that when we were translating scripture? Their religion is fair, considering that they have never been introduced to the true faith."

He was the lightest of the four of us. He was younger than the rest, had gleaming green eyes, and came from an enormously wealthy family of Madrid.

Brothers Rodrigo and Pedro nodded in agreement. All he had to do was to propose an argument, and these two could be counted on to agree with it, even if it made no sense and would cost them their lives. My life.

THE SAINT STOOD WITH HIS HANDS CLASPED TOGETHER, beatifically nodding. The four Indian merchants stood in the cathedral, singing. It was dark inside when yet another storm came. Dark clouds surrounded the capital. The Indians smiled, especially the short dark one who stood nearest to the incense. I could see him sniffing the air to take in more. It looked as if he was trying to experience heaven on earth by sniffing incense.

All the priests, monks, and sisters gathered together to hear the concert. This was to be our send off to them. They would sing; we would approve; they would go to the Land of War and be beheaded. Everyone approved. Everyone smiled.

The acoustics in the cathedral were such that a lamb being slaughtered would have sounded like God's sigh. Take them outside, and we would have heard cats fornicating.

There was such an outpouring of applause as they finished, I worried these four humble servants of God might have thought they could actually sing. One of the sisters stood to express her admiration.

We left the cathedral. There were more congratulations and general hand shaking and hugs. The four thought this signaled them to sing again. They stood with their backs to the cathedral's great wood door and sang.

It was awful. Any god who could allow it to pass as a salutation would have to be tone deaf.

Again, there were clapping and hugs. Again, they sang. As they finished, I quickly suggested to The Saint we continue with the ceremonies. Every time these people received a hug, they thought it was a signal to disturb the souls anguishing in hell.

The Saint presented them with jewelry. Well, not really jewelry. It was more like junk. These miserable wretches loved anything shiny. So in his humble saint-like way, he handed Spanish garbage to each: bells, mirrors, beads. Anything bright that could reflect the sun. Then he added things useful: scissors and knives.

I thought this last was a horrible mistake. A light rain covered us. As I watched the Indians accept them, I saw myself lying prone at the top of an Indian pyramid with this same Indian, dressed in glaring feathers, jabbing open my rib cage with the gift knife instead of an obsidian blade.

Off they went, singing and dancing, to death by the Rabinal. I was not sure if they were celebrating their deaths or ours, but surely it was to somebody's.

WE WAITED. I thought The Saint would give birth to a cow. Saints are supposed to hear the celestial bells. This saint worried, fretted, anguished, and made our lives miserable. More fasting. More prayer. More reading of scripture. I thought it would never end.

He must have had celestial balls.

I admit there is a part of my soul that complains. I think this is permissible. Do we not live in an imperfect world? If the world is in error upon occasion, does not the human notice and wish it better?

Brother Luis could not understand this slight philosophy. He sat next to me at all our meals. He would say his prayers slowly, so that no one could eat until he had finished.

"Brother, do you think you could abbreviate your prayers before we eat?" I suggested to him as we ate.

He stopped eating and turned to me. "It is difficult to understand you when your mouth is full, Brother."

I swallowed. "I am just suggesting your prayers are diligent. Perhaps they would be best delivered in the privacy of your room or in the chapel."

Everyone at the table looked at us. They had also stopped eating.

"Brother, we are in this land to convert savages. There is no other reason to be here. We are not here to eat or to enjoy ourselves."

"I understand that, Brother. But there is a time to pray and a time to eat."

"The time to pray is *all* the time. Our very lives should be an expression of prayer."

"Of course, Brother," I said. "Certainly. But the Good Lord would like us to have time to eat." Out of the corner of my eye, I could see The Saint enter, sit down, and listen. It was time for a change of tone. Brother Luis spoke first.

"Don't you believe in God?" There was silence at the table. The other monks' mouths dropped open. Instead of a quibble about eating and prayer, Brother Luis was treating me as if I were a Turk. There was nothing I could say.

Silence.

If I said I believed in God, it would look like as if I were trying to cover up doubts. If I said I did not, that, of course, would be a lie. If I were silent, it would seem he had uncovered a deep truth about me.

I am afraid all that came from my mouth was a sputtering "How dare you?"

Brother Luis nodded as if he were a great teacher and I a disappointing student who had finally gotten one answer right. "Yes, of course you believe in God. And of course the Good Lord would want us to pray to His infinite greatness. Is this not true?"

"Yes, Brother."

"Let us continue with our meal, then."

At that moment, I began to plot against Brother Luis.

22

ROTHER PEDRO RAN INTO OUR DINING ROOM. "They have returned! They have returned! They have brought Indian royalty with them!"

I had never seen The Saint jump so high or so fast. "Where are they?"

We ran outside to greet them. First The Saint, then Brother Luis, then the rest of us. I was the only one who carried his supper with him. Who was to know when one might eat again in that God-forsaken land?

Our four merchants stumbled along the road. I looked for physical damage. Nothing apparent. Alongside them was an Indian dressed in the most ridiculously colored beads, feathers, and jewelry. He was no taller than they, but he walked the road as if he owned all of Europe.

The four smiled and waved. They pointed to their new friend. Then, of course, they stopped in the middle of the street and broke into song. Their sojourn into the Land of War had not improved their singing.

After they finished, The Saint approached each, looked down, and blessed him. Each of the four smiled and giggled. The Saint ordered us to prepare a great feast to celebrate their return and to honor our guest.

I was not displeased by that turn of events.

That night we sat and ate and celebrated. We, again, were treated to the music of the cosmos by our four tone-deaf missionaries. They told us stories of their adventure.

They had left us with much courage. God was going to protect them. But along the way, they had regretfully lost some of their fearlessness. In fact, they had realized this Land of War, as we called it, was the site of the Great Abyss of Carchá.

They had decided to turn back.

"What if we continued and fell into the Abyss?" the small one said. "We would fall into Xilbalba. There we would have to face evil bats. How could we face these things? We could even fall into Blood River."

I didn't care. This time they could talk as much blasphemy as they liked. It is amazing what the Christian soul can tolerate when there is beef feeding it.

During the night they had seen a partial moon. In the sky, they could see Blood Woman, the mother of the twin gods. Of course, this was all they had needed to see. They had continued on their way.

Did that make sense? Did anything those people said make sense?

They had been frightened when they arrived in the Land of War, at first of the Great Abyss, then afraid of the people. Even though they knew the language, these were traditional enemies of all peoples.

"My sons, you had nothing to fear." Brother Luis made a grand gesture. "Jesus Christ will always protect you."

I had not expected that one. Brother Luis was not only sounding like The Saint, but he was talking when The Saint should have. I glanced at our True Saint. He was not upset. In fact, he nodded in approval. Had they conspired for new leadership when The Saint left?

Our four ambassadors were treated with tremendous respect. They had told the Rabinal of the new religion, then sung them Christian songs. The Rabinal people had told their royalty. The king had granted them an audience, where they sang again. The king asked about the priests of this religion, Christianity. They told of the robes, the haircut, and how clean we were. He was impressed with this last. All the priests he had ever known were dirty, smelled, and walked around with blood matted in their hair.

The king had decided to send his brother as emissary to us. The man dressed in beads and feathers nodded when our four minstrels pointed to him.

"My brother, the King of the Rabinal, would like to meet one of your priests," he said through the translation of the tall merchant. "He would like to know about this new religion our little singing friends have been bragging about."

I thought The Saint would give birth to a cow right on the spot. A Holy Cow. His face turned red; he started to speak but could not. Finally, he said, "This is Our Lord's Fate. We shall have a Mass to celebrate your arrival here. You can see the mystery of our faith. We shall make plans to meet the king, your brother, and begin the great Conversion."

While we were performing our chores, I thought about the impending loss of Father Bartolomé. He was our Saint. He was relentless in austerity, but he was not Brother Luis. He would not return from the Land of War, and we would live under the rule of

Brother Luis until we all turned old and gray.

The next morning The Saint announced his intentions. Light cascaded onto him as he stood on the pulpit. It gave him a brilliant yellow halo.

His voice was soft at the beginning, barely discernible. I thought of my fears in the seminary about sermons. Stand up in front of old men and tell them they are sinners? Preach to beautiful young women about evil thoughts while thinking what I was thinking?

"Christ is not content with hearing our words," Father Bartolomé said to the congregation. "Christ is not content hearing our prayers. Christ is not content seeing us in church on Sundays. We could utter His truths throughout eternity, but he would still not be content. He would only be content if we put into practice the Word."

His voice squeaked. The feathered royal Indian from the Land of War picked his nose in his sleep. The colonists looked angry. One silently raised his fist at the saint.

"The moment for action in the Americas had arrived. The Land of War has been given to the Lord. The cleric Bartolomé de Las Casas has received assurances that he could travel to the Rabinal for their conversion." I never understood why he spoke of himself in the third person. I heard laughter.

The Saint continued, "There is only one method of attracting all people to the true faith. It is not by the sword."

More laughter. At first I thought it was because he had referred to himself in the third person. It was not that. They were laughing too hard and with too much viciousness. Someone cried out from behind me, "Best of luck, Father!" There was more laughter. The nose-picking, snoring royal Indian awoke with a snort.

He ignored them. It was as if he had not heard them. "Slavery is wrong. The *encomienda* system is wrong. Slavery is wrong. War is wrong. War violates Christ's commandments. If you wage wars with heathens to make them accept the Lord, you will teach them to depreciate religion and avoid those who are teaching the faith."

He droned on. The high pitch, the squeak had gone. Now he was just trying to complete the sermon.

"Peace is such a great good that nothing men yearn for is more beautiful, more precious, more pleasing, or more useful."

He ended, and the chatter and snickers ceased as people got back to the business of the mass. I asked myself how they could heap ridicule on this obviously holy man.

As the colonists walked down the aisle to leave the cathedral, I found myself beside Don Alejandro, a gray-haired older gentleman. I had known his nephew in Spain. He had not laughed, but he had smiled throughout. As we walked down the front steps of the church, he pulled me to his side.

"Your priest knows how to get into one mess after another," he said, shaking his head. "Do you know what it is like up there? I was there on the third attempt to subdue them. The land is impossible. Too many mountains. Too many unfordable rivers. The animals and snakes attack when you least expect it. There is no salt, and the monkeys are as big as men. The Indians are crazed. They have no sense of propriety in war. They attack and attack without sense."

I began to sweat. My robes became damp with it.

"I don't understand why the congregation laughed at him."

"It is a perfect solution for everyone," he said, shaking his head again. "Everyone has heard his sermons on saving the poor Indians by peaceful means. For months they have been telling him that he is a hypocrite. Save the Rabinal, they told him. Go to the north and save those savages. Now he is going to try it."

"I don't understand."

Don Alejandro smiled and looked up at the light rain. "If you return, you will understand."

"If *I* return?"

"He, you, and all the Dominicans will become martyrs. This will please the cleric greatly. The colonists will not have to hear themselves berated. Wonderful solution. If, by chance, you live, then all will return in total defeat. The congregation will be spared these sanctimonious sermons."

The old man shook my hand and walked off into the Guatemalan drizzle.

I stood by the cathedral gate, thinking of my death. He had not seen another possibility. The Indians could be converted and spend all eternity running around believing that the Trinity is the Father, Son, and Holy Ant.

On my way back into the cathedral, I asked for a minute of The Saint's time.

"Father, I have thought mightily about the Land of War. I have considered what it means to the dreams of the Church that these savages be converted. This is the single most important moment in our lifetime. These heathens must be converted. Father, the one who goes to these lands must be conversant in their languages, must have fortitude, must have courage, must be able to accept pain without flinching. And he must be young to take on these perilous, but sacred, challenges. I would like to accept this task."

The Saint looked shocked for the second time in one day. "Thank you, my son," he said. "I must pray on this."

THE SAINT GAVE A MASS AT THE MONASTERY. This was the Mass to celebrate Christ's entry into the Land of War. He was to announce the procedures of the Order for this pacific crusade. The Mass was perfect except when the four choir-boy merchants sang. But it was a short Mass. One would think after my conversation with The Saint that I would suffer waiting for The Saint's decision. Not really.

There was not one doubt in me.

He rose to give the sermon: "We have the greatest pleasure known to man. We have the pleasure of the opportunity of conversion. Those who cannot hear shall hear. Those who cannot see shall see. Who can fail to see what He meant? The Faith shall be as bright as the sun. His Word shall be as clear as a child's song."

The Indian emissary ignored him. The feathered creature was picking his nose again.

"Therefore, one of us shall have the greatest pleasure of all. I had planned on this all my life, but through the kindness of one of us, I have come to see that I am not equipped to perform this most holy of tasks. I do not speak their language. In great sorrow, I must tell you I am not the one to travel north to convert these people. It must be another."

He looked at me. Up until that moment, I felt no fear. At that moment, my robes turned wet.

"Brother Luis, you know the language better than any one of us. Brother Luis, you have shown your holiness. Brother Luis, will you travel to the Land of War for Our Savior?"

Brother Luis turned white. I let out my breath. He, of course, said yes. The Saint said, "I know this must be a great disappointment to you, Brother Domingo." I looked down in profound sorrow and imagined the obsidian blade with wings, flapping away from me.

That's what you get when you want to be a saint. Someone might accept your offer.

THEY LEFT, AND HE WROTE. Morning, noon, and night, The Saint wrote. His mood was foul. Every time he left his library, the rest of us ran and hid. There would be another order, another argument, another scolding. We were not working hard enough for the Conversion. Brother Luis's life was at risk, and we were the lazy ones. Did you really want to go, Brother? It is not too late, you know.

Another shipload of his books came in. Indian after Indian carried his sacred books. In particular, he needed Aristotle. The great philosopher would explain it all. His Indians were exhausted as they carried the Greeks and the methods of their freedom.

A letter came from Spain. It bore the royal seal. We ran around breaking the order of silence as we guessed its contents. The Saint disappeared into his library. Hours later he came out. He looked much older than when he went in.

"Brother Luis is making the first step to the right conversion of New Spain," he said with a cracking voice. "The world is changing before our very eyes, and now we are attacked by our own.

"The Franciscans have written to the court about our work here. They have requested they become the sole priests of New Spain. They have said that we have turned the conquerors and the settlers against The Faith. They say we have done this by insisting that all who receive the sacraments be of pure heart and not have Indians as slaves.

"And they have attacked Father Bartolomé personally. These Franciscans say that Father Bartolomé has hundreds of Indians carry his books for no pay; that he refuses Indian baptism unless the Indian is perfectly prepared; that he proclaims the evil deeds of a few Spanish were performed by all."

His foul moods increased, as did our work. I had by then become known as the Chief Complainant of the order. But, with his worsening attitude, the others began complaining, too.

"Nothing we do is right," Brother Pedro said.

"This cannot continue for much longer," Brother Rodrigo said.

"We do not eat enough," I said.

"This morning when I brought in the vegetables," Brother Pedro said, ignoring my comment, "he stopped me and looked into the basket. 'They are not arranged correctly. If we truly listen to the philosophers, we know how to behave correctly in every matter.'"

Brother Rodrigo shook his head. "He is upset because of that letter. Brother Luis has not returned yet. When he comes back, everything will return to normal."

"I don't think he is coming back," I said. The other two were shocked.

"What do you mean?" Brother Rodrigo asked.

"Of course he will return," Brother Pedro said.

"Not necessarily. How do we know the Northern emissary was not sent merely as a trap? We know these creatures sacrifice humans. Maybe they've become tired of sacrificing their own. Maybe they wanted some new blood. Their ranks might be thinning."

"No, that is not possible."

"These savages have been known to eat people," I continued. "Brother Luis is probably in their stew by now."

Brother Pedro's mouth fell open.

Brother Rodrigo was not convinced. "If that is the case, you should be worried the most," he said. "If the cannibals eat you, they would not have to sup for a month."

IN OUR SMALL COLONIAL TOWN of Santiago de los Caballeros de Guatemala, the capital of Guatemala, the colonialists laughed at us. Even at Mass, their sneers and guffaws could be heard. The Saint preached to them about the Northern emissary, the chief he represented. They laughed even louder. He threatened them with excommunication. They threatened him with letters to the Crown.

Again, after Mass, I stopped Don Alejandro. I was happy he had not laughed at us in the church. Nevertheless, he smiled and shook his head.

"Your leader, your saint, is confident now. There is nothing that can hold him back. He will make the younger colonists' lives miserable with this paltry success."

"But the chief of the Land of War sent his brother. Doesn't that mean something? Couldn't we be on the edge of a great change?"

"That is what your leader would have us believe. I do not understand you Dominicans. When I was in Mexico, we never had these problems with the Franciscans. They, at least, tried to get along with the soldiers and the people in the towns. You Dominicans are better educated. For some reason that fact gives you the right to assume your are absolutely correct in your efforts. There is no compromise." He shook his graying head. For some odd reason I liked and trusted him. Secular wisdom was different than sacred wisdom.

"I occasionally have my doubts," I whispered. He did not hear me.

"The chief sent his brother," he continued. "Of course, the chief sent his brother. The younger colonists were surprised. They should have seen the campaign at Zaculeu. There were all sorts of negotiations going on throughout the siege. This was simply to buy time. They are savages, but they are not stupid savages.

"The younger colonists see the rabble hanging around our capital. They believe all Indians are lazy and fearful. They have not seen the wars. All they want is to build commerce without the requisite sacrifice." He shook his head again. The smile was peaceful, as if he had seen it all.

"I hope you don't mind me making a suggestion. It really is none of my business. I swore I would stay out of all this. I have my encomienda and my family to care for now."

"Don Alejandro, I am most open to your ideas. Please."

"You want to preach the gospel to these savages. That is commendable. The voice of the gospel can be heard only after the Indians have heard the sound of guns. Go to our governor. He will listen. Right now he thinks your leader may be making some progress. Go to Captain-General Pedro de Alvarado and tell him the truth. Tell him your saint is a confused old man. That he will kill and make martyrs of you all if he is not stopped."

Standing outside of the church, I saw visions of escape. I shivered. There was a fresh drizzle in the air. I thought of the light of my island home, Minorca. I shivered again in my cowardice.

"That would be a betrayal of all that has gone before me."

"Your work will be betrayed by your death."

"Why are you trying to save me?"

"In fact, I am trying to save my family. If your mad priest continues, he will have so many Indians agitated we could be at war for generations. My sons will never see peace."

THAT NIGHT I PRAYED IN THE MONASTERY GARDEN. I felt I was praying in the Garden of Gethsemane. I knew I was petulant. This is my nature. I am also a coward. Do I have a choice about this? I do not think so. I was born that way. The greatest sin would be to go against my own nature. Why would He put us here only to change what he had created.

I was asked to perform a heroic act. Going to the governor would be an act of courage. An act of courage in the name of cowardice.

I could never be the great soldier my father wanted me to become. Riding horses, attacking hordes of Moors plaguing our country. Attacking the Turks. Destroying the pagan civilizations of the Indians.

In the morning I found myself in exactly the position I expected to find myself: in bed, hungry. There are many colors of courage, cowardice has but one.

23

THOUSANDS OF FLOWERS OF EVERY COLOR and hue were twisted and turned into the creation of entry arches," Brother Luis said. "As we walked under them, the Indians of the city chanted and sang for us. The chief and his retinue were standing at the end point of the tunnel of flowers. They were dressed in the most resplendent colors, covered from head to foot in long green feathers and gold and silver."

There was nothing to do except stand with the others and listen to the New Saint tell us of his glory, which he was quite to ready to do. Our Old Saint sat next to him, his eyes became great pools of tears.

"Over by the great pyramid I saw their priests. It is true. They were dirty and covered with blood. They looked at my entry with scorn. Indeed, they are a dangerous bunch."

This man had become the first priest to make peaceful contact with the Indians. It was unbearable.

"Father." He turned and looked directly at The Saint. "The chief eagerly welcomed our faith. Father, he asked me to build a church. He asked to hear a Mass. Father, he commanded his people to tear down and destroy their idols. Father, I baptized him."

Now, Brother Luis was crying. I looked around the room. Most of the monks and priests were crying. I cried, too, for different reasons.

What a disaster I had created.

There was no question but we would all be in the Land of War in no time at all. Brother Luis would be in the history books, not in bold print like Saint Father Bartolomé, of course, but at least for a good sentence or two. If The Saint had to carry on his good works in Spain, our new leader would be Brother Luis.

Father Bartolomé scrambled off to his room. There was no time for a proper celebration. He had to write letters to the governor, the soldiers, and especially to the court. Each letter cried out that New Spain could be conquered by the cross rather than the sword. He was vindicated. The whole world would soon find out.

As The Saint left the room, Brother Luis managed a look at me. If our Saint was vindicated, he himself was as scornful of me as the Indian priests were of him. I had become less than an Indian servant. I hardly existed except to prove beyond doubt he was glory and I garbage.

We waited for the rainy season to end. We would all go. The tone, the atmosphere, of our small community changed rapidly. Instead of fearful missionaries, we were now fearless spiritual conquerors. The rain flogged our people, but there was singing day and night.

Especially by the four merchants.

At the Masses, The Saint ranted on about the success. The townspeople stopped laughing. During the prayers, during the silence, during the meditation, I saw the obsidian. A black blade descended into my chest, and I was blood.

As our departure date came closer, I became ill. At first it was a slight cough. That was not very difficult. Then I spit up much phlegm. As the mysterious disease spread through my poor body, I appeared to be overwhelmed with aches and pains.

God, did I suffer.

"Father, though you are stricken with illness, it is wonderful you are able to make it to supper every day." Brother Luis was always one to see the nuances of life.

"I find if I eat some tiny morsels, the pain lessens," I said as I placed a piece of mutton in my mouth.

"Yes, Brother. I am sure that is true. And it appears you must believe if you eat great amounts you will never experience pain again."

"No. All I am trying to do is feel some slight relief from the onslaught of anguish."

"We were taught that to feel pain is a good thing. It is good if we offer it up for the souls in purgatory. Perhaps if you offer your pain to Our Lord for the conversion of the Indians, then the suffering might have meaning."

"Brother, that is a wonderful idea. Right after dinner, I will return to my room and do that very thing."

I hobbled to my room, lay down, and dreamt of Marta. She wore a light brown dress. I wanted to touch the hem of her skirt. I wanted to touch her brown hair.

Brother Luis entered. "You seem more in rapture than in pain."

"I will return to health soon, Brother. I was just praying to the Virgin Mary that I shall be healed in time to fulfill my mission here."

He looked down at me, smiled, and shook his head. "You have been a great tribulation to me since we met. You are a great tribulation to our leader. You have no business being a monk. I suggest you take your rotund body and return to Spain. There you can lay about in the safety of your mother's arms."

"Brother, if I did that I would never be able to complete His holy assignment." Also, my father would have me turned into a soldier: a possible death by obsidian or a certain death by a Turkish blade through the eye.

I groaned and held my stomach.

"You are in pain, my son."

"Yes, Brother."

"I will talk to Father Bartolomé about returning you to Spain."

"No, don't do that!" I jumped off my cot.

"That is the one place that you can heal."

"No, please. I feel a little better."

"Good enough to make the trip with us to the Land of War?"

I saw crazed Turks slashing at my body. "Yes."

EVERY NIGHT BROTHER LUIS REGALED US with stories of his success. The savages had built a chapel for him before he arrived. Its walls were made of the trunks of trees. Its roof was thatched with palmetto leaves. The chief had chosen John as his baptismal name. He lectured his people on the importance of conversion. Chief John had accompanied Brother Luis on visits to other cities and insisted they convert also. When we arrived, we were to treat him with great respect and formality.

"Brother, did they give up their pagan ways?" I asked.

"Yes, many of them. They were greatly impressed with our priestly robes. Instead of feathers, they saw these white and black robes. Many of the Indians looked at me in awe. They wanted to touch the hem here." He pointed to the lower edge of clothes.

"You mean they no longer practice the heathen religion?"

"Not all of them, but many," his voice took on a frustrated tone. "The children wanted me to lean over so they could reach up and place their tiny hands on my bald head. Their priests do not shave their heads as we do. They have long, dirty hair."

"That is wonderful, Brother, truly wonderful. Now, is it true that they still practice the sacrifice at the altar? I do not mean the sacrifice of Our Lord through His body and blood with the bread and wine. I mean that they sacrifice real people on an altar and gouge their hearts out with obsidian knives. Is it true this is still their practice?"

Father Luis shook his head in dismay. "You know, you never should have become a monk. I am still amazed your parents could have been so thoughtless. You would have served humanity far better as a nun."

I was gratified to see the nasty Brother Luis return. Where had Saint Luis gone?

I answered, "Brother, it is extraordinary that you have been able to convert so many of them. It is truly spectacular. Yes, Brother, spectacular. But I still wonder if they have given up this one tradition."

The Saint was not in the room, and the others were becoming anxious about the conversation.

"You say the word 'truly' several times. I gather you are asking about the truth. Well, Brother, I believe the truth is that you are afraid to gather your tremendous girth up and accompany us to the Land of War."

The others were shocked at Brother Luis. They had not seen his beast within. He seemed not to notice.

"I grant, Brother, if they were to eat me they would have no concerns about their children's culinary welfare for eons. I grant that. Since you mention it, do they still eat people?"

"No."

"Yes, that is right. They do not need to eat people. They have human hearts to eat. That is the tastiest morsel of the human, isn't it, Brother?"

He was in a rage: "How *dare* you?"

"It is true these so called people have been known to eat each other. It is true there are enclaves of young men who prefer young men to young women in this group. It is true they worship rocks. And most frightening, it is true they carve out each other's hearts. They sound more like beasts than a lost tribe."

"You are worse than the soldiers. They, at least, have some respect for the Indian's military prowess." He had lost his facility for nuanced condescension. "You are despicable. You see them as not even human."

"Brother, I can see you are getting red in the face. I am truly sorry if I have upset you. That was not my intention. All I am saying is that this race is not exactly human. I am not sure if they are animal, but they are quite assuredly not human."

His face by then was no longer red; it was crimson. He began to sputter, "You have no *right*. I have risked everything. These *are* people. Father Bartolomé would understand."

"How can one define as human a thing that will eat its own? Few animals practice that. Or have sex with its own gender?"

"But they don't. . .some do, but most don't. Those who do merely need to see Christ. They have not been taught. You have no right to say this. I have risked my life for these. They are less than— well, not less than us, but they have not been taught. The reason for the human sacrifice is that the. . . well, they don't know any better."

"You mean it is human nature, when untouched by civilization, to practice witchcraft and cannibalism. I thought they would be in a state of grace, being so far from the evils of the city."

Brother Luis stopped talking. His face remained crimson, but now all that could be heard was a gurgling from deep within his throat.

In fact, I did not care if they were human or not. It mattered not a cucumber to me. When a blade crashes through your chest, you do not care if the knife is held by Aristotle or a frog.

"You are a pig!" he screamed at me. I thought he was going to hit me, but just then Father Bartolomé appeared in our humble dialogue.

"Brother Luis!" The Saint was properly shocked. "Stop that immediately. This is a holy place."

"Father," Brother Luis began, "I—" he stumbled. "No. He . . .we were—no, I mean to say, this man is trying to. . . ." He stopped. Brother Luis had lost his God-given ability to be articulate. I, on the other hand, sat there exhibiting the very face of innocence and holy solitude.

"I am sorely disappointed in you."

THE NEXT DAY THE SAINT HAD A LITTLE MEETING WITH US. Brother Luis looked down at his shaking hands, which held a trembling rosary.

"I have prayed and fasted on this matter all night. This has not been easy for me. But the one certain thing is that it is God's will we tend to these people the best we can. There is nothing more important. This is true, especially now. This is the time we have been waiting for. The violent suppression of the Indians can end. We have see it is possible to bring them to a peaceful resolution with the Spanish.

"Therefore, I have to put certain human feelings aside and do what is best for these people. Brother Luis, I have to ask you not to return to the Land of War with us. Brother Rodrigo, Brother Pedro, and Brother Domingo will be the apostles who bring the faith to these children."

Brother Luis was devastated. But he only thought he was devastated. I could have shown him devastation.

This was to be my end. Created by myself.

THE CITY CELEBRATED AS WE LEFT. There were banners and songs. Those who had jeered The Saint now stood in the streets and cheered him. There would be no more war in the Land of War.

Finally, Guatemala would find peace.

The Saint smiled as we rode out of the city on the burros. To my surprise, it was not the kindly smile he had for the Indians. This was the look of someone who had been right all along. I do not think the colonialists noticed. They were too happy.

In his haste to be slaughtered, The Saint had us leave at the first sign the rainy season had ended. Where there had been roads and possibly even trails, now there were streams and rivers. Mud everywhere.

He did not mind. He had the four merchants sing as we traveled. The noise and racket echoed through the land. He smiled a smile of bliss. He was the father, and these his children.

Each night he asked them to tell us stories of this land. They all nodded and smiled at the request. Every morning we heard their songs, every night their stories. I understood how our saint, Father Bartolomé, could stand to hear their singing. He was tone deaf.

But he could not fail to be horrified at their butchery of the stories of Christ. Still, he smiled his benevolent smile.

THE FIRST NIGHT, AT OUR HUMBLE DINNER, the short one began his stories. The Jews had captured Jesucristo. They tied him up and threw him into the corner. Then they wanted to have a feast. They killed a rooster and cooked him. They all looked in the pot to see how the rooster was cooking. The rooster came alive and flapped his wings. Chile flew out and got into their eyes. Jesucristo escaped.

As he finished the story, all four of these masters of the bible nodded and smiled. I looked over at our Saint. My God, he was smiling and nodding, too.

"Where did you learn this story?" I asked.

"We learned this from an Ixil. He had learned the story in his town of Nebaj."

I turned and looked at Father Bartolomé. "Father?" I started.

"It will take time my son, it will take time."

"But, Father. . . ."

"Who are we to know?"

The four continued nodding and grinning until they fell asleep.

We woke before the sun came up. The cool air was crisp, and my skin was cold. I looked at the four Indians. They were frightened. Images came to my mind of early morning attacks by rampaging savages, some wearing feathers, some wearing nothing.

"Father," I said to The Saint, "the young men are disturbed."

The one who had told the story the night before was the most upset. His eyes were wild.

"I dreamed, Father," he said. "My intention was not to dream, but after I told that story last night I dreamed."

"What did you dream of, my son?"

It would have been impossible for Our Saint to have said, *Go back to sleep, you little idiot.*

"Father, I dreamed of an owl." The others shook their heads and began to look around our camp in fear.

The Saint began, "My son, dreams are only—"

"Father, it was an *owl*."

"Yes, of course, an owl," he said. "Tell me about this owl."

"I was asleep. An owl passed over my head. I could hear it. It screeched as it passed over. Father, I know what that means. My own father interpreted dreams. He made his living that way. He raised our family by interpreting dreams. When the owl passes overhead, it makes a sound. It screeches and lets us know death is near. This is a favor to us."

I thought the other three would die on the spot. They held each other.

"An owl may mean a lot of things,"The Saint began.

"No, Father. It means death. It has always meant death."The others nodded.

"I am supposed to go out and protect myself now. The owl told me that death is near."

"What are you supposed to do?"

"I have to find a dog and grab it. Then I should pinch its ears. That will defend me against the owl. The owl said that death is near, very near. I have to find a dog, but there is no dog near here. The Spanish have dogs, but we are a long way from the Spanish. What shall I do, Father, if I cannot find a dog?"

"We must pray, my son." So there in the mud we knelt and prayed. We prayed for protection from owls. We prayed we might find a dog somewhere around there. Then the others had fears they wanted to pray about.

We prayed that we would not dream about coyotes, for coyotes trick you; not dream about opossums, because you will be robbed if you dream about opossums; not dream about deer, because they leap and are free, and so is death; not dream about rabbits, because they will steal your daughter; not dream about eagles, because they will bring sickness that will kill you; not dream about snakes, because they will bring lies against you; not dream about fish, because fish will watch you; not dream about crabs, because crabs will bring soldiers; not dream about horses, because horses represent caskets and your time to die has come; not dream about pigeons, because that would mean that your spirit is ready to leave your body; not dream about dirty water, because dirty water will bring illness and death to you, and if not to you, to your wife; not dream about the sun falling down, because that means death is very near, that everything you own will die; not dream about entering darkness, because entering darkness means you will lose what you love, your wife, your husband that you love—someone will die, they will die, and that is very sad because they were very good to you and you took them for granted and did not tell them when they were alive you loved them, but after you have that dream you must hurry and tell them you love them, because if you don't hurry, it will be too late.

We also prayed we would dream of stars shining brightly. This means that you will meet another woman.

She will be beautiful and rich.

We finished. The Indians seemed happier; they were not so frightened. I, on the other hand, was overwhelmed. I wondered what our brothers of the Inquisition would have done do to us if they heard our prayers.

The morning air was clear with almost a touch of warmth in it. I listened to the howling of monkeys fighting in the trees, to the songs of the parrots, to the leaves shaking. I wondered how the Indians would interpret my dream.

I walk alone in the jungle. My robes are darkened by the journey. I am afraid of the sounds and cries, but I continue on. I have a meeting with the obsidian.

From the green comes grunting and squealing. The leaves and bushes part. A snarling boar runs out at me. I run, but the bushes slow me. The harder I try to run, the slower I go. I run in mud. The boar bites at me from behind. I am to be his dinner, rather than he, mine.

He snarls and slashes at my flesh until I turn to face him. He stops. He looks up at me. He is transfixed and cannot move. I do not understand; then I look down at myself. I am no longer me. I am tall. I am thin. I am dark and I am splendid. The boar is not afraid nor is he enraged.

I pet his repugnant body. There comes purring from the beast.

All through the day our four Indian minstrels serenaded us. This was good and bad. The music was a horror, but at the same time it offered us complete protection from the wild things of the jungle.

As we left the jungle and descended into a long valley, they stopped singing. At first I thought they were tired, but they were never tired of singing and chanting and creating disaster among the harmonies. They were serious. In fact, they looked frightened and sad.

Our Saint, in his ultimate wisdom, failed to notice. No doubt his mind was lost in the mire of Aristotle, Saint Augustine, and the other intellectual giants. The shadows were long. We began to look for a place to spend the night. Again, our four little Indians surprised me. Each shook his head and told his new representative of God, No, they would not set up camp here. This was not a good place.

We walked along the bank of a swirling, angry river. They still would not let us camp. We turned up, away from the river, and looked for shelter. I saw the reason for their reticence.

First were the trenches. These are the sort the Indians used to stop the soldiers. They had been there for many years; they were overgrown. Nevertheless, they were dangerous. If you were to step into one, you would be speared by stakes set up from below.

Our four minstrels led us around them. A few had been used before. Bones lay scattered around the bottom. Here and there, I saw Spanish armor. We climbed another hundred feet and came to a great pit. The four Indians began blessing themselves rapidly.

"The Abyss of Carchá," the small one said, his mouth open in terror.

"The entrance to Xibalba."

They refused to move. The Saint and I approached to the edge of the pit. I looked in and saw hell. The bottom of this great hole was covered with bones.

I thought the Indians must have massacred thousands of Spanish. The vultures had picked the bones clean. But there was no armor. There were no metal breast plates or helmets. I tried to turn away, but, in horror, I could not stop looking into that great pit. There was tattered rags of color. Indian clothes. Not just Indian warrior's clothes, but women's and children's.

Quietly, quickly, the Saint climbed down into the pit. The Indians cried out for him not to. He did not respond. I don't know why, but I followed. Perhaps to protect him.

Bones crunched under our feet. At the bottom, we stopped. All around were bones. He stooped over and touched them. He picked up something. It was a skull, a tiny skull. He placed both hands around it and held it to his chest. His head shook. Tears streamed down his face. He gently placed it back with the others, then made the sign of the cross over the mass of bones.

As we emerged, mist from the river flowed into the pit, covering the bones with white. I had not noticed before, but there had not been a sound from the relentlessly noisy jungle.

24

I SAW THEIR PYRAMIDS—BLOODY, GORY, AND RELIGIOUS. This was their sacred place to murder. All around us, Indians were celebrating our arrival. Flowers and singing surrounded us as we entered the city. Brilliantly colored and beaded warriors waved and smiled. Children hid behind their mother's bright skirts. The city was alive with the greeting. All I could see was the pyramid. In front of it stood a rack with twenty small spears pointing to the heavens. Each spear had turned brown from the blood.

A skull rack.

These were The Saint's children. How happy he was. This was the moment he had fought for, prayed for, perhaps lusted for. They were all around him, touching his garments, looking up at his smiling face, babbling in their strange tongue. The smiles could not erase the horror of the pit that still could be seen in his eyes.

I wondered why he had revulsion for the pit but not the pyramid.

We sat through ritual after ritual: feathers, gold, and dancing. They brought out no headless victims, nor did they threaten us in any way. The Saint was thrilled. I was terrified.

In the morning, The Saint told me he would meet with their leaders and nobles. I would meet with their priests. This was the last group I wanted to see or think about. They are simple murderers, I thought. Their hands stink of blood. Then I thought, Know your enemy. And I was still terrified.

EIGHT OF US SAT IN A DARK ROOM next to the pyramid. Four of the eight were Rabinal musicians. Two were the ancient priests. One was a slave from another tribe. And then there was this rotund monk from Spain. I thought of the wonders of sound that could be created if the four Indian musicians could play background for our four singing Indians.

After the musicians finished their clamor, the slave brought gourds into the room. I looked at his face in the orange candlelight. He had clear skin, almost completely untouched by pox.

He walked around to the two priests and handed them gourds. They chanted to the gourds: *Ixtatzunin, Ixtatzunin.* I thought this was the name of the drink. They handed one back to the slave. He brought it to me. It was warm to the touch. I sniffed it. Smelled like fermented corn.

The musicians were not given any. The priests drank and looked at me. Terror flashed through my mind. I had never heard of these people poisoning a poor soul, though they had worked out a variety of other ways to relieve people of their souls. But poisoning? They did not need to. They had obsidian and skull racks.

But still?

I thought of The Saint. His entire life had been built on this Great Conversion, these Indians, at this time. Who was I to inhibit that? But then again, I had not intended to sacrifice my life in a darkened room with seven savages. If I were to die, I thought, at least it would be in public atop the pyramid.

I spilled the drink.

Of course, I spilled the drink. It was a gourd. It did not have a proper way to sit itself down. The bottom of it was not flat, but rounded. I expected no end of trouble at that moment.

The slave smiled, shook his head knowingly, and left the room. He returned with another gourd and handed it to me.

"Who are you?" I asked in mutilated Rabinal.

"A servant," he said.

I drank.

The musicians started their symphony of disharmony again. An old man came into the room. He was quite small, with wrinkles covering his face. He stood in front of the musicians and nodded in time to the music. He was dressed far more simply than the others. No gold, feathers; no jewelry of any kind. Just white pants with a few small triangles woven in, and a bright red coat.

There were no introductions, just smiles and nods. He was clearly aware of my presence. A look, a glance—each look hostile. Who was I dressed in white robes and a black cover, a Spanish monk to come here to persuade his people that their religion was wrong?

He looked at me, or rather looked into me. It felt weird. "Men have come to our city before; they wanted to trade with us. Really they wanted to trick us." As he spoke his voice seemed to leave his body and take its own shape in the dark. I looked at the words. In amazement I realized he did not speak in Spanish. But I understood the words. He spoke slowly and clearly. I wondered if I had been poisoned.

"These people want our souls, they want our spirits. They need them because they do not have souls and spirits of their own."

His words became multicolored in the blackness. My body and my soul separated.

Great trees everywhere. I am a part of the green and the land and the flowers and the other animals and I have no worries and no strain; I am just who I am and am not afraid.

I hear the sounds of the great jaguar. I hear his feet walking through the grass. I hear his great growl. I smell his foul breath. I am not afraid.

I jump on a giant armadillo.

Armor covers him. He has no fear of the great jaguar. I wish for an instant that I could be an armadillo, so that I could have that armor and never be afraid again.

"Get moving, mule," I say, "Get moving because Judgment Day has come."

We come through a thicket of brush. The jaguar had waited for me at the edge of the river. I ride the armadillo to a bee hive. I buy honey. I cover myself with it. I am completely sticky and roll over and over in the leaves and grass. I am now a huge mass of leaves and vines and grass. I climb on the armadillo and ride to the top of a small hill above the stream.

I say goodbye to the armadillo. The armadillo says good-bye to me. I purposely fall off the hill. I roll down the hill to the jaguar. I roll over and over, and land right next to the jaguar. I land with a loud noise, a frightening noise.

This scares the jaguar. He does not know what such a huge animal could be. The size of this great animal, and the horrible sound, scare the poor jaguar. He runs away. He runs away from me. I know the jaguar will not soon return to the river. He is frightened.

I have tricked that stupid jaguar.

I awoke to the sounds of Indian children playing. It was still dark, black as night. I was sprawled out on the floor of the miserable room beside the pyramid. The rest had left. In the minimal light, I could see ten or fifteen empty gourds lying on the ground, lying on their sides as if Spanish soldiers had stayed too late at a tavern.

They had succeeded far more than Father Luis could ever imagined: I had been rendered a complete and abject fool. I wondered if they had brought in their fellow priests from surrounding areas to laugh at this outrageous fat priest dressed in black and white robes, falling on the ground, thinking he rode armored rats from the jungle. With trepidation I wondered if they had brought The Saint to see my excruciating downfall. No, he would have stayed to help me and made me feel even worse.

As I crawled out of the room by the pyramid, the Indian children ran off, obviously afraid. They were the early risers. The sun had barely risen. I stumbled away from the pagan rock, then looked up to see a huge mural painted on the side of one of the houses of royalty.

The colors stopped me. What kinds of dyes were the Indians using here in the New World? I wondered. Maybe it was the morning light. There were blue beasts everywhere: monkeys, tigers, rabbits. The one that caught my eye was the bat. It was a rusty red and ascended from a deep black cave. Its wings were spread out, maybe five meters. Its face looked to the right. I could hear a screech, a grinding, crying sound. Out of the bat's head came lines and circles that I took to mean the sound that I had just heard.

It moved.

What was wrong with me? What had happened?

I looked away. Brother Pedro appeared. I had ignored him on our journey to this land. And now here he was looking at me in my time of despair and confusion.

"It is beautiful, isn't it?" he said.

"Yes, in its way."

Indian women passed in front of us, on their way to set up the morning market. Each was dressed in the spectacular way of these people. Jagged lines of blue and red and green and yellow and purple and all of the other colors descended in different directions from their necks down to their waists. From there, the lines of their skirts were straight, falling to their lovely brown calves.

One woman stopped to look at us. She turned to the mural. The morning light set her clothes on fire. She wore the usual colors and a brilliant tapestry covering a basket she carried on her head. The garment, this tapestry, would have looked splendid in the greatest castles of Europe, but she wore it over a basket. On her head.

The background was pure white. In patterns projecting out at Brother Pedro and me were multitudes of hues and shades, symmetrical and perfect.

"Marvelous," Brother Pedro said, shaking his head in wonderment.

"How do they do it?" I said. "How is it these savages, unlearned and ignorant of God's laws, as well as God Himself, are able to create something that expresses God's perfection?"

Brother Pedro turned to me. "I thought you were the one who thought these people were less than human. I remember something about the 'importance of slavery.' Didn't you talk about that when Father Bartolomé was absent?"

"I don't feel very good," I said. And it was the truth. All that riding of armadillos. My stomach challenged me and I had to find a place to throw up. Brother Pedro took me back to the rooms that were set up for us. I lay down.

I dreamt immediately upon falling asleep.

I am dressed in the Indian dress. I stand on the pyramid and dance in my colors. I turn and jump and hear the music in my soul; I fall from the pyramid, fall toward the ground below, and, as

I fall, I turn into a bird, a bird whose plumage is the colors of all the rainbows of the world. Then I fly.

The next morning I awoke with horror and terror in my heart. I had become a savage. Revulsion swept me. For all my inattention to the details of our faith, my chronic thoughts of Marta, my pettiness, I had never approached the sinfulness of the previous twenty-four hours.

What would become of me? I thought of my corpulent self roasting in hell. Hell was red. Tiny scarlet demons danced around my cooking body, screaming in delight. Hell was eternity, pain infinite.

Quickly, I ran to The Saint. I needed to attend to confession. I knelt before him and cried like a baby. I told him everything, every nuance of my humiliation and disgust.

"Have you harmed someone?"

"I don't understand, Father."

"Have you enslaved, hurt, killed, destroyed, taken the property of anyone?"

"No, Father."

"Your sins are venial, my son. You could do more for Our Lord and His Wishes, that is true. You could be a more competent brother. That is most assuredly true. But these sins you have told me with such relish are not of the same aspect as those that send sinners to hell."

"But, Father, when I was with those savages, I saw hell. I participated in their savage religion. I became one of them."

"And for this you believe our Good Lord will punish you? My son, for this, He will bless you. In fact, you certainly have my blessings for what you have done. Can you not see this is a step in the direction of the conversion of these people?"

"Father, forgive me."

"My son, there is nothing to forgive."

"Could you forgive me anyhow?"

So with great strain, The Saint forgave me for something he did not see as a sin. I thanked him and left. Walking through the doorway, I could hear him giving me his blessing again.

I hurried out.

I BEGAN TO NOTICE DIFFERENCES IN THESE INDIANS from the others. At first, they had all been a rainbow of confusion. Gradually, I could see the Rabinal had their own patterns of clothes different from those of the Indians of Santiago de los Caballeros de Guatemala. The Rabinal loved red and green flowers woven into their clothes. The Indians of Santiago wove diamonds into theirs.

After a few months they became comfortable with us. The stares, and the constant pawing at our black and white robes, decreased. Even their priests seemed to get along with us even though we had challenged their roles.

Their chief accepted The Saint's suggestion to build a church. We explained to the Indians how to build a Christian church. They were attentive and accomplished. We built a small wooden church. The Saint celebrated mass. All the Indians came in their finest feathers and gold. Brother Pedro and I assisted The Saint. He cried in joy throughout the service. He had converted them all, including the priests. The slave who had given me the corn drink was baptized as Francisco. The priest in the red jacket became Lazarillo. They had become Christians.

As The Saint held up the silver chalice, I looked out at them. They were praying, all right. But these were prayers we Europeans had never heard. They were praying to The Saint. They were praying to him as if he were already dead and had been canonized. The man isn't dead yet, I thought. You will have plenty of time for that afterward. But still they stared at him and prayed directly to him.

He had joined the Indian pantheon. He, of course, in his humility, did not notice.

After the service, their leaders and priests gathered around us. They were so enthralled they could not speak directly to him anymore. I became their intermediary. I was low enough for them. I could send messages to the superior being.

They wanted to give him a gift. This was mandatory in their civilization. I told them there was no way he could accept anything from them except their souls. They would not hear of it. They had to give him, or his representative, a gift. I knew he would not hear of it. At the same time, we could not risk offending these people. I had not lost my fear of the pyramid and their obsidian. I told them I would accept the gift for him.

Gold, I wondered.

They brought the gift to me. It was Francisco, the Indian slave. He was dressed differently than the rest. The colors on his jackets and pants were darker, dangerous. He walked proudly.

Lazarillo headed the gift-giving group.

"You may take him. He is not one of us, but he has been a strong and proud slave."

"Slave?"

"This was Belehé Qat," Lazarillo said. "Now he is the Christian, Francisco. He came to us years ago to negotiate a treaty. He became our slave. Because of his heroism in our wars with the Spanish, we have not sacrificed him. He is a great gift to you."

I graciously accepted for The Saint.

I quickly hid him.

He was polite. Francisco looked after me and smiled graciously. He quickly learned Spanish. But he was an enigma to me. He would look, smile, then turn away as if I were dismissed instead of he.

One day he asked about horses.

"Why don't you have any?"

"That is what the soldiers use for war," I said. His dark eyes gave me a look I could not comprehend. It said something like *I am a warrior. Do I really have to put up with these people?*

Yes, you do, I thought.

"MY SON, THAT INDIAN has been very helpful to you," The Saint said one morning.

I looked down.

"It is almost as if he is your servant, or even more."

"Yes," I mumbled to him. "He has been of great help. I have asked him time and again to desist in his attention to me, but you know how some people can be so devoted."

He paused. Yes, it was true these people could be devoted to him. He had worried about that. But that had been a sign of Christ's spirit infiltrating into their minds.

"You have been blessed that this Indian loves you and loves Christ so much that he seemingly has given his life to you and to our holy cause."

"Yes, Father, and I have addressed the Lord in my prayers about this."

The Holy Saint-In-Waiting, Bartolomé, would have strangled me with his beautiful blue rosary beads had he found out the truth.

I had another dream that night. I put great faith in dreams. Before I had come to this land my dreams were pleasant. My favorite was the one with Marta serving me her wonderfully cooked duckling. It was smothered in gravy and oranges. She placed it in front of me, then made her way to the front of the table to dance a slow, carnivorous waltz in my honor. That was a nice dream. Occasionally, I've rushed to bed in the hopes of having that one.

But that night, after The Saint had words with me, it was different. I found myself in front of the pit of bones. As before, there was fog everywhere. Only this time it was not fog.

Yellowish gases seep up from the pit. They flow through the bones and rise up to me. I attempt to turn from the pit rim, to run from this yellow fog, this pernicious gas, but The Saint holds me in place. I cry out to him to let me go, but he will not. He holds me from the back; I cannot see him. I am held in place. The yellow steam floats through the air in gentle waves until it reaches my nostrils.

I try not to breathe as the gas floats around my face. I hold my breath until I think I will explode. I have to breathe. There is only this gas. I let it in with a whoosh. I have inhaled death. I fall headlong into the pit of Indian bones.

The morning light came to my eyes. I was alive, lying in my bed in this pagan Indian city. Francisco had brought fruit for me as he did every morning.

25

THE SAINT, FATHER BARTOLOMÉ, CAME THROUGH the doorway beaming. I had become frightened of him and felt nervous twitches throughout my body when I saw him approach. They would roll up and down my belly. Guilt?

He didn't notice.

"More and more of the Indians are finding Christ," he said as I put the green fruit back on its tray. "A new tribe came out of the jungle this morning to be converted."

"You've shown the world they can be converted," I said. "You've proven Alvarado absolutely wrong."

"That's not important."

"I meant they can cease their cause now."

"Of course. Last night during the rosary I realized we have completed our task with the Rabinal. It is time we returned to the capital."

I was mixed with great relief and internal laughter at calling that mud-drenched piece of ridiculousness a capital.

"We've accomplished the goal of our journey. This has been a success beyond belief."

"I know you have been greatly taken with these people," he said. "I'm sorry, but I've asked Brother Pedro to be the monk here. Upon our return, I will ask Brother Luis to join Brother Pedro. Together they will convert the jungle beyond this land to the ways of Our Lord."

I thought of Brother Luis trying to convert one of the green snakes I saw on the way to this fortress in the jungle.

"I have told the king of the Rabinal of our plans. He wants to celebrate our departure with a pageant." The Saint was beaming again. "We will be expected to sit front and center. He wants your fellow, the one who serves you all the time, to play a major role. This is quite strange, but he insisted I ask your permission. I told him there was no need to ask. He would not relent."

"Very strange, Father, very strange."

"Yes, but certainly you have no problems with his participation."

"Of course not."

I TOLD FRANCISCO ABOUT THE PAGEANT. His eyes did not deviate from mine. There was no expression on his calm face.

"Francisco, what is this ceremony?"

"A tradition, Father."

"Brother," I corrected him. "What is this pageant?"

"It is the great dance of the Rabinal. It is known throughout the world of man. It is from the time when the people of my wife had a war with the Rabinal. It is the great story of the K'iché Lord's confrontation with the Rabinal king."

Francisco nodded. There was a sadness in his eyes, a hint I understood nothing. These people were never direct. I could not understand that. All you have to do is to say something. Make it clear. If you have to be subtle, if the situation demands it, I appreciate that. But these people were like that about everything.

The entire city began to prepare for the pageant. The musicians practiced, workers built great structures in the square, painters created great murals on the walls of the city.

And then a strange thing happened.

Francisco brought me a new servant. He said this woman would be able to help me. Again, this indirectness. There would be much packing and carrying. This woman could help handle the tasks. I thought Francisco would have been more than enough to help us travel.

The new servant was a great woman. Almost as large as myself. She was a Rabinal. She wore the traditional cloak of blues and greens, but there was something different about her. She immediately set about getting everything ready for the trip. She picked up and hauled things that were impossible for one person to budge.

I quickly gained respect for her. For some strange reason thoughts of Marta faded into the background. Her converted name was Antonia.

She was impossible to hide from The Saint. He asked about her. I said she had volunteered to help. I had never seen him smile like that before. He shook his head with an air of wisdom, but not of patronage.

And still she packed and carried and prepared food for me. She was everywhere and did everything. God, I was grateful. There was nothing for me to do except enjoy her stoutness. And there was no lack of that. Francisco and she would laugh and joke as they worked.

Then it was finished. Everything was ready to return to the capital. The next morning would be the pageant. We would see the celebration, stay in the city one last night, then return. I was eager to return, but there was something about the city and its people that had captured me. The mural. The way they received us.

The fact that they had not stripped us, stretched us out on the stone temple, and crushed our chests.

My chest.

For this I was grateful. I felt something peculiar that night. I could not quite name the feeling, but it impelled me to leave our sanctuary and walk around the city. This would be my last unaccompanied walk. Tomorrow would be the pageant. The next day we would leave.

The work on the platforms and stages was complete. There was silence in the city. The full moon cast a light haze on the smoke surrounding the strange pyramids and temples. There was something extraordinary about them. That night they and I were different. They were beautiful.

Each building was light blue in the moonlight. The temples were enormous. I had not seen such magnificent buildings even in Madrid. They seemed to jut out from the earth, protrude from the ground to the sky, aiming directly at the moon. The stairs were such that I could not imagine humans actually being able to walk up them. It would be like walking straight up into the night sky.

Great flags flew from the four bottom corners of the pyramid. There was a breeze, so they waved gently in the night. As I watched the flags, I changed my opinion about these people. There was something extraordinary, enticing, about them and their civilization. I walked back smiling. I laughed at the thought that The Saint had finally converted me into an Indian lover.

As I got into my cot I was still smiling. I had survived. No obsidian blade had broken into my chest. There had been peace. The Saint had been right. Somehow through this, I felt different about myself also. I was at peace.

I ride the armadillo again. I find myself in the green grass, tall grass surrounding me. I look up, and here is the jaguar again.

Only now there is no trickery, there is no fear, there is no confusion. There is only the jaguar and me.

The jaguar slowly comes to me. I graciously hop from the armadillo onto the jaguar. We stop, look, then curl up next to each other.

The jaguar turns into Marta.

In the morning, the yellow light fell onto my eyes. I happily remembered the dream. But then I felt something. I was crowded on my cot. My robes were gone. There was a great figure snoring next to me. My God, I thought, what have I done? Antonia.

I jumped up, grabbed the bedclothes. She tried to jump up also. The cot crashed to the floor with a great resounding thud.

"Oh, my God," I said as I fled to the corner. I clutched the blankets to cover myself, and wheezed.

"Thank you, Brother," she said. I heard her laugh as she left.

THE SAINT, BROTHER PEDRO, AND I had raised seats that were reserved for honored guests and gods. A brilliant canopy of colored textiles hung over our heads. Next to us sat the king and his royal family. I had never before seen a range of colors and fantastic jewelry like that. I was dazzled.

All around us in the ball court were the people of the Rabinal. They wore the finest clothes. This was their most holy of days. Their new spiritual leaders were leaving. They had been converted. Happiness at their redemption had to be celebrated. But they were also sad. Many pointed to The Saint and cried. He had saved them, and now he was leaving. War with the Spanish had been averted.

The day began with a ball game. The Saint leaned over and told me this was a spiritual experience for them. This was the site of the beginning of their religious cosmology. Their mythological twin gods had played ball at this spot, and the gods of the underworld had become upset. They were too loud. The twin gods had to go to the underworld.

"Is that their hell?"

"Something like that, I guess."

The ball game began. I could see no religious significance or symbol in the play. But the game was fast and hearty. There was no lost movement. Each player was agile and splendid. The game was completely captivating until I saw Antonia. She was sitting by the stairs, smiling at me. The ball went through the ring. Suddenly the game was over. Cheers rang out through the city. It was deafening.

"They have honored us again,"The Saint said to me.

"How is that?"

"They did not sacrifice the winning team."

"Just so they don't sacrifice the guests of honor."

The Saint shook his head and sighed.

The players left the field, and the musicians entered. The Rabinal musicians and our four singing Indians took their places at the end of the stadium. I tried not to look at the fat lady who had uncovered me during the night. What a great woman she was. Proud and large. The best of the Rabinal, I thought. As I looked at her, I felt things that had not been available to me before. I think it was love. I glanced at her. She smiled a great front toothless grin. She waved at me.

Mortification. The word that came to me, mortification. From the Latin *mortificus*. I remembered that from a class at Salamanca. *Mortificus*, death-making. Yes, this was certainly the feeling of death making. This was close to death.

I would die if The Saint saw my embarrassment. I refused to look at him.

I looked down into my lap. I saw moving memories of the morning. No, I could not look there. I looked at the crowds. I thought I saw her again. No, it could not be her all the way over on the other side of the stadium. I glanced at where she had been sitting. She was still there. Waving and toothlessly smiling.

Inevitably, irrevocably, I looked at The Saint. I had to see if he had seen. He looked at me, then at the fat wonder of the world. I don't know what he said or how he looked because I looked away. *Mortificus. Mortificus.*

I brought out my beads as the musicians began. Hail Mary, full of grace and then other words came to me. Latin words straight from hell: *futuere, fustis, battuere.* Striking and copulating. In Egyptian: *petcha.* This was the male member in action. I had learned these words in Salamanca from the boys who laughed and yelled them. They said these words were hidden in the books.

There was music and singing. Some chanting. The players came out onto the field. The drum beat again and again. I saw Francisco. He was dressed in the most splendid Indian garb. There were green feathers everywhere. Around him, what appeared to be his servant actors were dressed in humble dark clothes.

On the other side of the field, more Rabinal royalty and priests paraded in. They were dressed in gold and silver. Bells sounded as they moved. They danced in a slow rhythmic dance.

I looked back at Francisco. He carried a rope tied into a noose. He danced up to the Rabinal. He sang, yelled, and chanted at them.

I had practiced enough Rabinal that I could understand some of their chanting and singing. "Before the face of Heaven, before the face of Earth."

The Rabinal king danced close to Francisco and sang to him. He also had a noose which he swung around the air.

"You have delivered yourself up to my Toltec club, my Mexica ax, my white earth, my magic herbs, to my strength."

The Rabinal tossed the noose around Francisco's head. The music stopped. The city was silent. Nothing moved. I looked for

Antonia.

Her face was round with deep black eyes. I thought I could see tears left on her round cheeks. I did not understand what was wrong. She looked away from me. She stared intently at the play. I looked back at the actors.

They chanted at each other. The Rabinal yelled at my Francisco that he was a captive. "It is here you shall pay for your excesses, here under Heaven, above Earth. You have addressed your mountains, your valleys, for the last time. Not again, by day or by night, will you go forth from your mountains, from your valleys, for truly it is here you shall die, shall end, here under heaven, above earth."

I became transfixed by the thing. The words were slow and clear. I was amazed I could understand every word. Perhaps it was the gems, maybe the relentless chanting, possibly the monotonous drum and music of the Indian musicians. I was enchanted. I forgot my fat Indian friend, The Saint, and the place we were. I had joined the Indians as an audience of the compelled.

The music echoed back from the tall buildings; there was a faint second beat to everything played. The scene shifted to the Rabinal King's palace. A huge canopy of green feathers protected him and the queen. Around them were men and women servants. And around the servants were warriors dressed as Eagles and Jaguars.

A Rabinal warrior danced in front of the canopy. He told, sang, chanted, that he had captured the K'iché prince.

The king was pleased. "Praise to Heaven, praise to Earth, that Heaven has given him over to you, that Earth has delivered him up to you. Here he must be shown regard, must be done honor, within the great walls, the great palace."

I thought of some of the passion plays I had seen at the university. I had ignored them as much as possible.

The Rabinal dancers unbound Francisco and sang to him that he was a proud warrior but must bow in submission and bend his knee. Francisco sang back that as a proud warrior he would not bow into submission.

"I've come from the great walls, the great fortress, the corn-city Iximché."

I felt some anxiety here for my servant-slave, Francisco. I worried about the line of the K'iché dying. I asked The Saint, "Is there sacrifice in this play?"

"They would not offend us with a human sacrifice."

By now Francisco was facing the Rabinal king. Francisco, as the K'iché prince, sang out. If he were to bow down in submission, he would bow down into submission with his arrow and shield, with which he would strike down the king.

The Rabinal king chanted, "But here is where you shall pay, here under Heaven, above Earth. So you have addressed your mountains, your valleys, for the last time, for it is here you shall die, shall end, under Heaven, above Earth. May Heaven, Earth be with you, man of K'iché."

I glanced to The Saint. He was smiling at the play; then he saw me looking at him. He waved me off as if I were a schoolchild asking a ridiculous question.

I looked at the stairs, at Antonia. She was still crying in that dignified way. And I understood. She was not crying because she was leaving this city. She was crying because she was going to lose her friend, Francisco.

A great tapestry was brought out to Francisco. It was full of brilliant colors and the soft motion of gods and animals. Francisco draped it around himself. He challenged the king to bring his musicians. Out they came. Francisco danced to their cadences.

I began to panic. The Saint did not understand. This was real. There would be no symbolic execution. By the end of this play, Francisco would be dead. I looked at the back end of the Indian stage.

Priests.

Obsidian.

Francisco continued: "Lend to me the Mother of the Green Birds, the Brilliant Emerald, that I may dance with her, that I may meet death, my end, under Heaven, above Earth."

Francisco and the Mother of the Green Birds danced with the Rabinal, trumpets blaring.

"Father Bartolomé," I said to The Saint. "They intend to kill Francisco. There is no other way for this to end."

He shook his head at me in anger and contempt.

Now Francisco was dancing with twelve yellow Eagles and twelve yellow Jaguars. Francisco yelled out: "Look upon me, Heaven. Look upon me, Earth." Antonia put her hands over her eyes.

I scrambled out of my seat. The Saint grabbed my cloak, but I yanked it away.

"Look upon me, Heaven, look upon me, Earth. Is it true I must die here, must end here, here under Heaven, above Earth?" Francisco chanted.

I stumbled through the seated Rabinal nobles.

"Aaaah, Sky! Aaaah, Earth!" Francisco chanted, cried.

I reached the field, chanting my own chant: "My God, my God, what am I doing?"

"I await only my death, my end, here under Heaven, above Earth."

I ran toward the platform.

"Come, you Eagles, come, you Jaguars, come then, do your work."

The priests moved out onto the stage. The Eagles and Jaguars began closing in on Francisco.

"Sink your teeth. Sink your talons. Get it over with in one moment."

I climbed onto the platform.

The Eagles and Jaguars lifted Francisco and placed him on a sacrificial stone. The priest's black knife was in the air as I barreled into them. I was like an avalanche from Heaven. Feathers and gold flew everywhere. Priests and kings sprawled on the stage. Eagles and Jaguars fell onto the field.

Francisco lay stretched out on the rock, his chest, his skin smooth; his body intact. He looked at me, shook his head, and smiled.

26

THE JOURNEY HOME WAS BITTER. I think he was horribly sad they had not completely accepted his teachings. In a quiet dark place in myself, I hoped he would have appreciated my act. Instead, he seemed angry and hurt every time I approached him. I had revealed the sad truth.

We stopped again at the steamy pit of bones. Yes, it had been the Spanish who had committed this atrocity. There was no question.

A day before we were to reach the muddy new capital, he began to question my behavior.

"How did you know they were going to kill Francisco? So what if Antonia was crying? That could have been her response to the ceremony."

"I thought they were going to kill him."

"The black knife held high in the air could simply have been part of the ceremony, like in the theater of Madrid. Did it have to mean they were going to gouge the poor man?"

I gave up. He would inevitably change the Rabinal of reality into the Rabinal of his mind. They would again become good, peaceful people who had a few vices. And the Spanish would again become the assassins.

I think he hated me.

Along the way home, the colonialists greeted us with cries of joy and thanksgiving. There would be no war in the Land of War. Our people were tired of fighting. There would be peace.

I FELT THE SAFETY OF A MUDDY OLD HOME when we returned. We created servants' quarters for Francisco and Antonia.

At the morning mass, The Saint lectured on the courage of the Rabinal. He described in horrible detail the pit of bones. He asked the Spanish to open their hearts to the Indians.

He left out the obsidian dance.

AFTER MASS, IN THE VESTIBULE, I spoke with the old colonialist who had delivered me those grave warnings. He congratulated me on my survival.

"I thought I had seen the last of you, Brother."

"And I you."

"They are not such savages as we have been led to believe. They must have changed in the years since we attacked them."

I wanted to tell him of the blade and Francisco. Why didn't I? Perhaps I felt a need to protect the dream The Saint had created.

"They are wonderful people, my son," I said to him. "The Lord has given us a great opportunity to bring souls into his mansion." My son? Good Lord, I had become sanctimonious. Too much time around The Saint.

"Since you left, there have been changes. Captain-General Alvarado has sold off his fortune and borrowed from everyone. He built a fleet of thirteen ships, then bought equipment, food, and horses for over a thousand soldiers."

"He's not going to attack the Rabinal in the Land of War?"

"No, not at all. He has renamed it 'Land of Peace.'"

Father Bartolomé will be canonized, I thought. Probably within five years after his death. Maybe two. I wondered if the Vatican would call me as a witness to his miraculous deeds.

"Alvarado is going to search for El Dorado."

"Are you going?" He looked too old for war. These old fighters never knew when to quit.

He opened his arms in pride. "Not now. I am an *encomiendero*. I have land, and I have slaves. I know your order would not approve, but this is the time to build the land. I have no wish to run off and get killed by strangers."

THAT NIGHT FRANCISCO LEFT US. I had thought he would be with me the rest of my life.

The Saint tried to explain to me. "The Captain-General has requested new servants for his young wife. I told Francisco to go."

"But, Father, this is slavery," I objected.

"No, not at all. They have agreed he will not be a slave. He will be her servant. And as a servant, he may serve the Lord in two ways. He will show them with his gentle heart that the Indians are good people."

"There are others doing that."

"He also trusts you. He will tell you what happens, and what is going to happen, in that household."

When The Saint made up his mind, there was the end of the conversation. I said good-bye to Francisco. He reflected no emotion. It was as if I had not saved his life. Maybe he had thought he was supposed to die in that Rabinal charade.

After he left, I had to relearn how to do things for myself. This unpleasant task soon became tiresome. Gradually, almost without my knowledge, and certainly without my permission, the large toothless Rabinal woman began to look after me.

Antonia was thoughtful even into the late evening.

I worried about a scandal, and there was one. But I was not the central character, merely an observer, which I prefer anyway.

It began with Brother Luis. He hated me. He was clear and honest about this feeling toward me. I had participated in the Conversion of the Rabinal while he tended to the petty births, mundane marriages, and burials of the colonialists. I was a fat baboon; he a latent saint. How could I have relieved him of his rightful place? Believe me, that had not been my plan.

"Something is wrong with Father Bartolomé."

"There are always celestial happenings with a saint."

"I wish you wouldn't call him that. If he ever heard you, he would be hurt."

"He will never hear unless you tell him."

"Brother Domingo, I know there have been differences between us, but I intend you no harm. There is something wrong."

I chuckled at his lack of harmful intent and asked him to go on. Curiosity is never a safe approach to life. I had survived the Land of War and felt stupidly secure.

"He is visited by a woman. At night. She comes in black robes, carrying a lantern."

"Brother Luis, I am not gullible."

"There is a black hood covering her head. The orange of the lantern reflects off the black."

"And you are suggesting what, Brother Luis?"

"I am not suggesting anything. I have seen this vision two nights. Last night, she walked, or closer to the fact, crept along the sides of the buildings until she reached our monastery. I watched from my window."

It was true that his window was directly over the side door.

"I leaned out and saw Father Bartolomé swing the door open. As he allowed her entrance, the hood fell from her head, revealing her black hair and features."

I could not forestall a laugh. "Are you trying to tell me The Saint has a concubine?"

"I am saying nothing like that at all. There is something going on that is dangerous."

"This woman in black is not a mistress?"

"She is not like your toothless joy, Brother. She is beautiful. But I don't know who she is, or what she wants."

That night I stayed in Brother Luis' room. I begrudged him the loss of a night with my Rabinal friend, but curiosity is powerful. And stupid.

It was very late when Brother Luis woke me. I rushed to the window. First, there was orange light; then I saw a figure sliding along the sides of the buildings. She wore a black cape wrapped around her, which covered her head as he had said. An Indian accompanied her. We couldn't see his face.

She stopped at the door below us. From his open widow we could hear her tapping on the wood. She let her hood drop as The Saint opened the door. Her face became visible for an instant as she entered.

Both of us had seen who she was. Neither of us spoke. We stared out into the blackness. Brother Luis whispered the words, "Doña Beatriz." She was the beautiful young wife of Captain-General Alvarado.

The door below us slammed. We looked out the window again. She was running back down the street. I thought I could hear her crying. I recognized Francisco following her.

We agreed not to speak of this again. Normally, I enjoy gossip—I thrive on the slight, the innuendo, the hint that the great and holy are not. But this was The Saint, and I needed him to re-main saintly.

"THE CAPTAIN-GENERAL IS LEAVING." Francisco had told me the obvious. This is what The Saint had asked us to do. Francisco had spied and reported it to me. I had reported it to The Saint. But this news was weeks old.

"My Father," said Francisco, "there are great discussions and ar-guments in the palace. Alvarado is going away."

"It's 'brother' you call me, not 'father'. . . . What came of the discussions?"

"Captain Alvarado conquered this land. He is leaving, and the Spaniards have had great talks about what to do."

"What to do about what?"

"He is leaving this land and going away." I've never understood why these people talk in circles. I remained silent, hoping that Francisco would get around to telling me what was going on. He stood in front of me, nodding. Then he was still, and I was still. I waited.

"Francisco! For Christ's sake, what is going on?" I cried in im-patience. His tranquil black eyes and silence had unhinged me.

He was unmoved. "Captain Alvarado is leaving, and there are matters that are not finished."

"And?"

"He is going to another land, and they have had discussions with the Council. They met in his front room, and they are served there."

"You brought them what they needed?"

"They have met on the day 2 Ah and the day 13 Ganel. They have had these two meetings, Father."

"Brother," I corrected him again. "The Council and Alvarado met, and you served them? You overheard them."

"Captain Alvarado is leaving Guatemala. The Council has requested that he do something about our people. The Council fears that, with him absent, the kings will revolt, and the country will be lost to the Spanish."

"Kings?"

"They are our kings and brothers. They have been held in captivity since Captain Alvarado destroyed the Kaqchikel nation in the fields below the volcano. The Council is afraid of them."

Finally. I had never imagined that Francisco could say so much. This was a revelation.

"What does the Council want Alvarado to *do* with them?"

"They begged him to take them away in his fleet or to punish them, if they have given cause."

I told The Saint about the Council, then watched his anger and indignation.

"Tell Francisco to hide. They may hang him for telling us. I will write at once to the crown and ask for dispensation. They must not be killed."

THE NEXT SUNDAY AT THE SERMON, he was relentless. "All people must be treated with respect if we expect the blessings of the Lord. There can be no confusion over what is right and what is wrong."

I watched him in his efforts to save the Indian leaders. A sadness came over me. I thought he would be canonized in my life time. That was assured. But he was pathetic in this life. By humiliating the Council at Mass, they would know he was moving to have the Indians saved. Now, they had no choice. This was the moment of their death sentences. He had no idea.

The next morning, after the Mass dedicated to the honor of Captain-General Alvarado and Doña Beatriz, the first Indian was found. On a small road just off the plaza, he was found hanging from a tree. Then the others were discovered. They had been hanged at street corners away from the palace. I suspected that Alvarado did not want his beautiful young wife to become upset.

Antonia told me what had happened.

It was the chiefs of the old city who had been hanged. The Indians were furious and planned retribution, but many others of their royalty were in the Spanish prisons. They would be also be hanged if there were rebellion.

In the land of the Rabinal, I had felt fear, persistent fear. Now, I did not feel fear. The Spanish would never attack the clergy. No, it was not fear.

It was despair. Anger, fear, lust, even shame I had felt, but, by my nature, despair is foreign. But this was despair—for my people, for the Spanish in this new land, for the Church. And most especially, for the Indians. Not even a saint could protect them.

Throughout the city, the hangings were discussed. Some thought they had deserved it. Others felt the city would be safe now, because Alvarado was leaving and the Indians were properly afraid. Don Alejandro, the old colonialist, was worried. He said that he did not like secret trials.

The Saint refused to leave the chapel. He lay prostrate in front of the cross, arms spread in supplication. He prayed and cried and prayed some more.

We heard that Alvarado had named Castellanos, the treasurer, as acting governor and captain-general. As both, he would have total power.

The Saint struggled to his feet to write more letters. He met with Alvarado and Castellanos at the Council chambers. He returned and again lay prostrate in front of the crucifix.

The next morning we found more hangings. I thought The Saint would go mad with grief and rage. There was nothing to be done. The following morning there were more hangings. And more the next. The Indians refused to look at our faces. The next morning there were more.

The Saint became pale and thin.

I COUNTED EIGHT HUNDRED AND FIFTY Spanish soldiers as they marched out of our capital. Alvarado was at the lead on his great black horse. He scratched his red beard as he passed me. I wondered what kind of man this was. I had a sudden impulse to pick up a rock.

Now, I thought, the slaughter will come to an end. The rest of the Indian chiefs were found. Alvarado had hanged all the Indians held captive and left them swinging from trees in a forest north of the city.

The next morning there were more hangings. There was no trial. There was no debate. Just hangings of Indians. Castellanos had continued the executions. These Indians were found further from the city, though. Each morning there were ten to twenty Indians found hanging from branches.

The Saint decided to return to Spain. Brother Luis and I knew that was the only choice for him. He would go mad here in helplessness. There, he would at least have the ear of the court.

AS HE LEFT OUR CAPITAL, I knew he would never return to Guatemala. I waved and, I think, cried. He looked down. He had conquered the souls of the Indians, he had saved the lives of the Rabinal, he had turned the Land of War into the Land of Peace, but he could not save the souls of the Spanish. He could not prevent the destruction of all that he had worked for.

The number of Indians found hanging from trees fell. There was no need to continue. All the Indians that could be considered dangerous had been hanged or had fled. The remainder cowered or smiled. During this time, we at the monastery took in many fearful Indians to live with us. This had been my idea, and Brother

Luis had readily agreed. It taxed our ability to find enough food for everyone, but Father Bartolomé would have wanted it that way.

I cannot say Francisco and I became friends—I do not think any Spaniard and any Indian could be friends at that time, or perhaps any time—but on Wednesday evenings he visited. He saw what we had been doing with the refugees from the hangings. He talked about comings and goings at the palace. He had a good sense of palace politics. I began to wonder if he had lived though intrigues before.

One Wednesday night, he told me Doña Beatriz hated her husband's child by an Indian. This was Leonor. "The Captain-General's wife looks at her with disgust."

With this information, I began to notice Doña Beatriz closely during Mass. It was true. The look on her face when she glanced at her stepdaughter was one of royalty looking at the droppings of a horse that had been found on the finest plates of the palace.

Her brother, Eduardo, Leonor's husband, ignored his sister. He treated her as if she did not exist. To add to the mess, the royal treasurer, Castellanos, had become arrogant with power.

"This man acts like a usurped brother," Francisco said.

Bishop Marroquin was more interested in the nuances of who got along with whom in the palace than in the Indians. This surprised Francisco. He had come to expect that the clergy would act as protectors of the Indians.

"I thought the older priests," he said, "would have either wisdom or, perhaps, a sense of humor."

As the violence ended, we began to settle into a routine. The other brothers and I worked to make life bearable for the refugees in our monastery. Once a week Francisco would come by for dinner. We would hear the palace gossip.

Antonia and I became even closer. Who is to say I sinned? After what I had seen, I did not believe God handed out hellish punishments for love. This was an era of dark hate and horror, death by hanging, and life by scarcity. She touched me, scolded me, and chewed on my ticklish skin. If that was a sin, what was the slaughter of countless Indians?

27

THE RUMORS BEGAN. First, I heard from Don Alejandro. He had heard from a trader from the north. Alvarado had not found El Dorado. He had stopped to fight Indians. There had been a fierce battle. A frightened Franciscan came to the capitol. He said the captain-general had been killed. Some believed the rumors, others not. Francisco reported that the palace was worried.

A letter came. It was from the Viceroy Mendoza. There could be no higher authority. Alvarado was dead. There had been a fight. His horse fell, then rolled over on the captain-general. An inauspicious death.

The Indians quietly celebrated. I could tell. No one said a word to me, no one acted relieved, no one cheered. Their eyes smiled.

The first Wednesday night after we heard of Alvarado's death, Francisco told us the palace had become chaos. There were no more rivalries, no more gossip, no more chatting and scheming. It was as if God had died.

"Doña Beatriz, at first, did not believe the letter," Francisco said. "She said it was impossible. When she read the letter, she asked me what Muchitiltic, the place where he died, meant. I told her it meant 'all black.' She ordered us to paint the palace black.

"With the oil from the spring, we did. At first we thought painting the inside walls would suffice. But then she wanted us to paint the outside walls black. We did. She wanted us to paint the roof black. We did. She wanted us to paint the stone pavement in the courtyard black. We did. She commanded us to hang long black curtains throughout the palace. We did. All day she walks through the palace, holding her unborn baby in her stomach and talking to herself."

I shook my head in sadness. "She has become mad."

Francisco looked at me with curiosity, almost as if he was thinking, It's not just she who is mad.

"The Bishop and the council visited her late last night. Bishop Marroquin tried to comfort her. She dismissed him with a wave of her hand. Castellanos told her she had gone too far. He told her that grieving was important, but God could have sent an even greater disaster. She screamed at him. She said he had wanted her husband dead for years. She said there could be no greater calamity than the death of her husband."

I could imagine the bishop's shock at the degrading of Calvary. Nine days of mourning were declared. The bishop held services every morning at six. Every evening bells rang out in sorrow.

"SHE TOLD THEM SHE WOULD BECOME THE CAPTAIN-GENERAL," Francisco said to Brother Luis and me. "Tomorrow the Council will provide her with an answer."

Francisco enjoyed all this. He had changed in the brief time we lived in the new Spanish city. Even after all the hangings and fear, he seemed contented. I did not understand why.

The next day, Doña Beatriz became the new captain-general. She insisted on being called "Unfortunate One." Don Alejandro shook his head in dismay. The Indians did not know what to make of it. They seemed to think she would end their brutality. They stood around the black palace and looked at the painted black cobblestones and painted walls, pointing and touching, talking among themselves.

Now, I wonder why I had not noticed the storms. There had been much to do. We had released many of our refugees. They began to feel safe. They were slowly returning to their homes and villages. Many had to be taken care of—babies, the old, the confused.

The storms came in waves. Black clouds passed over our city, some so low that they touched the peaks of the tallest buildings. The mountain volcano above the city was completely covered in black clouds for days.

Great raindrops fell out of the clouds. They were unlike anything I had seen in Spain. Each was large, falling in unison with the rest, creating a torrent.

That was the sign from the sky. There had been signs from the earth. At times there were low groans and shakes. We had become used to this. There were volcanoes all around and one great one above us. We assumed the earth around the great volcanoes had always rumbled. We were new to this land.

FRANCISCO HAD JUST COME UP TO ME under the porticoes of the cathedral when the shaking began. I grabbed a pillar to steady myself. I noticed that he looked up at the volcano. The shaking stopped.

"What is up there?" I asked.

"That is the Volcano Hunahpú. At the top there is a great lake.

In the lake is the spirit of Hunahpú. It has been said that, when his nation perishes, he will return and attack all foreigners."

"Even the priests?"

Francisco smiled, then shook his head in the Indian style. He looked at me with a sad silence.

"There is going to be an insurrection," he said. The rain beat on the walls of the church.

"Your people?"

"Not the Indians, not us," Francisco said, shaking his head. "Castellanos. He wants to be the permanent captain-general. My son works as a servant for the Castellanos family. He heard them plotting. Doña Beatriz has tried to treat us fairly."

Francisco had a son? Here? The mysteries of Guatemala.

"There is no guarantee that Beatriz will be any better than Alvarado or Castellanos," I said.

"Not much better," he said, "but better."

"Tell her," I said. "Be careful."

LATE THAT NIGHT, WE FELT THE HAND OF GOD. You could feel His touch. It was as if He were dormant all my life, then with a suddenness and capriciousness, He became known to man, known to me. He erased all the questions and provided one answer.

I lay in bed in fear. Brother Luis banged on my wood door. I thought to hide Antonia. Then I thought, if I were to die tonight, God would have seen anyhow.

Brother Luis took me to the doorway, where there was a young Indian man. He was tall and handsome in the candlelight. We brought him inside.

He told us he was a servant of Castellanos. "My father told me," he said, "to tell the Dominicans if anything were to happen."

"Who are you?" Father Luis asked.

"I am Lord Cotuha, adopted son of Belehé Qat," he said. "You know him as Francisco Hernández Arana Xajilá." He looked to be young. His nose was straight and narrow, while Francisco's was short and blunt. He did not look at all like his father.

"Castellanos has gathered together many soldiers," the boy said. "They are going to attack the palace tonight. They have guns. They are going to kill the new captain-general and all her servants. Everyone in the palace will be slaughtered."

Antonia built up the fire. I thought of Francisco. I thought of all of us.

"If I attempt to enter the palace, they will kill me," the young Indian said, pleading. "My mother is Doña Beatriz's maid, Xtah. They call her Lucía."

The mysteries of Guatemala.

There was no other choice. I put on a warm blanket and ran out. I had to lean against the rain. It pushed and pounded at me, so that I thought that I was not moving at all. I stopped to catch my breath under a portico. I leaned against the wall, trying to breathe. Under my feet, the ground became water. It began to pitch and roll as if I were on a boat. There was no substance to it. A deep growl rose from the ground.

For some strange reason I thought of my time at the university in Salamanca. They told me the New World would be turned into a Utopia for God's greater glory. The great drama would be the beginnings of this Utopia.

This was not Utopia. It was its antonym.

The earth stilled. I ran to the palace. It was too late. The battle had begun. In front of the gates, there were guns going off and sabers flying in the dark rain. Castellanos and his men attacked the guard. The guard was not holding. I watched; then knew I had to be inside with Francisco. How can a Spanish priest be friends with an Indian? I wondered as I made my way to back door. Friends to the point where I would risk my life to save his life? Again? Saving him had somehow given me responsibility for him. It made no sense.

Inside, the palace was dark, darkened even more by the black paint and long black curtains reflecting black in the few candles that were still lit. All that could be heard was the relentless cascading of the storm outside. The guard had not alerted the family and servants of the attack.

I acted like a madman. Again. I ran to the servants' quarters first, yelling and screaming, "We are under attack. They will try and *kill* you. Wake up!"

Some had been awakened by the earthquake; others were still sleeping. I ran up the stairs to the family of Alvarado. I had no choice. Someone had to awaken them to the danger.

Halfway up the stairs, the earth shook in ways I thought not possible. The stairs rolled and swayed. I fell and tumbled back down to the ground floor. The shaking refused to stop. It was as if the Lord had taken the Earth and swirled her like a cup of broth. The Indian servants had begun to run from their quarters. There was fear in their usually impassive faces.

I heard one cry, "Hunahpú!"

There was a rush of people everywhere. Those sleeping upstairs tried to hurry down the stairs to escape the building. Indians sleeping downstairs ran upstairs for unknown reasons. There were cries of fright in the darkness.

The shaking stopped. I looked up from the stairs. The earthquake had a knocked a hole in the ceiling. Water was streaming in. I followed the Indians running upstairs, looking for Francisco, looking for the boy's mother, looking for Alvarado's wife, the new captain-general.

In the dark, in the blackness, there were screams and cries emanating from everywhere. Then, in front of me, was Doña Beatriz. Her face was the face of terror. In her hands she held a golden goblet.

This was a child filled with fear. That's all she was, barely a young woman, a pregnant young woman. She turned from me and ran into the chapel. I expected to hear her scream, but I think she was so frightened that not a sound could come from her mouth.

Leonor, the Indian princess, ran along the balcony. There was little fear in her face. She commanded her maids to follow her downstairs to help the children. I did not know where Francisco was, but I could see the pregnant widow of Alvarado hiding like a small, fearful child in the chapel. I ran toward her.

There was a great sound like the rushing of millions of eagles flapping their wings. It was a tearing, crushing sound. I looked through the darkness to the bottom of the stairs.

Where I had just been was covered with water. It was as if the Great Flood was occurring before my eyes. The crushing water was filled with ice and chairs and pieces of wood. Children were floating in the water, screaming. Everything was moving in the black torrent away from the stairs.

I turned again toward the chapel. There was another earthquake. Previously, the stairs were unmovable; I felt secure holding on to the banister with one hand and grabbing at the passing children with the other. In this earthquake, the stairs began to roll as if they were made of string. The stairs crumbled. I fell into the torrent of water. Above me, I could see the chapel roof falling.

In the water, matters became quite simple: Find the direction of Heaven, and move one's arms in that direction. Around me were the roar and crush of the flood. The current carried us rapidly through the remains of the palace and then outside. I could see there were no more battles for the palace. All was covered with this vicious flood.

We were swept along. I bobbed above and below the chaotic waters. I had no strength in my arms. My robes pulled me into the depths of the icy river. The water completely covered me. I knew God had chosen this time and this place for the conclusion of my story. There was some peace in knowing that my screaming and squealing had stopped. I breathed in the ice-black water.

IN THE GRAY MORNING LIGHT, I found myself on a muddy bank. A soaked Francisco sat next to me. He looked over and smiled. "The black rain is for the wooden men, not human beings."

"What?"

He stood up and made his way through the mud toward the destroyed palace.

Everywhere below the bank was destruction. Trees were knocked over. Chairs and palace furniture lay embedded in the mud. And there were bodies. Arms and legs stuck out of the mud at random. Here was a head covered with black mud. There was a back, because the person had died face down.

I turned toward the monastery. I could not tell who was Indian and who was Spanish. Most of the time I could not tell who was male and who was female. It mattered not to God. I knew, in the rubble, both the rebels and the defenders of the palace would be found. It made no difference to Him.

That was the one answer: It made no difference to Him. Good or evil, male or female, Spanish or Indian, child or adult, it made no difference. Live your life with its petty pursuits, or live it robustly. You will still end up in the mud. It makes no difference.

All the buildings except one had fallen. His house, the cathedral, still stood. Everything else displayed His random touch. Arms and legs protruding from the mud. Here was a head, covered with mud, looking skyward. I almost laughed that this dead body had sought help from Him.

I FOUND MY RABINAL FRIEND, ANTONIA, and Brother Luis. Francisco returned to the monastery with one of Doña Beatriz's hand maidens. Francisco told me her name was Lucía. She quietly embraced the boy servant of the Castellanos family, Cotuha.

Francisco smiled when I tried to thank him for saving my life.

"We are going back to the origin, to the blue lake of the beginning—Lake Atitlán," Francisco said. I watched the three of them disappear from the muddy ruins into the forest.

I never saw them again. The wonders of Guatemala.

THERE WAS NOTHING LEFT OF OUR CITY. As I had feared, death covered every inch. Beatriz was found in the palace chapel, holding onto her gold cup, crushed by the walls. Don Alejandro wanted to place her body in the woods, so wild beasts could devour it. The Indians wanted to place her on a raft and sail her down river to the ocean. They believed she had brought this destruction by her indiscretions. The bishop would not allow it. She was buried with the others in a mass grave.

Bishop Morroquin, sick of us and her, gave her gold chalice to our order, the Dominicans.

All the rebels and all the defenders were dead, found in strange and bizarre positions in the mud.

It made no difference to Him.

I LEFT THE CAPITAL AND BEGAN MY JOURNEY to the Land of Peace. My great friend, the Rabinal woman Antonia, came with me. My brother monks stayed to help rebuild the capital—this time, they said, at another site, a safer place. I knew they had been fooled. It would make no difference to Him.

We carried goods and religious materials to set up a small church near Antonia's people, the Rabinal. My poor mule pulled a cart laden with bibles, The Saint's books, and the Queen of the

Americas' glorious and muddy Spanish wood cabinet. Maybe this was my final attachment to my homeland. Covered in her linens and undergarments, I found her writings and a strange Indian manuscript. I vowed to read them and to write my own account of the strange occurrences at Santiago de los Caballeros de Guatemala.

And that would still make no difference.

Along the way we stopped at an ancient pagan pyramid. It was huge and far larger than any building I had seen or heard of in Europe, including the Vatican. Trees and vines grew over and from it.

Antonia led me down a tree-lined path behind the pyramid. The narrow path ended at a small, round green lake. She called it a *cenote*. She said this was where the ancestors made offerings to the gods. She knelt and burned copal by the water.

I ran from the *cenote*. I made my way past the monkeys, past the vines, past the ruined pyramid. In the packs, tied to the burrow, I found the gift I wanted to offer this puddle. I rushed back to Antonia, back to the *cenote*. I stood on the edge of the water holding Beatriz's golden chalice. This cup had nothing to do with Christ. This was the gold of conquest and enslavement. His gold has nothing to do with that.

The chalice left a yellow arching trace in the blue sky before it splashed into the green water.

Epilogue

THE END OF THE EXPERIMENT IS CHRONICLED in a sad letter sent by the friars to the Council of the Indies on May 14, 1556. They were writing, says the report, in order that the King might clearly understand what happened. For years the friars had worked strenuously despite the great heat and hardness of the land—they had destroyed idols, built churches, and won souls. But always "the devil was vigilant," and finally he stirred up the pagan priests who called in some neighboring infidel Indians to help provoke a revolt.

The friars and their followers were burned out of their homes, and some thirty were killed by arrows. Two of the friars were murdered in the church and one sacrificed before a pagan idol. One of those to die was Friar Domingo de Vico, a zealous, learned missionary, who was able to preach in seven different Indian languages.

Subsequently the King ordered the punishment of the revolting Indians, the Land of Peace became even poorer, and the possibility of winning the Indians by peaceful means alone faded away.

—Lewis Hanke,
The Spanish Struggle for Justice in Colonial America

ACKNOWLEDGEMENTS

It is said that history is written by the victorious. In the case of the Spanish invasion of the Americas, that is not completely true. *The Popol Vuh:The Sacred Book of the Ancient Quiché Maya* reaches back in time far before Europeans landed in the "New World." It describes the origins, cosmology, and world view of the Maya. Translations by Adrian Recinos, Delia Goetz, and Sylvanus G. Morley, and then Dennis Tedlock, are invaluable. Less well known, but crucial to understanding Alvarado's war on the Mayan civilization, is *The Annals of the Cakchiquels*, written in the 16th century by Francisco Hernández Arana, and translated by Recinos and Goetz. Also, the *Rabinal Achi* is a key pre-Hispanic Mayan choreographed drama that informed this novel. There are several translations and recordings of the work. For understandings of Alvarado and Beatriz's point of view, John Eoghan Kelly's *Pedro de Alvarado: Conquistador* was crucial.

The complexities of the Maya language can be glimpsed in *Language of Guatemala*, edited by Marvin Mayers. Likewise, *Gramática Del Idioma Kaqchikel*, published by P.L.F.M. in Guatemala, allows a peek into the Mayan linguistic structure.

The splendid archeology of Robert Carmack, seen in his *The Quiché-Mayas of Utatlán:The Evolution of a Highland Maya Kingdom* and *The Historical Demography of Highland Guatemala*, gave this writer a shot at recreating that historic landscape.

Gaining entrance into the worlds of the Maya and Guatemala was made possible through the deep understandings of the Familia Paniagua of Guatemala; Xalapa, Mexico; and San Francisco, California. Any and all failures of this understanding are mine and mine only. My thanks *por vida*.

I am deeply grateful to Emanuel Paniagua for his permission to use his painting, *Creación del Serpiente (El Quetzal)*, for the cover of this book. Certainly, many thanks to Barry Sheinkopf at Bookshapers for his good work and patience in editing and book design. *Matiox*, Barry! Tanya Vlach's literary and media platform consultations have been invaluable. And, of course, this book would not have been possible without the love, support, and guidance of my partner, Norita Vlach.

ABOUT THE AUTHOR

William Vlach's poetry has been published in the United States and the United Kingdom. Both his playwriting and parody have won writing awards. William has published essays on diverse topics such as police psychology, the history of health care ethics, film noir, and the psychology of genocide. Currently he is completing his second historical novel, *The Naked Greek*. His web site is *williamvlach.com*. He continues his practice of clinical psychology in San Francisco, where he lives with his wife, Norita.